Demon Dawn

The Resurrection Chronicles

M.J. Haag

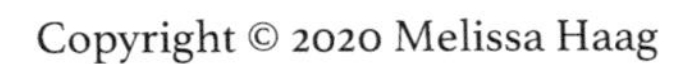

ISBN 978-1-943051-48-9 (eBook Edition)

ISBN 978-1-943051-54-0 (CreateSpace Paperback Edition)

ISBN 978-1-943051-55-7 (Paperback Edition)

Editing by Ulva Eldridge

Cover design by Shattered Glass Publishing LLC

© Depositphotos.com

To google drive and champagne,
Without you two, there'd be no book.
Thank you!

DEMON DAWN

Survival requires sacrifice.

The world irrevocably changed after the hellhounds and fey appeared. Most people didn't survive that first night. Dad had said we were lucky we did. I'm not so sure about that anymore.

With her father murdered before her eyes and her faith in the remaining humans shaken, Brenna reluctantly accepts sanctuary in Tolerance, a safe zone managed by the fey. The wall keeps the infected out. But it also keeps the humans in... with the very creatures that caused the world to break.

Big, grey, and ruthlessly deadly, the fey strike fear in the hearts of men and women alike. But Brenna finds one more intimidating than all the rest. Scarred and angry, Thallirin watches Brenna with an intensity that makes her relive the events that followed her father's murder. She knows what Thallirin wants, and she's never going to be used like that again.

Tormented by her past, Brenna sees no possible future for herself other than eventual infection or starvation. There is hope, though. Her community is abuzz with a newly discovered way to protect women against the disease that's turning people into zombies. However, it doesn't come from a needle.

It comes from sleeping with one of the dark fey.

WHAT HAS HAPPENED BEFORE...

More than two months ago, earthquakes unleashed hellhounds on an unsuspecting mankind. The bite of a hound changed humans, turning people into flesh-craving infected.

The hellhounds weren't the only things to emerge from the earthen caverns. Demon men with grey skin and reptilian eyes had been trapped underground for thousands of years. They, alone, possessed the ability to kill the hellhounds and help bring a stop to the plague. They had only asked for one thing in return: a chance to meet women who might be willing to love them as they are.

CHAPTER ONE

RESTLESS, I WALKED ALONG THE WALL AND SEARCHED THE barren trees for any sign of movement. Dawn's early light was barely creeping over the horizon. Usually at this time of day, infected roamed among the trees, but everything remained still just like it had yesterday and the day before that. Breach day. The day the infected had fooled me and gotten inside Tolerance.

Bitter regret filled me quickly, followed by frustration. Although I'd been the one the infected had fooled, I didn't blame myself. I put the blame where it was due. On the damn infected. They were getting smarter, and we'd all been unprepared for that. It didn't make me less angry about what had happened, though. The infected had taken so much from us already. Our sense of safety. Our ability to go anywhere. My eyes once again swept over the wall that protected as much as it imprisoned. This was the world we were living in now. A dangerous, scary place filled with things that wanted to kill humans.

A sudden burst of panic hit me. The feeling wormed its way into my chest and tightened so hard and fast that I could barely breathe. I paused on the grille of an upturned SUV and took one slow, steady breath while counting to eight in my head. Then I did the same thing on the exhale, repeating the process until the panic eased.

I continued along the wall again, pacing my section as if nothing had happened. I tried not to think of the reason for my attacks. Ever. It was easier to focus on the task at hand: watching the trees for infected. I found it ironic that trying to spot an infected was soothing.

In an odd way, it made sense though. The infected I could kill. My past...well, there was no killing memories.

I took another calming breath. Since the quakes, watching for infected was the only way to survive. I could barely remember my life before the world went to hell a few months ago. I didn't really want to. It would just make my current life more hellish.

Focusing on the trees, I paused.

"Where are they?" I said softly to myself.

"Brenna," a voice called from behind me. "Do you need more arrows?"

I glanced at the fey standing below me. He was big and had to be close to seven feet tall. While I was appropriately bundled against the cold, he only wore a pair of jogging pants and a t-shirt that stretched tightly over his broad shoulders and expansive chest. Not all of the fey liked wearing shirts. I appreciated that this one was covered.

His lizard-like eyes swept over my face, and I briefly wondered if he was seeing our differences in my blunt teeth, rounded ears, and pink skin. Or was he looking for something else?

Inwardly, I cringed and hurried to answer so he'd go away.

"No. I still have them all." I reached back to touch the feathered ends sticking from my quiver.

He grunted.

"Are you hungry?" he asked.

"No, I'm fine. Thank you."

He repeated his previous grunt, and I started moving again before he could come up with something else to say.

The fey loved talking to women. Like they would cut off their grey, pointed ear kind of love. I found their intensity a little disturbing, but they weren't bad. Not really. Even if they were constantly trying to talk to me, they respected when I said no to something. Well, most of them did.

The sun rose higher as I continued pacing back and forth on my section of the wall. Tolerance, once a small suburb hidden in the Missouri trees just outside of Warrensburg, was far enough out that the infected still roaming Warrensburg didn't always hear us. But we'd never gone this long without attracting attention, especially with the wall's lights flooding the sky at night.

Near midday, I saw a fey farther along on the wall, scrutinizing his section of trees. I followed his gaze and saw movement. My hand automatically flew back for an arrow as another fey stepped from the trees and shook his head.

Since the fey had returned from Tenacity, the other fortress-like camp only a few miles away, my presence on the wall wasn't required. Not that it ever had been. But after the breach, the fey had put more emphasis on having men patrolling outside the walls for unusual activity. Unfortunately, the only thing unusual at the moment was the complete absence of infected.

Giving up on finding something to shoot at, I waved to the fey on the wall and headed for the ladder. The fey waved back, jogging toward my section as I descended. I dropped the last three rungs so he wouldn't jump to the ground and try helping me down. The fey liked touching women more than they liked talking to them. But only with permission. They didn't take what wasn't offered.

Unlike human men.

I immediately shook off the thought and started home.

My shoes crunched on the fresh layer of snow that now covered all traces of what had happened only a few days ago. The carnage had been severe. More so because the humans from Whiteman's military base had been here as a result of a breach at the base. Maybe that was why the infected weren't outside our walls now. Maybe they were checking out Tenacity, the new walled-in location for Whiteman's survivors.

A group of nearby fey caught my attention. They were surrounding a woman, trying to coax some conversation out of her. Based on the way she was glancing around as if looking for a route of escape, she didn't seem to enjoy the attention. Between that reaction and the scowling fey standing just off to one side, she had to be one of the few Whiteman survivors who'd decided to stay. If I had to guess, she was assigned to live with the scowling fey but wasn't interested in being his valentine. And, he didn't like seeing the other fey swarm his roommate.

She saw me and waved.

"Brenna," she called, wedging her way through the wall of muscle to hurry in my direction.

I begrudgingly slowed to wait for her. It was no mystery how she knew my name, but I didn't know hers. As the girl with the bow who liked to guard the wall, I kind of stuck out in this very fey dominated community that liked to shelter women. Besides, the fey talked. A lot. Especially about their favorite things. Women and women's parts.

All but one of her admirers scattered to find other prey. Thankfully, that prey was never me. As a minor, I was off limits to them. It didn't matter that my eighteenth birthday was only a few weeks away.

"Hey," she said, nearing me. "I'm Cheri. Would you know where I can find Hannah?"

"Sure." I gave her the house number.

Cheri waved, ducked her head, and started walking. If she thought keeping her head down would keep the fey away, she was in for some disappointment. I'd no sooner had the thought when a fey stepped out from between two houses to intercept her.

I shook my head and continued home. It still felt weird thinking of my family's assigned house as home. There were pictures of another family in the basement, carefully packed away by one of the fey who had helped clear the houses out when they first decided to make this place a safe zone. I never let myself think of what had happened to the people who lived there before us. It was probably the same thing that happened to most of the people on the planet. Hellhounds and infection.

The house was quiet when I let myself in. That likely meant that Zach, my brother, was out following one of the fey around, and Mom was reading one of the books Julie had brought her. Standing in the mud room, I stripped from my winter gear and hung everything up so it'd be ready for when I went out again.

The kitchen was already cleaned up from breakfast, so I went to check on Mom. She was in her room, but not reading. She had her chair pulled up to the window and was peeking through the curtains with a pair of binoculars in her hands.

"Dear God, he's hung like a horse," she said softly.

My mouth dropped open.

"What in the hell are you doing?"

She jumped and fumbled with the binoculars as she swiveled to look at me. When she gripped them securely once more, she scowled at me.

"Watch your mouth. I don't care if the world's going to shit. I'm your mother, and you will respect me."

I crossed my arms, not buying her act.

"I will respect you until the day I die, and you know it. But

I won't ever stop calling you out when I see you doing something wrong. Just like you wouldn't ever hold back on me."

She was quiet for a moment.

"Fair enough. Are you hungry?" She set the binoculars on her lap and moved her wheelchair forward.

"Are you going to tell me what you were doing?"

"Nope."

"Then I guess I'll just need to walk across the street and tell whoever is in that house that my pervy mom was eyeing up his meat stick. I wonder how that will go over?"

She sighed and stopped wheeling forward.

"Probably with him asking if he could see places only your father saw."

That robbed me of my irritation with her. Uncrossing my arms, I went to sit on her bed.

"I miss him, too," I said softly.

"It's not just missing him, Bren. It's being practical. Molev was right. I need to start thinking of you and Zach."

Her use of Zach instead of Zachy didn't escape my notice. She'd been treating us both differently since we'd arrived here weeks ago. Molev, the fey's leader, had taken her aside to talk to her not long after. I wasn't sure what he'd said, but that was when she'd changed.

I didn't let myself think for a moment that she'd changed because of what had happened to me.

"What do you mean?" I asked. "All you ever do is think about us."

She shook her head and looked down at the binoculars.

"No, sweetie. I haven't been. Not really. We live in a different world now. The rules of parenting are changing. Keeping you clothed and fed isn't enough. I need to do everything I can to keep you safe."

"You have. You are."

She started shaking her head again. It wasn't like her to hold back.

"Whatever is eating at you, just say it. I hate when you dance around the subject."

A grin pulled at her lips.

"I think you and I should start dating."

"What? Why? Who? Are you insane? Zombies are outside the wall, doing God only knows what, and you're worried about our love lives?"

Her tired brown eyes met mine as she tucked a short strand of hair behind her ear.

"Three days ago, I was lucky. So were you. We could have been bitten and changed."

I stared at her, my mind pulling me back to the horrifying moment when the infected used their makeshift ladders to climb the wall. I'd watched them run through the streets, unable to nock arrows fast enough to put a dent in their numbers. While I'd fought for my life and everyone else's in this place, I'd thought of my mom alone in this house. Bound to her wheelchair.

And suddenly, I understood what she was trying to tell me.

It was a topic I couldn't get out of my head since it became known.

"You don't want to date," I said. "You want immunity from infection."

Thanks to Eden and her run in with infected, the fey and most the humans here now knew what it would take for humans to become immune to infection. The human men were screwed. Actually, that wasn't right. The human women would be screwed. By fey, the only creatures immune to infection.

"Sleeping with one of the fey is no guarantee for survival. Sure, you won't turn, but you saw what the infected did to some of the people they got to. There's no living through that, either."

Her gaze searched mine for a moment, and she gave me a small shrug.

"It's not just for immunity, Brenna." She took a deep breath. "I want a partner. I want to know that someone will be there for you two when I'm not."

My chest squeezed painfully at the thought of losing her, too. Dad had been there for us through the quakes and the chaos that followed. He'd been the one to get us out of the house to look for supplies. We'd survived the worst of it, or so I thought, because of his steadfast presence. Then, in an act of unwarranted violence, he'd been taken from us by humans looking to expand their numbers with healthy, young people like me and Zach. That group had revealed the truth of the world to me. A truth from which my dad had tried so hard to protect me.

My expression must have given my thoughts away because Mom pushed toward me.

"I will love your father until the day I die, Brenna. And if I had a choice, I'd give myself more time to mourn him. But time is a finite thing, and we never know how much we have. You and Zach are more important than my grief or my pride." She took my hand, holding it firm. "It's time I find someone. Someone who will look at me with respect. Who will see my intelligence and not my wheelchair. Someone who will cherish what I am and what I have to offer. Someone your father would approve of."

"That's what you were doing, then? Visually interviewing the candidates?"

She chuckled and swatted my hand.

"You know me better than anyone. Everyone might think I'm tough and ornery..."

"But you're worried. Nervous," I said in understanding. "They are big."

"All over," she said with a glance at the window. "But not dangerously so." She patted my hand again. "And they're gentle. Kind. Very respectful. If you say no, they'll listen."

"Why does it feel less like you're pep-talking yourself and more like you're pep-talking me?"

"I want you to date, too, remember?"

That had kind of purposely slipped my mind.

"I'm fine. There's no need. I'm as good of a shot, if not

better, than most of the fey. I don't need to tear off infected heads with my bare hands. A decent vantage point, and I'm just as lethal."

"Until you run out of arrows," she said. "I wasn't the only one lucky three days ago."

I shook my head, feeling the weight of panic settling on my chest.

"No, Mom. I'm not. I won't."

A noise in the hall drew her attention. Zach stood there, flushed, but not angrily so.

"It's Brenna's choice, Mom. Don't guilt her into anything. She's done enough." Our gazes met and held. Guilt reflected in his eyes. He swallowed hard and started to turn away.

I sprang off the bed, grabbed him, and spun him around for a fierce hug.

"Don't," I whispered as he held me just as tightly. "Don't even think about it. The past is behind us. We both need to look forward. We watch out for each other. Always. No regrets. Got it?"

He nodded even as he trembled. I continued to hold him until the shaking stopped and he moved to let me know he was done. When he met my gaze, his lashes were wet and his eyes red.

"Find a fey to teach you any moves today?" I asked.

He grinned.

"No, but I found one making a bow. I helped him for a while. He didn't talk much but showed me how to make arrows."

"That's great. If we stockpile them, I can start placing caches along the wall."

"That's what I was thinking, too." Some of the regret and sorrow left his gaze, replaced by excitement.

"Why don't you start lunch?" I asked. "Mom and I will join you in a bit."

He nodded, glanced at Mom, then left.

When I turned, Mom was watching me.

"It's always your choice," she said. "Never doubt that. I will castrate any man or fey who believes otherwise."

"I know."

She nodded, set the binoculars on the bed, and started wheeling toward the door.

"Take a peek," she said, glancing over her shoulder. "That way you'll know what you're getting into before you decide."

I stayed in the room and sat on the bed, but I had no intention of peeking at our neighbors. Big or small, I knew what I'd be getting myself into with one of the fey. They didn't date. They obsessed. Some of the women here had found real happiness with the level of devotion from their chosen fey partners. And, I couldn't deny that Drav was amazing with Mya. But the way he told her what to do...the way they all liked giving orders at certain times...none of it sat well with me.

A memory pulled me in before I could fight it. That first night at the bunker, Zach sat at the table beside me. Strangers were filing past us with their plates to get their portion of the food. I'd nudged Zach. He'd stood with me, and we'd done what the others had. However, when we got to the front of the line, the old guy had shaken his head.

"You work to get fed. You haven't worked yet, so you don't get a portion."

"You took us but don't plan on feeding us? Why?"

He had nodded his head for someone to take the plate from my hand.

"We plan on feeding you," the younger guy had said. "You just need to work first."

The memory of the man's blue eyes burrowed deeper, switching from the first day to the second when he'd lingered in the kitchen after I'd begged to do the dishes. I'd been begging for something to do to guarantee a portion of the evening meal for Zach. At fifteen, he'd been hungry all the time before the quakes. Afterward, when food was scarce, he appeared almost skeletal.

"There are other ways to work, you know," Van, the man with the blue eyes, had said while he watched me.

"What?" I'd asked. "I'll do anything."

The slow smile he'd given me still haunted my dreams.

"Have you ever given a thought to the future? With so many of us dying, who will be left if we don't start doing our part?"

I'd understood what he'd meant.

"No one is going to force you. But every time you let me do it, I'll give up my portion of food for you."

For Zach, I'd lain still under Van in a bunker filled with people. Some had pretended to sleep. Most of the men had watched. Van had acted like I was the love of his life. He'd petted me and promised to make sure I was ready so I'd enjoy it.

Van hadn't physically hurt me. I'd been embarrassed, ashamed, resentful, and angry. But Zach had eaten the next day. Me too.

My stomach twisted as the memory faded, and the familiar weight of panic settled heavier on my chest. I picked up the binoculars and turned them in my hands while taking my slow breaths.

Van and his father had called it a choice, but it hadn't been. Not really. In a system where the men with guns didn't work but made up the rules for those of us who hadn't had guns, what choice was there between starvation and letting someone use my body?

I was never going back to that way of living.

Setting the binoculars down, I joined Mom and Zach in the kitchen.

"What do you think?" Mom asked.

"I think that you're making a decision based on fear and that you should stop and consider the long-term consequences carefully."

Zach stopped stirring whatever he had cooking on the stove to look back and forth between Mom and me.

"What are we talking about?"

"Mom wants to hook up with one of the fey so she doesn't have to worry about being turned."

"And," Mom added while shooting me a look, "so I know,

should anything happen to me, that someone will be here to look after you two."

Zach remained quiet for a moment, studying me then Mom.

"I want to be mad," he said. "The resentment is right there. But I remember how scared I was when the infected were running around. How useless I am to keep either of you safe."

"Zach," Mom said in a tone that promised she had a million reassurances ready, but he quickly held up his hand.

"Dad was the bravest man I knew. One of the strongest, too. He died keeping us safe. The fey who rescued us from the bunker didn't die. They were shot and attacked by hellhounds, but they lived. Well, almost all of them. They're stronger, faster, and immune.

"Since the beginning, Dad told us we needed to stick together to survive. But we know we wouldn't have lasted out there without him, and he wouldn't have wanted us to take that risk. That's why we're here." He focused on Mom. "If you want to give one of the fey a reason to care, a reason to stick by us no matter what, I understand. But, you need to care about whoever you pick in return. They're good people and don't deserve to be used more than they already have been."

I looked at Mom. Her scowl might fool some people, but not us. She was doing her best not to cry.

"Your dad would be so proud of you," she said, her voice husky. "Both of you."

Zach went to give her a hug. I took over stirring the stew on the stove. It looked like a can of soup, a can of peas, and a can of dog food. I cringed, knowing that we had to be getting to the bottom of the supplies to be cracking into the dog food.

"No making faces," Mom said, smacking my hip. "Food is food. Go get the bowls."

We ate lunch together, and when Zach and I started bundling up to go out, Mom pulled me aside.

"I'm set on my decision," she said. "But I'll need your help."

"Name it."

"When you're out there, talk to the fey. Find a few who'd be willing to come over for dinner. Make it clear it's not a promise for anything more than conversation and food. Zach is right; I need to feel some affection for whoever I choose. It wouldn't be fair otherwise."

"Wait, are you asking me to be your—"

"If you say pimp, I'm serving dog food soup for the next week."

I snorted.

"We'll probably be eating dog food for the next week no matter what I say."

"When you mix it with the chicken noodle soup, it's not so bad. Tastes like stew," she said with a grin.

But behind her humor, I saw her worry. She didn't like feeding us dog food. She didn't like depending on others to bring us supplies. There was a lot in life not to like now. I hoped she wasn't adding to the list by looking for a fey.

"Fine. I'll do it. And I'll be picky. I promise. But I refuse to do physical inspections for you. You're on your own there."

CHAPTER TWO

THE BRISK WINTER WIND SMACKED ME IN THE FACE AS I LEFT THE house. It robbed me of my breath, and I ducked down into the brown scarf I wore. Winter was easily my least favorite season. It made my fingers cold, which didn't mix well with my love of archery.

"Hey, Brenna," a voice called.

I looked up at the passing fey's welcome. Usually, I nodded and continued on my way. Sometimes I said hey back. This time, I reluctantly stopped.

"Hey. How's it going, um...I forgot your name."

The fey froze like a deer in the headlights. His gaze swept the area around us then landed on me.

"My name is Newaz."

"Newaz. Right. Sorry."

"There is no need for an apology. There are many of us."

I smiled. The fey really were nice. Well, most of them.

"And I'm glad for it. Without all of you, none of us would still be here. Would you like to come over for dinner tonight? My mom's hoping for some conversation. It's not to hook up or anything. Just to talk and get to know each other."

He frowned, and his gaze swept the area again. I looked around as well, wondering if there was something weird going on outside the walls again.

"I cannot come over for dinner tonight. Perhaps you should ask Thallirin."

My gaze whipped back to Newaz.

"What? Why would you say that?"

Only two days ago, Thallirin, the biggest, scariest fey I'd ever seen, had gotten in my face and yelled at me for putting myself in danger. Then, he'd ordered me inside Mya's home like some errant pet that'd peed on his floor. He was the exception to the fey niceness rule.

Newaz's face darkened.

"No reason. I must go speak with someone else."

He hurried off, leaving me staring after him in confusion. That had to qualify as the shortest conversation with one of the fey, ever. Well, shortest where I didn't walk away first. And weird. Why in the hell would he bring up Thallirin? That was the last fey I wanted over for dinner.

Shrugging off Newaz's oddness, I resumed my walk to the wall, not going far before I ran into another possible dinner invitee.

"Hi," I said, slowing.

"Hello, Brenna."

I repeated the same invitation. Like Newaz, this fey started acting weird, looking around, flushing, and hurrying off after giving some lame excuse.

It happened three more times before I gave up and went to my spot on the wall. Uan, a fey who often guarded the wall near me, was there and nodded when he saw me coming up the ladder.

"Hey, Uan," I said. "Do I have something on my face?"

He tilted his head to look at me.

"Your nose, mouth, and eyes."

I rolled said eyes and laughed.

"Thanks. I thought maybe I had lunch on my face."

"Why would you think you have lunch on your face?"

"Because I invited five different fey over to dinner, and they all acted like I nutted them with my bow." I flicked the bow playfully at Uan's midsection, and he backed up hastily.

"Yep. Like that. I thought you guys liked conversation and food." I paused for a beat. "Is it because my mom's in a wheelchair? I thought that didn't matter."

His expression turned from wary to serious.

"Brenna, your mother is a strong and beautiful woman. Her wheelchair does not matter. It's you."

I sputtered in indignation.

"What's that supposed to mean?"

He looked around, just like the other guys had.

"I swear if you tell me that you have to go talk to someone else, I'm going to beat you with my bow then make you find me a new one."

He chuckled at my threat, this not being the first time he'd heard it, and met my gaze.

"You are too young to ask anyone to dinner."

"Oh." Robbed of my indignation, I had nothing else to say.

"When you are eighteen, you may ask someone to dinner."

"I'm not asking you to dinner for me. I'm asking for my mom. She's lonely and just wants someone to talk to."

Interest lit his gaze.

"Just talk," I reiterated. "Zach and I will be there, too."

"A family dinner," Uan said. "Yes, I would like one of those."

I couldn't help but feel a little bad for him just then. Locked underground before the quakes, without any women of their own and no chance for families, the existence of human women offered something the fey had never known to want. Now that they did know, they wanted families of their own very badly. But their wanting was like Mom's, not Van's.

I stopped my line of thinking and smiled at Uan.

"I can tell my mom you'll come to dinner, then?"

"Yes. I will come to your family dinner when the sun sets. I must share this news with Thallirin."

My mind shuddered at hearing that name again as Uan turned and waved to a fey farther down the wall to come guard his section of wall.

Before Uan could jump down, I grabbed his arm.

"Please don't take this the wrong way, but Thallirin's not invited."

Uan grinned widely, showing his sharp teeth.

"Of course not. You're too young for dinner with Thallirin."

My grip tightened on my bow.

"Uan, you're making my head hurt. Why are you telling Thallirin that you're having dinner at our house?"

"He must know you were asking on behalf of your mother instead of yourself. Some will be disappointed you were not interested, but they will be glad to hear they did not steal your attention from our brother. Thallirin will be pleased as well."

It took a second for his words to click. He thought I was interested in Thallirin? Worse, it was sounding like they all thought Thallirin was interested in me.

"Eh?" Uan's replacement asked as he came up to us. "She is not interested in the others?"

"I'm tempted to push you both off this wall."

The new guy glanced at the other side.

"But there are no infected to kill."

Uan swept his arm out, forcing his companion to take a step back with him.

"Do not provoke her," Uan warned. "She will poke our testicles with her bow."

The other man made a pained noise and turned slightly sideways.

"That is not how I want my testicles to be touched someday."

Uan grunted in agreement.

I struggled with my frustration at how easily our conversation had spiraled out of control.

"Uan, I'm going to say this very plainly. I am not interested in any male, be he fey or human."

"Yes. That is good. When you are eighteen, then you can be interested. Thallirin is patient."

I pivoted and started for the ladder, unable to deal with another minute of their naïve fey bullshit. I wasn't mad. They didn't know any better. But, communicating with the fey was often like talking to toddlers, and I didn't know toddler-speak for "leave me the fuck alone." I needed expert help.

"I will see you at dinner," Uan called as I jogged away from the wall.

I debated between going to Mya or going to Eden. Mya was sick, and I hated to ask for her help when she wasn't feeling well. But, I didn't want Eden thinking my request for help to set the fey straight had anything to do with what had happened in the bunker. Because it didn't. Well, not the way she would probably think.

Turning the corner, I saw more than the usual number of fey lingering on Mya's street. They watched me approach her door and knock. A moment later, Drav answered.

"Hi, Drav. Can I talk to Mya?"

He grunted and moved aside. He was a good guy. Easy to like. Which was a good thing since he was in charge during Molev's continued absence.

Stepping through the door, I saw Mya and Drav weren't alone. Matt Davis, the man in charge of Tenacity, sat in the living room along with Eden and Ghua.

"I didn't mean to interrupt," I said, already retreating. "I'll just come back—"

The door closed behind me.

"Stay," Mya said. "These aren't closed meetings unless you ask to see my baby. Then, I'm kicking you out."

I grinned and shook my head.

Since announcing her pregnancy, Mya's fame among the fey had gone from protective-sister-they'd-always-wanted to baby-bearing-rockstar.

She gestured to a chair and focused on Matt.

"The fey *are* helping," Mya said. "Without their escort, Tenacity would have no supplies."

"You're right. And I'm not asking for more fey help. You and I agreed that after the walls were up, humans would be responsible for standing guard. That's why I'm here. I'm looking for human volunteers who would be willing to take on a few guard shifts at Tenacity so I can send more people out for supplies."

I unzipped my jacket and took a seat as I listened.

"If everyone were able-bodied, I'd have the numbers I need for guarding and supply runs. But I have kids. Elderly. Injured. And, I'm not asking for volunteers permanently. Cassie's trip to find her son proved there are still survivors out there. With the planes still on base and some fey help," he added with a cringe, "we can start looking for more people. Bolster our numbers."

Mya remained quiet for a moment, glancing at Drav then Eden. Eden shrugged, but I could see she wasn't overly interested in helping Matt.

"Any trouble since settling in?" Mya asked him.

"None. I established a seventy/thirty system for supplies. Anyone who goes out keeps seventy percent of what they bring back, and thirty percent goes toward the community storage, which feeds those who can't go out. But, I have more who can't work than those who can."

Eden snorted.

"Don't forget those people lived here with us. I think you mean won't work, not can't."

Matt said nothing. He didn't need to. The weary droop of his shoulder said enough.

"Fear is as debilitating as many physical ailments," I said. "Can't. Won't. If you put either of those types of people outside the wall, the result will be the same. People will die. It makes sense that you don't want to risk those who are actually willing by forcing those who aren't."

Mya nodded.

"It doesn't change Matt's problem, though. Or my answer. If we keep enabling them—"

"I know," Matt said. "It will only get worse. Yet, I can't stand by and just watch people starve because they're too afraid to do their part."

I understood why Mya was refusing to allow the fey to help. They'd give up anything to possibly impress a female survivor. Even their lives. I saw their longing on a daily basis. They lingered for even a scrap of feminine attention. It wasn't fair that so many of the humans at Tenacity were willing to use that to get the fey's help.

Especially when the majority of the Whiteman survivors had made their negative feelings regarding the fey very plain.

However, the humans living here were a different story. We liked the fey. We were able-bodied. And we didn't need Mya to protect us from being used by the other camp.

"There are a lot of good people here, in Tolerance, who'd be willing to take a few shifts if you let them know what's going on," I said, thinking of my family and Mya's brother.

"Fine," Mya said. "We'll put the word out that you're looking for human volunteers to guard Tenacity while your people go on supply runs, Matt." She looked at Drav. "Everyone who's willing should meet at the north wall at first light."

"Thank you. And about the planes?"

She looked at Drav.

"We will help," he said. "But when the planes are above, they must look for signs of Molev, too."

Molev, the leader of the fey, had been missing for several weeks. Everyone in Tolerance was concerned about his fate. He'd been amazing when Mom, Zach, and I had first arrived, spending time with Mom and assuring us we were welcome and safe. If he were here, he would have been the first one I would have invited for dinner with Mom.

"Agreed," Matt said easily. "Perhaps this is a perfect opportunity to continue building better relations between some of the survivors and fey."

"How do you mean?" Mya asked.

"The fey have far better eyesight than we do. We should pair a pilot with a fey each trip."

Mya nodded slowly, looking at Drav.

"Many will want to see the world from above," he said. "You will have no shortage of volunteers."

"Good. It's settled." Matt stood and offered his hand to Drav. "We'll welcome the help from any human who volunteers and will start looking for Molev and survivors tomorrow."

After he left, Mya turned to me.

"Sorry for making you wait," she said.

"I don't mind." I glanced around the room at Drav, Ghua, and Eden.

"Did you want to talk alone?" Mya asked.

"No. It's okay. Nothing I have to say is a secret. Mom's lonely and interested in some company, so she asked me to invite someone over for conversation and dinner. When I started asking, the fey got weird. I just found out that they all think Thallirin is interested in me and that I was asking them to dinner for myself, which freaked them out because they all thought they were stealing Thallirin's woman. When I tried to explain that Thallirin has no claim on me, they agreed...but only because I'm not eighteen yet."

Mya frowned slightly.

"I'm sorry. I'm going to blame the pregnancy on this one, but I'm not following. What's the problem?"

I focused on three slow breaths before answering.

"No fey should be allowed to call dibs on any female. Ever.

Unless we truly don't have a choice."

"Ah. I see. I don't think Thallirin has called dibs." She looked at Drav.

"Dibs means to choose," he said. "Are you saying no fey should be able to choose? Only the females can choose?"

"No, I mean it needs to be mutual," I said. "Just because Thallirin likes me, doesn't mean I need to like him back. And it doesn't mean that everyone else needs to stay away from me."

"They must until you're eighteen."

I looked at Mya.

"That's why I'm here."

"I understand." She looked at the others. "Would you mind giving us a few minutes to talk alone?"

Drav grunted and Ghua stood.

"I'd like to stay if it's okay with you," Eden said.

I shrugged. She'd been my second pick for help, so why not?

Once the men cleared out, Mya sat up a little straighter.

"They mean well," she said. "Their way of thinking is often so different from ours it drives me insane."

I breathed a sigh of relief that she really did understand. She plucked at her blanket a moment, and I could tell she was struggling with something. I hated when people didn't just say what they wanted to say.

"When my mom first found out she'd be in a wheelchair for the rest of her life, it was hard," I said. "On all of us. It almost tore our family apart because each of us was so worried about sparing everyone else the anguish we were feeling that we kept it all inside. We have a rule now. If you're feeling something...thinking something...whatever, you just say it. Don't beat around the bush. Don't pull punches. Just say it. Because most of the problems in our lives stem from misunderstanding and miscommunication."

Mya smiled slightly.

"I appreciate that more than you know," she said.

"Good. I'm here asking you to make it clear to the fey that I'm not interested in anyone. And my lack of interest has nothing to do with my age. Pairing up with someone, if it ever happens, will be on my terms, not someone else's."

"I agree," Eden said. "Not everyone wants to be matched up, Mya."

"I get that. It's just hard after seeing where the fey are from and knowing they had nothing before this. A stone slab for a bed, a gourd to carry water, and endless darkness. Seeing their delight in learning there's more to life than they ever knew...it's hard to take that hope away. And, that's what I'd be doing when I talk to Thallirin and tell him you have no interest in him." She exhaled slowly and fidgeted with her blanket again. "Are you opposed to Thallirin because of his looks?"

I thought of the big fey, the scars marring his face and arms, and mentally cringed away from the image. It wasn't how he looked; it was how he looked at me that was the problem. How could someone look so stoic, yet angry and interested, all at the same time?

"I've honestly never looked at any of the fey too closely," I said. "I knew they'd take it the wrong way if I did, and I didn't want to cruelly give any of them hope that I would ever be interested."

"I didn't think I would ever be interested, either," Mya said. "Eden, too, I'm betting. But the fey tend to grow on you."

I stood and zipped my jacket.

"I've made my wishes clear. What you do now is up to you. However, if I'm faced with the choice of staying here and being paired up or going to Tenacity, I'll leave. I won't be forced to sleep with anyone again."

"Brenna, that will never happen here," Eden said quickly. "I won't let it."

"And that's not what I was suggesting," Mya said, looking pale and shocked. "I only meant that you might change your mind someday."

Instead of answering, I left. I'd said my piece and made my feelings on the matter quite plain. And, I was more than a little infuriated that Mya was obviously siding with the fey in this.

When I reached the house, I called out that I'd found someone to come to dinner before I retreated to the backyard. Looking at the various targets, I nocked an arrow then let go of my annoyance by releasing shot after shot. I already had excellent aim. What I needed now was speed, too. A lot of it.

My fingers grew sore, as did my arm. Trivial things in the big picture of life faded to a single priority: become better at killing infected. How many more infected could I have taken down if I'd been faster? I shook my head, ridding myself of the useless, self-deprecating thought. The past couldn't be changed, and I was doing what I needed to do to fix the issue I'd identified.

Not that I'd find myself in a position of needing to rapid-fire at infected ever again. Well, not if we stayed here.

Retrieving the arrows, I looked up at the fey lining the wall. Now that Tenacity's wall was complete, Tolerance was swarming with fey. I thought again of Matt's request for volunteers as I turned to retrace my steps.

I paused at the sight of Thallirin standing in the shadows of a tree. My chest and throat grew tight with fear, and I forced myself to breathe calmly. This wasn't the first time I'd noticed him watching. Before today, I figured it was because I was just an oddity. I mean, all the fey looked at the humans. We were still new to them. Me, more so because of my love of my bow, a weapon they knew how to use, too. Now that I knew the real reason for Thallirin's attention, that familiar panic tried to pull me under as I met his unblinking gaze.

Mya's question about disliking him because of his appearance echoed in my head. His scars didn't make him ugly. They made him as intimidating as hell. There was never even a hint of waver in his hard gaze. Half the time, he looked pissed. The other half, cold and ready to kill. And that was who liked me? No thanks.

Putting the arrows in my quiver, I forced myself to head straight toward him. My approach didn't change his expression.

"I heard you have me in your sights as a future love interest once I turn eighteen," I said bluntly. "I'm not interested. It has nothing to do with my age or you, personally. I have no interest in being matched up with anyone. And I'd appreciate it very much if you started stalking someone else."

My hands were starting to sweat, and my voice had started to quaver. Damn it.

"You wish to be alone." The harsh rasp of his deep voice made me want to wince as it did every time he spoke.

"Yes. Please."

He stepped out of the shadows, into the weak, cloud-filtered sunlight.

"You wish for something you do not understand."

"Um, pretty sure I do. Just go away, Thallirin." I turned to do the same, but he caught my arm. The massive expanse of his hand fully wrapped around my bicep. Yet, for all his largeness and strength, he held me in place gently.

I'd been held in place gently before and had sworn I would never allow it again.

Turning, I looked into his cold eyes.

"Let go, or I'm going to start screaming."

His expression flickered, and he released me.

"Do you still look for companionship for dinner?" he asked.

"No. Uan is coming over. And it's for my mom, not me, just so we're clear. I meant what I said. I'm not interested in any man."

"You are still young."

My hand tightened on my bow as he turned and walked away.

CHAPTER THREE

MOM WAS NERVOUS, AND IT HAD NOTHING TO DO WITH THE DOG food stew we'd be serving for dinner.

"You look pretty," I said, standing back to look at her.

She tugged at the skirt of her dress. She didn't often expose her legs, hating how they looked with so little muscle to them.

"You want to wear pants?"

She shook her head.

"It's better if he sees what he's getting into."

"I don't think he'll know there's a difference," I said. "Yours will probably be the first set of non-fey legs he's seen. He'll think we all walk around on twigs."

She snorted.

"You're right. Put on that other dress."

I groaned, and she laughed. Knowing she was serious, I grabbed the other dress selection she'd somehow acquired and stripped out of my comfortable sweatshirt and jeans.

"You're getting too thin," she said, watching me. That was another rule in our house. There was no shame in nudity. There couldn't be.

"If you're telling me I'm thin just to stuff me with dog food, I'll pass." I started tugging on the dress. "But if you're going to offer pizza or ice cream, game on. I'm a skinny bitch who needs some carbs."

She was rolling her eyes at me the moment my head popped through the neckline. The dress fell into place, and she studied me critically.

"I think he'll be able to tell now," she said. "Thanks, Bren."

"Any time, Mom."

"Now, let's go see what the master chef has prepared for us this evening."

She led the way to the kitchen, where Zach had the table set with a large pot in the middle.

"Made a double-batch," he said.

"Um." My tone conveyed anything but excitement.

Mom swatted me just as someone knocked at the door.

"I'll get it," I said, already moving.

Uan smiled at me when I opened the door. He wore a button-up shirt that hugged his arms and chest so snugly, I knew he'd bust a seam before the night was over.

"Hey, Uan. Come in." I stepped aside and closed the door behind him.

His eyes swept the space until they landed on Mom. They stared at each other for a long moment.

"Mom, this is Uan. Uan, this is my mom, Nancy."

"I know," Uan said. He moved to Mom, towering over her. "You are a very beautiful woman, Nancy. I will like talking to you."

She smiled.

"Dinner's ready. Let's eat."

Any earlier annoyance I felt toward Uan faded during our drawn-out dinner. Mom enjoyed talking to him, and Uan couldn't take his eyes off of her.

"Would you like to go for a walk, Nancy?" Uan said when I took his bowl.

"I would love to, but my chair doesn't like snow."

"I know. I want to carry you."

I glanced over my shoulder and met Mom's questioning gaze with a shrug. She'd known what she was getting into. The fey were handsy if given a chance. Did she honestly think her legs would stop that?

"I would love to go for a walk. Let me just change."

"There is no need. I will wrap you in a blanket." He was already standing and grabbing a blanket from the back of the couch. I wondered just how long he'd been thinking about asking her.

In two blinks, Mom was swaddled and in his arms. She tried moving her arms and gave me an annoyed look.

"You okay, Mom?" I asked, giving her a chance to speak up.

"Er..."

"She will be fine," Uan said.

"Okay. Don't keep her out too long," I said, opening the door for Uan.

"Brenna, we're going to talk when I get home," she said as they passed.

I laughed.

"Have fun, you two."

When I closed the door, Zach was there, shaking his head at me.

"That wasn't nice."

"I gave her the opportunity to speak up, and she didn't. And, she doesn't like when we baby her. I was trying to set a good example for Uan."

"Do you think she'll buy that?"

I grinned.

"I'm going to go change then go out back and practice."

He was waiting for me by the door with his own quiver when I reemerged.

"Has Mom said anything more about you finding your own guy?" he asked, following me outside.

"Nope. She doesn't need to. It seems like the fey are playing their own dating game."

My brother, who took after my father with his light brown hair and grey eyes, gave me a sharp, protective look.

"What do you mean?"

"When I went out to find a fey to come over for dinner, the ones I talked to ran off because they didn't want to upset Thallirin."

"I don't blame them. That guy's scary."

I nudged him with my shoulder as we set up.

"It's because Thallirin likes me and they don't want to step on his toes, not because they're afraid of him."

"Ah."

"Yeah. Ah." I let loose my first arrow.

"You tell him to piss off?"

"I tried. But you know what it's like talking to the fey. They don't actually hear what you're saying and only understand what they want."

Zach nocked two arrows, a technique he'd been trying to improve with little accuracy. I stepped back, giving him room.

"I saw Matt Davis today," I said. "He's looking for volunteers to guard Tenacity's walls tomorrow so he can send more people out for supplies. Only human volunteers, though. Want in?"

"You know it."

"Good. We leave at dawn."

Mom yawned widely, and I grinned.

"Late night?" I asked, knowing it had been. Uan had returned her hours after they'd left. Mom's face had been flushed with cold, and her eyes a bit glazed.

"Mind your own business."

I only grinned wider and leaned my elbows on the table.

"You are my business. Did you spend the whole time making out, or were words actually exchanged between kisses?"

She scowled at me.

"We talked the whole time. Uan took me to the wall where I could shoot and be useful. He's a great listener and makes me feel—"

Her tired surliness faded into true sorrow.

"Talk, Mom," I said gently. "Don't shut us out."

"He makes me feel like a whole person. Like your dad did."

"Then, I approve," Zach said. "Of Uan and of your choice, Mom. Dad wouldn't want you to face any of this on your own. You know that."

She nodded, giving Zach a sad smile before turning to me.

"You have my support as well," I said. "You were happy last night. That's worth fighting for."

"Good. I'm glad you feel that way. I want you to stop by Cassie's on the way back and ask about birth control."

"And, I'm out," Zach said, quickly moving toward the door. "I'll see you at the wall."

"Chicken!" I called after him.

Mom set her hand over mine.

"Be careful today. Come back to me in one piece."

I stood and kissed her cheek.

"This is just guard duty, Mom. I stand on the wall here all the time. It's just a different wall. Besides, I'll be safe on the wall in daylight."

"That's what we thought last week."

I gripped her hand and nodded. Nothing was ever safe anymore. But, that didn't mean we should just stop trying to live.

After leaving the house, I jogged to catch up to Zach. We followed the sidewalks in the pre-dawn light, heading for the north section of the wall. There were almost a dozen humans already gathered there and even more fey.

Ryan, Mya's brother, noted our approach and waved us over to the human group.

"I'm glad to see you two here."

"Thanks," Zach said. "We're happy to help out."

"Let's hope we still feel that way when we're done today," Ryan said. "I heard things aren't going very well at Tenacity. Our reception may not be as welcome as we think."

"After the way they acted here, I'm not expecting much," I said.

There was a reason Mya and the fey created Tolerance instead of staying at Whiteman: the Whiteman survivors hated the fey. It was an insane prejudice, just because the fey were different, and one I couldn't understand. The fey weren't just nice. They were nice to the point that it would be easy to use them for self-gain. Which is what some of those people had tried doing.

Ryan grinned at me and nodded in agreement.

"If we stick together, we shouldn't run into any problems," he said.

"Brenna will not have any problems," a familiar voice said behind me. "She will remain here."

Even as my throat dropped to my stomach with dread, I pivoted to face Thallirin. This was just like two days ago when he told me to get in the house. I'd listened then, and because of it, he seemed to think he had some kind of control over me. He needed to be set straight.

He strode toward the group, each step accentuating the domineering confidence that had been a pain in my ass since the moment he first saw me. I'd already told him, in no uncertain terms, last night that I wasn't interested. Why wasn't that enough?

"Will I stay here?" I asked. "I don't remember making that decision for myself."

Thallirin's gaze flicked to me. Not a hint of what he was thinking or feeling showed in his expression. Well, that wasn't entirely true. He looked as deadly as ever.

"It is not safe outside the walls. You take an unnecessary risk leaving."

"Since the earthquakes, everything is a risk. That doesn't mean I should sit in a house and stop living."

"You will not sit in a house. You will guard the walls and live here."

Unable to believe what I was hearing, I glanced back at Ryan. He raised his hands, a clear sign he wasn't going to get involved.

"Do you see any other females in this group, Brenna?" Thallirin asked, reclaiming my attention. "There are no females because no male would allow that risk."

"I heard that you learn words the moment you hear them," I said. "Here's a word for you. Chauvinist asshole."

"That was two words," one of the fey bystanders said.

"Your anger due to the facts that we are stronger, faster,

more agile, and resilient is misplaced. I do not think less of you for your weaknesses. I only seek to protect you because of them," Thallirin said.

"He doesn't get it," Zach said.

"Obviously," I said. I shook my head and turned away from Thallirin. "Whatever. I'm going."

"No one will take you," Thallirin said.

Ignoring him, I looked at Ryan.

"I can run a six-minute mile. I'll meet you there."

A growl rose behind me, and I felt a rush of cold fear. However, I knew better than to freeze because of what I felt. Turning, I glared at Thallirin.

"Animals growl, not intelligent people capable of communication."

"I am communicating, and you are choosing not to listen. It is dangerous for females outside the wall. You will remain here."

"Communicating means that both parties speak and listen. It doesn't mean giving orders and expecting the other party to obey. You're not my parent. Stop trying to tell me what to do."

He took a menacing step toward me.

"Sorry I'm late!"

Thallirin paused at the sound of the female voice. We all looked at Angel jogging our way. Although I'd heard the news that she was about six months pregnant, she didn't look it. But, it was hard to tell with all the layers she wore.

With a smile on her lips, she stopped beside Thallirin and looked at me.

"Hey, Brenna."

"Hi. I'm glad you're here. It'll be nice to have some female company."

I looked pointedly at Thallirin.

"I'm so relieved. When I heard you might be going to Tenacity, I didn't think teaching a pregnant lady archery would be as adventurous."

"What?"

She glanced at Thallirin.

"He didn't tell you?"

"Oh, he told me plenty, but nothing about archery lessons. Let me guess. This is an excuse to keep me safely inside the walls where Thallirin can continue to stare at me like a creepy pedophile stalker?"

His face darkened, and I knew I'd struck a low blow because all fey were super sensitive about this underage thing. However, I couldn't bring myself to care. The fey were the ones hung up on my age, not me.

"I think we better go," Ryan said. "Maybe next time, Brenna."

"I'm going," I said firmly. "I'll be home by dark, Angel. If you want to stop by my house, I'd be happy to teach you then. Although, I'm sure any of the fey would be able to teach you just as well."

I didn't miss the way she caught Thallirin's arm as I turned to go. Her soft words burrowed into my head as I followed the group to the wall.

"You're not protecting her; you're alienating her. If you

want to keep her safe, then you go with her. No female wants to be told what to do. She needs to be able to make her own choices."

Shaking my head, I stuck next to Zach as we climbed over the wall. On the other side, each fey paired up with a human.

"What's your carry-style, Zach?" I asked. "Princess, wild game, or backpack?"

He made a face at me.

"Why do you have to ruin it?"

I chuckled and walked up to a fey.

"I'm Brenna. Thanks for taking us."

He glanced at someone behind me.

"You're welcome, Brenna. Would you like Thallirin to carry you?"

"No, I would not. Thank you for thinking to ask instead of assuming. Are you okay with carrying me? Or are you too afraid of hurting Thallirin's feelings?"

"His feelings will not be hurt if I carry you. He knows I understand you belong to him."

"I think I'll go princess-style," Zach said. "How about you, Brenna?"

My brother's attempt at distracting me from my anger did more than that. It helped put things into perspective. I didn't need to address my very large problem right then or solve it alone. I had Zach and Mom. Using a wheelchair had only increased her mama-bear tendencies. Thallirin wouldn't know what hit him.

"Carry me however works best for you," I said to the fey watching me.

He grunted and picked me up.

As soon as he started running, I turned my face into his chest. Over his shoulder, I saw Thallirin. He ran directly behind us. Our gazes locked, and the undeniable urge to growl at him had me closing my eyes.

Several minutes later, the fey landed with a soft thump on the other side of Tenacity's wall. He immediately released me and stepped away.

Ignoring him, I looked around at the expansive neighborhood. Like Tolerance, the wall extended farther than I could see. House after house lined the roads inside the wall. The sidewalks were snow-free, and narrow golf cart tracks marked the dusted road.

A large group of people was already gathered just inside the wall. Before I could wonder why, Matt stepped forward. He shook Ryan's hand then addressed the rest of us.

"Welcome to Tenacity. We're glad you could make it." He turned to his people. "The volunteers from Tolerance will fill some of the day shifts on the wall so more people can go on today's supply run."

Matt began calling out names for wall assignments, and a few people grumbled when they stepped forward. He looked at the remaining people.

"Anyone can go on the supply run. Remember, the fey are not on this run to gather for Tenacity. However, they'll help keep you safe while they gather for Tolerance. You keep seventy percent of what you bring back; thirty percent goes to the community for redistribution.

"A party is also going out to Whiteman Airbase to secure a plane to look for more survivors and new areas safe for supply runs. So don't let the sound of something in the air distract you from what you're doing. Stay safe. Stay alive. Come home."

With that, the humans Matt assigned to the wall took their positions, and a trickle of people started climbing over the wall on the waiting ladders. But not as many as I expected, given the number gathered. I couldn't tell if Matt was disappointed more weren't going, though. Instead of focusing on the people staying, he watched the people leaving with the fey.

While the humans used the ladder, the fey neatly scaled the wall made of vehicles and other big machinery. It always amazed me how the fey could clear the barrier in seconds, their feet finding footing while their hands remained free.

The running engines outside the wall sounded so loud and out of place in the otherwise quiet neighborhood. I itched to get up there to see if they drew any infected. I hadn't heard a single call on the way here, and that wasn't normal.

"We have marks on the wall," Matt said, drawing my attention. "Climb up the ladder and pick a section to patrol. Someone will come to relieve you every two hours for a fifteen-minute break."

I started for a ladder but noticed Thallirin still standing inside the wall. I wished he would have left with the others.

"Want me to stay close?" Zach asked.

I loved my brother for his protectiveness, but he knew as well as I did that there wouldn't be much he could do about Thallirin.

"No. I'm fine. Go where you're needed. Not that I think we'll see much. The infected seem just as quiet here as they do back home."

"For now," Zach said. "Enjoy it while it lasts."

He climbed up the ladder, his bow over his shoulder. I shouldered mine and did the same. It was such a part of me that I didn't even notice I had it. It felt just as normal as a hat in winter.

"Thallirin," Matt said. "I can't stop you from going up there, but you do know that Mya doesn't want you to help guard the wall, right?"

"I am not guarding your wall. I'm guarding Brenna."

I rolled my eyes as I reached the top and walked to an unmanned section much farther away. Even though I didn't hear Thallirin, I knew he followed me.

"Don't you have anything better to do?" I asked when I took my position and saw him several yards from me, staring out at the trees.

"No."

"I find your constant attention smothering and would like it if you left. I've guarded walls before, without you standing ten feet away, and can manage again."

"But when you needed me, I was close enough to protect you."

I knew he meant the day the infected breached the walls. If

not for Thallirin, I wouldn't be alive, and I was big enough to acknowledge it.

"Yes, you saved me. And I've saved countless other people. That doesn't give me the right to force my unwelcome presence on them or try to tell them how to live their lives."

He grunted and crossed his arms, not looking at me but watching the trees.

This was going to be a long day.

"YOU SHOULD EAT SOMETHING," Thallirin said when my stomach growled yet again. It wasn't delivered in a nice, considerate way but in an angry, impatient tone he'd been using on me every time he spoke.

"I will when I get home. You should go away."

"I will when we get home."

I breathed through my nose. He'd been like that all day, annoyingly present and unbothered no matter what I said. I wasn't trying to be rude, just like I was sure he wasn't trying to be a pain in my ass. Why couldn't he understand not all human women wanted a man in their lives? I'd made my opinion pretty clear when I told him I wanted to shoot every arrow in my quiver at him. The ass had opened his arms and told me he would hold still...as if I needed his cooperation.

"I still want to shoot you."

"I know."

The distant sound of engines drew my attention to the

road. Three trucks drove down the center of the unplowed lane, escorted by fey on all sides.

"Are any missing?" I asked, knowing Thallirin's sight was far better than mine.

"No."

I believed him, but that didn't stop me from adding, "Are you sure? Maybe you should go check."

He grunted and remained where he was, ten feet away. That was the maximum amount of distance he'd maintained all day even when I was given a break to go to the bathroom, which is why I threatened to shoot him.

The trucks rumbled to a stop in front of the wall. The back of one of the trucks opened, and humans jumped out, moving toward the other two trucks to help the fey unload the supplies. Boxes and totes filled with clothing, blankets, and food were carried over the wall and taken to a large storage shed. The bay door stood open, and I could see long tables set up inside.

Matt watched over the proceedings, directing where things should go.

"You and your grey monkey can go," a man said as he climbed up to join us on the wall.

I put my foot on the ladder and shoved it off balance. The man gave a startled cry and clutched the rung as he started tipping sideways. Thallirin caught the end of the metal rail and righted the equipment, his cold gaze landing on me.

"Brenna, no tipping ladders."

CHAPTER FOUR

I LOOKED AWAY FROM THALLIRIN TO SEE THE MAN CRINGE AT THE sound of Thallirin's deep, angry tone.

"Did you hear him?" I asked the man. "Even after you insulted him, he's sticking up for you. Learn some respect or next time, it's an arrow, not a ladder shove. Got it?"

The man glared at me, but remained mute as he climbed the wall.

"And for the record, he isn't *my* anything."

I climbed down without fear of retaliation because Thallirin remained on the wall until my feet touched the ground. How could that fey be so smart about some things and so annoyingly stupid about others?

"What was up with the ladder drama?" Zach asked, jogging up to me.

"Darwinism."

Zach laughed.

"Looks like you survived your day well enough. Was your section of the wall as quiet as mine?"

"Not a single infected. Kind of weird, given the noise of the trucks."

"Take it as the blessing it is," Ryan said, joining us. "Come take a look at how Tenacity does things."

We followed him to the shed and watched as all of the scavenged items were laid out on the tables. Meats were separated from veggies, and all of the other home goods were stacked on shelves. The food was counted then thirty percent of the total was removed to the community pile. What was left was divided among the people who had gone on the supply run. By the time it was divided, each person was walking away with maybe two days' worth of food for a family of four.

Those gathered outside the building started shouting offers.

"I'll take your next guard duty for that frozen roast."

"I'll double that."

More than half the people ignored the trading going on and rushed to form a line in front of the community supplies. Volunteers took down house numbers and what was being given, which wasn't much.

"We should aim for Harrisonville tomorrow," Ryan said. "It hasn't been picked over like Warrensburg."

"I agree. But there aren't many who will be willing to go that far, and those who do go will be in danger here, once they get their share," Matt said.

"Danger?" I asked.

"Despite the rule that people will get kicked out for stealing, someone will try. And, someone will be hurt," Matt said.

"I'll talk to Mya," Ryan said.

Matt shook his head.

"There is no easy solution to this. The people here need to change. They need to figure out how to put their fears and biases aside. Until they do, the amplified frustration with those of us who don't agree with their fears and biases will only make them more volatile."

"Everyone is entitled to an opinion, but no one should ever disagree with it," I said.

"Hypocrisy at its finest," Zach said in agreement.

"Tenacity could really use more level-headed thinkers," Matt said. "Your family is welcome here any time. There's plenty of room."

"I'll let my mom know you offered," I said even though I already knew that living in Tenacity would be a hard pass for my family. We'd lived with these assholes for over a week. It had been enough to realize we never wanted to do it again. Yet, what I'd said to Mya the day before hadn't been a lie. If she or the fey thought I was there for the fey dating game, I'd take Matt up on his offer.

"Thanks. If you're willing to come back tomorrow, we could use the help again. It'll take a while for us to regain the supplies we lost."

"I'll be back tomorrow," Ryan said. "It's been quiet enough for a few days that I should be able to convince Drav to send a bigger group of fey for Harrisonville, too. Maybe that'll help convince more of your people to tag along."

Matt agreed, and we climbed over the wall to join the waiting fey. The supplies they'd gathered for Tolerance were already divided into boxes, which the fey carried. Some of the boxes were filled with random things like movies and books. Others had kitchen gadgets and clothes. Very few had food.

As soon as Ryan climbed onto one of the fey's backs, they started to leave in small groups. I looked around for someone to carry me, pretending not to notice my very available shadow. The fey who'd brought me had a box of goods in his arms. Zach, standing by his fey, shook his head and waited to see what I'd do. I knew that no matter what I decided, Zach would have my back.

"Tell Mom I'll be home a little late. It looks like I'm walking."

"You cannot walk home," Thallirin said behind me. "It will be dark soon."

I turned and crossed my arms to glare up at him.

"The sooner you understand I'm not an ignorant child you can manipulate into getting your way, the better. I am not yours in any regard. I've asked you nicely, and then not nicely, to leave me alone. I'm not interested in some fey happily-ever-after. Not now. Not after I turn eighteen. Not ever. I don't know how much plainer I can say it."

For a moment, he said nothing. Just stood there looking at me. His cold gaze lingered on my face, and something in his expression shifted.

"Neither do I," he said finally. "Walk. I will follow and keep you safe."

I started jogging and waved to Zach as his fey passed. The crunch of my footsteps kept me company, soothing some of my irritation. Although I knew the danger of being out after dark, I didn't regret my decision. I'd picked life above all else once before, and although I kept telling myself I'd do it again, I wondered if I really could. To save Zach? Yes. My mom? Absolutely. But myself? I wasn't sure.

My thoughts didn't distract me from my surroundings. As I moved, I scanned every tree and every elongating shadow. My bow rested on my shoulder, but I could have an arrow nocked in seconds. However, nothing moved through the woods other than me and Thallirin. It took several minutes to clear the trees and follow the trail through the fields.

Neither of us spoke, and the light began to fade before long. As the silence grew, a seed of hope sprouted that maybe Thallirin had finally gotten the message.

The lights from Tolerance already shined into the dark sky by the time we reached the wall. One of the fey patrolling the top lowered a ladder for me. I nodded my thanks and climbed over, relieved I'd arrived safely.

Instead of going straight home, I remembered Mom's request and veered off toward Cassie's house. When I glanced over my shoulder, wondering if Thallirin was going to try to follow me, I saw I was alone. I hoped that meant I'd finally gotten through to him just as much as I hoped he'd recover from the letdown and find another girl to safety-stalk.

I knocked on Cassie's door and only waited a moment before her partner, Kerr, opened it.

"Hi, Kerr. Could I speak to Cassie, please?"

He stepped aside and motioned me in. The scent of roast made my mouth water. I wished we had real meat to eat, but I knew the cost of eating well. I glanced at Kerr, wondering if Cassie regretted her choice. Probably not. A lot of the women with fey seemed pretty happy.

Kerr led me to the kitchen where Cassie and her children were already eating.

"I'm sorry to interrupt dinner, but my mom wanted me to stop by. She was wondering if you had any birth control."

Cassie swallowed her mouthful of food and stood up, leading me away from the kids and back to the front door. Kerr followed us, stopping in the doorway to the kitchen so he could watch the children and us.

"I'm so sorry," she said quietly. "You're not the first one to come looking for birth control since the news. Let your mom know that the fey are looking for it when they go out for supplies. Nothing came back today, though."

Kerr shifted his weight ever so slightly when she said that. I glanced at him, his unwavering gaze holding mine. Given their love of children and desire for families, I doubted any birth control would ever come back with the fey.

"That's okay," I said, looking at Cassie. "I'll let my mom know."

I let myself out and hurried home. Warm air enveloped me as soon as I stepped inside. Instead of the welcoming scent of roast, I smelled soup and dog food again. I tried not to let it bother me.

“Come in here,” Mom called from the kitchen. “There's hot food waiting for you and a mom who's ready for conversation.”

“It's a good thing I'm hungry and ready to talk,” I called back, removing my layers.

When I walked into the kitchen, I saw Uan sitting at the table with Mom and Zach. Mom was smiling, but I could see the worry in her eyes.

“Everything went really well today,” I said, taking my seat. “I never thought I would see another place like this, but Tenacity is almost a replica. A little bit bigger. And if I'm not mistaken, I saw a school.”

“I heard they took over Leeton,” Mom said. “That’s a long way from here.”

She meant it was a long way for me to hoof on my own, and she was right.

“I’m pretty sure that’s strategic. Human foot traffic is discouraged, which means less risk of attracting unwanted attention for places that should be safe.”

She gave me a long look, reading into what I was saying.

“The place might look like this,” Zach said, “but the people are nowhere near as friendly.”

“So, no different than what they were when they were here,” Mom said.

“Not really,” I agreed before helping myself to my first spoonful of dog food soup.

I'd barely eaten half a bowl, joining in on the easy table banter, when someone knocked on the door.

"Let me get it," I said, already rising.

Zach looked at me.

"Are you sure?"

"Absolutely."

If Uan caught on to the undercurrent of our conversation, he gave no indication. I left the table and returned Eden's sheepish smile when I answered the door.

"Am I interrupting dinner?" she asked.

"Yeah. It's not a big deal, though. What's up?"

"I was hoping I could talk to you for a minute."

The way she stayed outside, even though I had the door open, let me know she wanted a private conversation. So, I grabbed my jacket and stepped outside with her.

"Thallirin came over," she said without preamble. "He wanted to talk to Ghua about how to deal with a stubborn child."

I groaned. I'd been so sure I'd gotten through to him.

"He thinks I'm just being stubborn?"

"What's funnier is that Thallirin thinks that Ghua is an expert on you." We walked around the house to the backyard. "I know it's none of my business, but I really want to help you. I know what you've been through. I also know that, although the fey are basically harmless, they're also very persistent. The combination can be extremely frustrating."

"You've got that right."

"Thallirin said you called him a pedophile. He's freaking out, thinking there's something wrong with him. I'm not saying that so you feel bad. I'm just letting you know so that you understand where he's coming from. Maybe it will help get through to him." She shrugged slightly and sighed. "I think you're going to need to be upfront with him about what happened at the bunker."

My chest tightened by slow degrees.

"What happened there has nothing to do with my refusal."

"It did for me," she said. "I left that place, swearing I wanted to spend the rest of my life by myself. That I didn't need anyone. When Ghua showed up, I was terrified. Not just because he was freakishly different or because he was ripping heads off of infected, but because he was extremely interested in me. And he made that interest very clear. You should have seen his face when I lied and said I was twelve. Complete devastation. They respect the no females under eighteen rule. Thallirin will leave you alone because of that. But, it won't stop him from caring about you or wanting you. You need to help him understand why you will never want him in return."

I looked up at the stars.

"What happened is in the past. I'm over it. And it has nothing to do with what's happening now."

"Sugar, that's not something you just get over."

"In this world, you do. There's no time for self-pity or doubt. That's the quickest way to die, and I'm not done living yet."

Eden remained quiet next to me for several long moments.

"I'm sorry we didn't get there sooner."

I turned to look at her.

"Don't carry the guilt for someone else's actions. Any decision that was made that might have delayed your arrival doesn't change who's responsible for what happened to me. It was the people at the bunker. It was Van."

I hated that I'd said his name. He didn't deserve any acknowledgment from me. Yet, I refused to let Eden carry the burden for what happened.

"And don't worry about Thallirin's fascination with me. Like you said, the fey are basically harmless to us. Just annoying. I'll manage."

She nodded and left.

When I went back to the house, I found Uan saying his goodbyes.

"I must guard the wall tonight. I will return in the morning, though."

He bent down and kissed Mom thoroughly before leaving. She stared after him, her eyes glazed, as I took my seat. Zach grinned as he watched her. It didn't take her too long to snap out of it.

"Spill it," she said, no-nonsense Mom taking over. "What really happened today?"

"I don't want to talk about it," I said.

"But I do."

Slouching in my chair a little, I gave in.

"The fey are insistent that Thallirin and I are going to get married and have babies and live happily ever after. They're not getting it through their thick heads that I have no interest in him."

"I don't understand what that has to do with you being late. Did he force you to stay with him?"

"No, Mom. Nothing like that. All the other fey refused to carry me, trying to play matchmaker and forcing me to deal with Thallirin. I chose my own two feet instead of his loving arms."

Her expression shifted ever so slightly. Our family didn't do pity. At least, it was our rule not to. But I could see it in Mom's eyes. She wanted to pity me for whatever happened in the bunker. I never really talked about it, and it was the one subject she hadn't forced. She probably hadn't needed to. Zach had been there, too.

"I understand you need to take a stance," she said, "but don't do it at the expense of your safety."

"I didn't. There hasn't been anything moving outside the wall in days. And we would have known if there had been any hounds nearby."

"Okay. I've said my piece. You know my feelings on the subject. If Thallirin does anything you don't want him to do—"

"I know. You and Zach both have my back."

She nodded.

"Now, did you stop at Cassie's?"

"Yeah, she says there's been a mad rush on birth control since the news. She doesn't have any. Supposedly the fey are out looking for more, but with their baby obsession, I wouldn't count on it. But, there's a supply run tomorrow that I'm willing to join."

"I'll go, too," Zach said. "Just don't look me in the eye when I hand you your birth control."

He started to get up, but Mom grabbed his arm and drummed the fingers of her other hand on the table as she gave Zach "the look." Zach made a pained face in return and sat again. She released him.

"As much as I want to run away from whatever conversation is about to go down, I'm staying," he said sullenly.

"I like Uan," she said. "And he seems to like me just fine in return."

"We couldn't tell," Zach said dryly.

"When I tell him I'm ready, he's going to want to live here with us."

Despite her stern tone, there was doubt and worry in her eyes. Not about her decision but about us. I reached out and took her hand.

"We're okay with that, Mom. We're old enough to understand what's happening. We know you're not replacing Dad. And it's okay if you have feelings for Uan. It won't ever change how much we love you."

She closed her eyes for a moment and squeezed my hand in return.

"I have the best kids in the world," she said softly.

"Given the current population, that's probably true," Zach said.

Mom laughed and smacked his arm.

ZACH and I walked toward the wall. Just like the day before, a group of fey waited along with a small group of humans. Ryan waved when he saw us.

"Wasn't sure you'd be back after yesterday," he said.

"What do you mean?" Zach asked.

Ryan's gaze shifted to my right, and I followed it to where he was looking. Thallirin watched us from his solitary position near the wall.

"There's a lot in life that will try to stand in my way and stop me from accomplishing what I want," I said. "That doesn't mean I should just give up before I even try."

Ryan smiled slightly. I noticed how cute he was, and it sent a jolt of panic through me.

Before a tell-tale flush could give me away, I glanced at the fey gathered.

"Am I going to have to take the slow way again today?" I asked.

"I will carry you," a fey said, stepping forward, "but not because I am interested in you."

"Thanks for clarifying," I said dryly.

With little drama, we made it to Tenacity before the sun was fully up. Like the day before, Matt waited in the street along with a large crowd. Everyone looked a lot less happy than the day before.

"I'm sorry you came all the way out here," he said. "There are only a handful of people interested in going to Harrisonville, which means I have more help on the wall than I need."

"It's okay. I actually want to go on the supply run," I said.

"Are you sure they're going to let you?" Matt asked with a glance at the fey behind us.

"I'm sure they're unprepared for the fallout from a temper tantrum thrown by someone my age," I said, embracing the stubborn child role in which Thallirin had cast me.

"Give 'em hell and keep 'em in line," Matt said softly.

"All right," Ryan said. "I guess we'll be going. Thirty percent to use your trucks seem fair to you?"

"More than fair."

"We'll fill the tanks up while we're out there, too."

When we went to the ladders, Thallirin was there, his arms crossed.

"You know it's not safe," he said in his typical low, stoic voice.

"Yep, and you already know I'm going to go anyway because nothing is safe about this world. Besides, I'm tired of eating dog food."

"Tell me what you want, and I'll get it for you."

"No. I'll get it myself because I'm strong, smart, and just as able to gather supplies as Ryan or Zach. My vagina isn't a disability. It's a body part."

His face darkened.

"What? That word bothers you?"

"Children shouldn't—"

"Just stop already. I'll be eighteen in a few weeks, if that. What excuse are you going to use to keep me a prisoner then?"

"Your safety isn't an excuse."

"It is. Infected got inside the wall. I could have been dead just as easily inside Tolerance as I could outside of its wall. You let nothing near me before. Why doubt your abilities now?"

I knew I had him, and by the way he blinked at me, he knew it, too.

"You will stay where I can see you."

"Since you stalk me everywhere I go, even to the bathroom, I doubt there's anywhere you wouldn't see me."

He grunted and motioned to the ladder.

Triumphant, I grinned at him and grasped the first rung toward freedom and understanding. His hands closed over the rungs above mine, and he leaned in close.

"This is not a victory."

CHAPTER FIVE

SAFELY TUCKED INTO A TRUCK WITH GARRETT AT THE WHEEL, I watched the road ahead as we approached Harrisonville's city limits. The drive had taken well over an hour. The first half had gone smoothly enough because the fey had cleared that part of the road the day before. The second half had slowed us down a bit while they removed a few cars here and there. The number of abandoned vehicles that clogged the way had increased the closer we drew to the city. All of what they'd cleared was nothing compared to the concentration of vehicles ahead, though.

Garrett pulled the truck to the side of the road and cut the engine.

"This is as far as the trucks go," he said. "We'll go on foot to clear out a few neighborhoods and get a feel for the infected population."

I looked at the buildings in the distance. As my first time

outside of Tolerance in weeks, scavenging those homes for supplies felt intimidating. Yet, I knew what to expect. A random infected lingering where they once lived. A few groups wandering the streets. A trap or two to avoid. All of that would have been daunting when it had been just my family. However, in a group this size, with this many fey, we'd be fine.

"Ready?" Garrett asked.

"Yep."

The door creaked as I pushed it open and jumped lightly to the ground. The fey were milling about, waiting for the humans to congregate.

"Okay," Ryan said, addressing the group. "Most of us know this drill. Humans stay with the fey at all times. Same room. Close proximity. Stay quiet. Stay alert. The first pass is to clear infected. The second is for supplies. Don't assume a house is clear. Ever. Any questions?"

Zach and I shook our heads.

"Let's go."

I started to follow, and a hand closed over my shoulder. Rolling my eyes, I looked back at Thallirin.

"Are we going to do this every step of the way? There's a roast in a working freezer out there somewhere with my name on it."

A momentary frown flickered over his expression.

"A group always guards the trucks."

"That's bullshit. I came for supplies, not guard duty."

"We split everything," Ryan said, and I saw he wasn't the only one watching the Thallirin-Brenna spectacle. "And he is right. We usually leave three or four behind to guard the trucks so we don't come back to a dead engine or a truck full of infected."

I was determined, maybe a little stubborn, but not stupid. When Dad had been alive, we would leave Mom to guard the vehicle while we went in for supplies. It made sense to leave the person with the most limitations behind. Mom, despite all of her independence, just couldn't make it into some houses because of her chair. Likewise, although I could shoot as accurately as most of the fey, I couldn't run as fast or carry as much. And, apparently, a vagina really was a disability.

Barely refraining from rolling my eyes, I conceded.

"Fine."

Zach gave me a questioning look.

"Go. You know what to look for. Just make sure someone's watching your back."

"I'll keep an eye on him," Ryan said.

"You better."

He nodded, and Zach and the others left in the arms of the fey. I wondered how Zach really felt about all the rides he was getting. I needed to ask him if he minded all the manhandling.

"You'll have a better view from the roof," Thallirin said. "It will hold your weight."

With an audibly aggrieved sigh, I scrambled up to the roof and used my scarf to secure my hood to my head. The wind battered at me as I carefully watched our surroundings. With the trees set further back from the road on both sides, I had a clear view of any immediate danger. Not that there was any.

The fields and trees here remained just as quiet as they had back home.

I felt myself getting cold despite my layers. When I guarded the wall, I moved. A lot. On the narrow platform of the truck's roof, there wasn't room to take more than a step or two.

"We need to guard the truck, he says," I mumbled under my breath. "More like uselessly freeze my ass off." I bounced lightly in place and blew on my hands.

"If you're cold, sit inside the truck," Thallirin said.

"Your common sense is useless on me. I'm just a child, remember?"

A grunt came from the other side of the truck, and I turned to glare at the other fey.

"You have some sage wisdom to add to this conversation?"

The fey shook his head and continued his walk along the trucks.

I stubbornly remained on the roof. I honestly didn't mind guard duty so long as Zach and I got a fair share of the supplies. And, despite Zach's teen boy weirdness about Mom wanting birth control, I knew that he would come through for her if there was any to be found. What I minded was being managed.

The bracing wind didn't let up for a second the entire time the group was gone. When a few of the fey started returning with supplies and left again with stacks of empty totes, I called it good and climbed into the truck and locked the doors.

Thallirin and the other fey left me alone for a while. The

amount of time I stared at the keys in the ignition bordered on insane. Did I really care if letting the truck idle would draw infected? They wouldn't be my problem. They would be Thallirin's; and in my state of glacial rage, I thought he'd earned himself a few well-placed bites for putting me in this position in the first place.

However, no matter how much the idea of warm hands and feet tempted me, I didn't reach for the keys. I pulled my arms from my sleeves and stuck them under my armpits while drawing my knees to my chest.

Thallirin knocked on my window, interrupting my daydream of sipping warm, dog food-free, soup.

"Are you hungry?" he asked through the glass.

"No. I'm cold because you made me stay here instead of letting me run for my life in the streets of Hasenpfeffer or wherever the fuck we are. Go away so I can succumb to hypothermia quietly."

I stuck my tongue out at him like the child he believed me to be then ducked further into my hoodie.

"Open the door, or I will break the window." He said it so annoyingly calmly that I had no doubt he would do it to get to me.

"I can't. My hands are in my armpits. And if you break the window, glass is going to come flying in here and cut me. That's not a very good way to show you care. Plus, no windows will make me even colder. If you'd told me I would have been standing still outside for hours, I would have dressed differently. More layers. Instead, I dressed as if I was going to move."

I pushed back the hood to scowl at him.

"You do realize I survived this shit storm before you showed up. I'm not some helpless female who just lucked out. I fought for my life. I went into houses, killed infected with a knife, and took supplies, just like they're doing in town now. How else do you think I ate?"

"You no longer need to fight. I will fight for you."

Angry, I shoved my hand back through the sleeve and slapped my palm on the window, right over his face. He didn't even flinch.

"You're frustrating the hell out of me. Please go away before I break the window myself."

He looked at my hand and lifted his own to cover mine through the glass. That I could immediately feel his heat, surprised me. As did the way he slowly curled his hand into a fist, then left me to shiver in silence.

Miserable didn't describe how I felt when I finally heard a voice call out. Like a turtle emerging from her shell, I peeked out of my jacket and saw the majority of the group jogging our way. The fey carried laden totes, and the humans carried whatever they could. Thallirin stepped up to relieve Garrett of his burden. Garrett nodded his thanks and made a beeline for the truck.

"Your lips are blue," he said when he climbed into his seat and shut the door.

"And my ass is thoroughly chapped."

He chuckled and started the engine.

"If it helps, we cleared at least four blocks of houses and found a few roasts that still look good."

"It helps a little," I said with exaggerated sullenness.

"Any trouble other than Thallirin while we were gone?"

"No." I stuck my hands in front of the heater vent, hoping for hot air, and looked in the mirror to see everyone loading up the supplies. "Why is our truck the only one running? Aren't they worried the noise will draw attention?"

"It shouldn't be a problem with all of the fey out there and us safely in here."

"You didn't answer my first question."

"Thallirin asked me to. He's worried you got too cold."

I groaned and thumped my head against the headrest.

"Not a Thallirin fan?" Garrett asked.

"Not an anyone-with-a-penis fan, honestly."

"Ah."

"No offense."

"None taken. I'm guessing you've tried telling Thallirin that?"

"I have. The fey hear what they want."

"You might want to try talking to Angel. She seems to have no problem speaking their language."

"I'll keep that in mind," I said, thinking back to how Angel had gotten through to Thallirin the first time he'd tried stopping me from leaving Tolerance.

After everything was loaded, we started home.

"What was it like in town?" I asked. "As quiet as everywhere else?"

"No. There were a fair number of infected, but none of the recently-turned, slow ones."

"Not sure if that's a good or bad thing."

"My thoughts exactly. I hope that doesn't mean we're all that's left of humanity."

"Me too." I kicked off my boots and put my toes directly over the vents. "Tomorrow, I'm putting hand warmers in my boots."

"You're coming back?"

"Yep. I'm grateful for the supplies that are delivered to our door every few days, but I want something more than dog food and chicken noodle soup. I want cereal again. Pancakes. Real meat. I'd kill for a piece of bacon."

"You sound like Angel. All she has to do is say she's hungry for something, and Shax manages to find it for her. You should leave a note for your admirer. He'll probably get you what you want."

I frowned at Garrett.

"What are you talking about?"

He glanced at me before watching the road ahead once more.

"Uh, I don't get supply deliveries. If I need something, I go for a supply run or check the food shed. That's where the fey put any extras. I usually trade whatever I have for whatever I want."

I stared at the road ahead and tried to ignore the sinking

feeling in my middle. When we'd arrived at Tolerance weeks ago, Molev had taken us to our new home and promised we would be protected and fed. There'd been food in the house already, and before we'd gotten too low, a supply box had appeared on the step. No one had told us about a damn food shed or that there weren't deliveries going out to all the houses. I'd never thought to ask. That there was a love-smitten fey responsible for all the food we'd been getting made me want to swear.

Glancing out the window, I looked at the back of Thallirin's head. His black hair was longer than most of the other fey but was decorated with the same thin braids at the sides. The first time I'd seen him hadn't been long after we'd arrived in Tolerance. A few days, maybe. How had I not realized before this? All the watching me. The food choices in the box. The timing of the deliveries.

"This has got to stop."

"What?" Garrett asked.

"Nothing. Never mind."

Thallirin glanced back then and met my gaze. I turned away and closed my eyes, already knowing what Thallirin wanted in exchange for the food he'd been giving us. He wouldn't get it. Ever.

For the rest of the ride, I seethed and plotted. When the truck finally stopped in front of Tenacity's wall, I was warm once more and ready to face off with Thallirin. He wasn't at my door waiting for me, though.

Jumping to the ground in relief, I walked around to the

back of the supply truck where Ryan directed the division of the supplies. It was the first time I really got a look at anyone who'd gone into town. Most of the fey were covered in blood and gore, and I knew Garrett's assessment of the infected presence had been downplayed.

Spotting Zach, I jogged over to him. Unlike many of the others, he was spotless.

"You okay?" I asked.

"Yeah. It was crazy in town but worth it. Look at these supplies."

I did. The totes weren't filled with random stuff like the day before but chocked full of all forms of food. There had to be close to two hundred totes on the ground when everything was unloaded

"Take sixty totes over the wall for Tenacity," Ryan said. "We'll divide the rest when we get home."

Sixty seemed like a lot, but given the number of people Matt was trying to feed, I knew it wouldn't last long. After the fey delivered the supplies, they started leaving, some with as many as three totes stacked in their arms.

"Zach, hold this," a fey said, handing my brother a tote. As soon as Zach had it, the fey picked him up.

"Give a guy some warning," Zach grouched. "The tote's sitting on my nuts."

Several of the fey around me made pained sounds.

"Sorry," the fey said as Zach shifted the weight and looked at me.

"You getting a ride?" he asked.

"I will carry your sister," Thallirin said from behind me.

I glanced at him.

"I do not have any infected blood on me. It's safe."

Facing Zach, I lifted a shoulder.

"No, no ride for me again."

"I can stay with you," Zach said. We both knew that Mom wasn't going to be happy with my choice.

"Nah, go with Ryan and watch how the supplies are divided. You can take our portion home so Mom can start dinner."

He nodded, and they took off. I didn't wait for the rest of the fey to leave but started out. Thallirin followed me in silence. Fey passed us with supplies, running at impressive speeds toward home. I watched the last of them with a scowl. They hadn't been carrying a damn thing and had looked clean enough to me.

Like the day before, the journey was long and quiet. The wind wasn't as bad as it had been at the top of the truck, though, and with a steady pace, I stayed warm enough. It was good cardio, too.

Before we reached the end of the third field, I spotted a shape running toward us. I lifted my bow off my shoulder and reached for an arrow.

Thallirin's very warm hand closed over mine.

"It's Drav," he said before releasing me.

Settling the bow once more, I watched Drav approach. His frown was more pronounced than usual.

“I will carry you,” he said, barely coming to a stop before scooping me up.

My weight landed wrong on my bow, which he’d picked up with me, and I heard the wood crack. Before I could react, he grabbed the bow out from under me, tossed it aside, and started running.

I didn’t think; I reacted. My elbow smashed into his windpipe with enough force that his hold loosened. As he wheezed for breath, I struggled free and tumbled to the ground with an oof. Not wasting time, I scrambled back to my bow and fell to my knees in the snow.

The shaft looked undamaged at first glance, but I knew better. I’d heard the crack and had felt the wood give underneath me. Too afraid to pick it up, I leaned over it and scanned the length again. A hairline fracture bisected the upper limb just above the grip. My chest squeezed at the sight of it. There was no fixing that. I sniffled.

It was dumb to cry over a bow. Nothing lasted forever. I knew that. But, that damn bow was my last connection with Dad. We’d picked it out before the quakes, and using it made me feel like he was still watching over me.

I looked up at the two fey who watched me warily.

“What the fuck is wrong with you people? What did I do to deserve being treated like this?”

“I will replace the bow,” Drav said.

“It was from my dad. You can’t replace sentimental value.” I picked up the bow in both hands. “I’m guessing there was a sense of urgency in getting me back before dark.

I'm ready now. I don't think there's anything else for you to break."

Drav glanced at Thallirin then picked me up again and started running. I didn't pay attention to the trees like I should have. I kept thinking of the broken bow. It'd been stupid to throw a fit. What if he'd been trying to save me from a horde of infected? Maybe it was for the best that the bow was broken. Being that emotionally attached to something was a dangerous distraction I couldn't afford. Yet, I still ached that it was broken.

When we cleared Tolerance's wall, instead of setting me down, Drav continued to run. A sick ball of worry formed in my stomach.

"Where are we going? Is my mom okay?"

"Mya wants to speak with you."

He stopped in front of his house and let me enter on my own two feet. Mya was sitting in the living room, a trash can at her side and a book in her lap. Nothing about her position or expression looked urgent.

"What's wrong?" I asked, moving into the room.

The door closed, and I looked back to see that we were alone.

"I just wanted to talk to you for a minute. How was today's supply run?"

I slowly turned to face her, my thumb smoothing over the fracture in the bow.

"I'm here for an idle chat?"

"Well, not entirely idle. Please, have a seat. I'm feeling

awkward enough, and you standing over me like that isn't going to make this any easier."

Despite my anger, I sat with my bow resting on my knees and waited to hear her out.

"The fey are upset about the way you're treating Thallirin. Purposely ignoring him. Saying rude things. Thallirin has sacrificed so much to be part of their brotherhood again, and they won't turn their backs on him. Not even for you."

That's why my bow had been broken? Because of fucking hurt feelings? I used my panic-attack method of breathing to calm down enough to answer rationally.

"I'm not asking them to turn their backs on anyone. I'm fine using my own two legs to get to Tenacity and back."

"They just want to see Thallirin happy."

"And I'm not caving to community preference and spreading my legs to make that happen."

She had the decency to look shocked.

"That's not at all what I'm suggesting!"

"It is. You know it is. I've tried to pull my weight. I guard the walls, doing my part. So does Zach. Molev said it didn't matter that Mom was in a chair. He promised we would be safe and protected. Instead, I'm being bullied into picking a fey for a partner."

I stood.

"Matt said we'd be welcome there. I think it's time I mention that to my mom."

I moved to leave then turned back to Mya.

"Oh, and as an example of the bullying, Drav didn't ask to

carry me here. He told me what he was doing then grabbed me, breaking my bow in the process. This bow was the last thing I had from my dad. Maybe you'll be able to understand the significance of that more than they seem to be able to."

"Brenna, I'm so sorry."

"Don't be sorry. Be different. I know you're pro fey, but don't forget they aren't the only people depending on you."

I left her house, and as I walked home, I considered my conversation with Mya and my options. Living at Tenacity wouldn't be easier for any of us. In fact, it would be harder. The last few days had proven that. Yet, I refused to continue like this. Where did that leave me?

Heat and the scent of dinner enveloped me when I walked in.

"I'm home."

"You're back early," Mom called as I started peeling off layers.

"Yeah. Drav carried me back. I broke my bow."

There was a beat of silence.

"Oh, honey, I'm so sorry. Can we fix it?"

"No. The upper limb fractured just above the riser. I'll need to use yours tomorrow." I finished kicking off my boots and entered the kitchen to find Mom silently crying as she cut meat into little cubes.

"Those better be tears of joy that we're having real meat tonight."

She shook her head at me, and I sat beside her, already knowing what was making her cry.

"Losing the bow hurts. But, we need to look at things practically. It's just a bow. It doesn't mean I'm losing any more of Dad than I already have."

"It does. We're replacing everything. I can't do this." She wiped her hands then her face. "I can't see Uan." She wheeled away from the table and went to her room.

Zach watched me.

"You okay?"

"I'm feeling like Mom right now. But I know it'll pass. You?"

He sighed.

"Losing is just part of life. You know?"

I nodded, understanding exactly what he meant. Life was a series of learning, loving, and letting go. You either got used to the letting go or gave up on living.

"Keep cooking," I said. "Tonight, we'll find out just how serious Uan is about Mom."

The stew was simmering by the time Uan knocked on the door. I let him in.

"Mom's having a rough day," I said. "She's missing my dad. She told us she didn't want to see you anymore, but I don't think that's true. You've made her happy."

He looked down at me for a long moment.

"She makes me very happy."

"Then go remind her of that."

He went back to Mom's bedroom and let himself in without knocking. Zach and I waited by the table. The low rumble of Uan's voice came from the room several times before the door opened and Mom emerged. Her face was tear-stained and mottled, but she didn't give us the Mom glare as she parked at the table.

"Thank you," she said simply.

"Anytime," I said.

We served dinner and sat down together. Before I managed more than a few bites, Zach reached into his pocket and withdrew several packets of birth control, which he set on the table without a word. I was surprised he handled it with so much dignity. And in front of Uan, too. But it was only right since he needed to understand what they meant.

I looked at Mom then Uan. Uan frowned at the packets of pills.

"Do you know what they are?" Mom asked.

"Medicine," Uan said. "Are you sick?"

"No."

Zach started eating in a hurry.

"Slow down, Zach. Even if you finish, you're not excused."

Zach groaned.

"I asked Zach and Brenna to go on the supply run today to find birth control. These pills will help prevent pregnancy. At my age, it's a risk to have more children. Do you understand what that means, Uan? If you choose to be with me, I can't give you kids. You won't have children of your own."

He looked at us then Mom.

"I will have children of my own. I will have Brenna and Zach."

CHAPTER SIX

I WASHED THE POT AND WONDERED WHAT WOULD HAPPEN NEXT. Mom had her pills and Uan's definite interest. Hearing that she wouldn't ever have his baby hadn't scared him off.

Glancing over my shoulder, I considered the pair as they sat on the back porch. Mom was bundled up in a blanket on Uan's lap. Their heads were close as they talked to each other. I was glad she had someone.

"How soon before she gives him the green light to move in, you think?" Zach said, taking the pot to dry.

"Probably not very long. A few days at most. She'll want to give him some time to change his mind."

"Do any of them ever say no?"

I snorted.

"Not that I've ever seen."

"What are you going to call him?"

"Uan for a while. Dad, if he deserves it."

"Really?"

"You heard Mom. We'll be the only kids he'll have. I think he'd like being called Dad."

Zach was quiet for a minute.

"If he deserves it," he agreed.

After we finished up with the dishes, I went through the cupboards to look at our supplies.

"Damn. This is amazing."

Zach grinned.

"Two full totes, one for each of us. And, I got to pick what went in them."

He'd organized everything by type, putting the canned goods in a lower cupboard and the boxed stuff in the upper cupboards. We even had two bags of flour and other baking ingredients.

My mouth started to water for the biscuits that I knew Mom would make.

I PACED the back of the truck, moving to keep warm. I'd gotten smarter each trip, not just about how I did things but about how the supply runs were handled in general. On the second trip to Harrisonville, we'd approached from the north. Garrett had explained that the group never came in for supply runs from the same direction twice because of infected traps. The infected were getting too smart. We'd left with more supplies than the day before, thanks to a supercenter, and I had managed to stay on the roof without freezing my ass off. To top my amazing day, Thallirin hadn't tried to talk to me during our trek home on foot, and Mom had made biscuits.

Thinking of the flaky treat, I pulled a wrapped biscuit from my pocket and took a bite. Even cold, it was amazing.

My footsteps were quiet as I turned, scanned the surrounding trees, and walked the length of the truck trailer. While two of the trucks were the canvas-backed military kind, the third was hard-backed. The cargo bay kept the humans warmer and safer, and the solid surface made it possible for me to move around when on guard duty.

A thick tree to the right caught my attention. I didn't stop to stare but kept moving, noting it again during my sweeping glance.

"An infected is watching us from the south," I said quietly. "It's standing against the tree."

Thallirin, who was on the south side, scanned the trees.

"I see it. Two others behind it."

He jogged over to the other fey and spoke quietly. That fey nodded and took off at a sprint toward the trees. The infected I'd noted didn't move, not even when the fey reached the tree line. It just stood still for its death. Frowning, I looked around. Nothing else moved.

"That was weird."

"Why?"

I looked down at Thallirin.

"The ones smart enough to watch us are also smart

enough to run. Why was it watching, and why didn't it run when it knew it was spotted?"

He grunted and continued to patrol the area.

I put away my biscuit, more alert now, and glanced at the position of the sun. It'd been at least two hours since the main group had left for town. My gaze shifted to the houses in the distance. It had been a long wait on the first two runs, too. But we hadn't seen any infected before. At least, not out by the trucks. Did seeing them mean it was worse in there?

My stomach twisted with worry, and I wished I was with Zach. We knew how to look for supplies. How to watch out for each other. I knew Ryan wasn't his sister, but I couldn't help but feel a little mistrust toward him at that moment. Would he place as much value on Zach's safety as I would? Probably not.

I stopped pacing and rolled my shoulders.

"Are you cold?" Thallirin asked.

"No. Worried. I wish I was with Zach."

"He will be safe."

I looked down at Thallirin.

"If you're so sure of that, then why am I up here and not out there?"

He didn't answer. He didn't need to. We both knew Zach's safety was no more a guarantee than mine.

Moving again, I paced with greater purpose, as if my effort would hurry the clock. When the first runner appeared, coated with steaming gore, my throat tightened.

"We cleared four blocks," he said, scooping up snow to rub

over his face. "There were more infected. Ryan wants us to bring two trucks closer to hurry the loading."

Two of the fey jumped into the driver's seats of the supply trucks and rumbled away before I could scramble off the trailer roof. I watched them turn, then back up toward the start of the neighborhood. Did they think we would need to leave fast?

I hurried toward the roof of the cab, sliding down the windshield to the hood. Thallirin hovered, ready to catch me if I fell. I ignored him and monkeyed my way down the grille and bumper.

"I don't drive stick," I said, "But I think we need to turn this one around, too."

Thallirin walked over and opened the passenger door, waiting for me to get in.

I could waste time and say I'd keep watch from the outside, or I could get inside so he moved it faster. Looking at the flurry of activity around the two distant trucks, I hustled toward the door. His hand rested on my back, helping me as I stepped up into the cab. I didn't complain. The step was slick with cold and snow, and I'd almost slipped.

"Do you think those infected were lookouts? Are more coming?" I asked as soon as Thallirin got in.

"You're safe."

I rolled my eyes at his placating non-answer, like I was some child needing reassurance, and watched as he started the truck and began the process of a Y-turn. How could a creature with no prior knowledge of vehicles already know how to drive a stick after a few months when I'd been on this planet for almost eighteen years and still couldn't drive one? The fey made me feel like such an underachiever at times.

As soon as the truck was facing the other direction, Thallirin got out, leaving it to idle. I swiveled in my seat to watch what was happening. As far as I could tell, the trucks were being loaded as fast as hell. Several fey were running our way with people in their arms.

I reached for the handle and opened the door an inch before it was closed on me. I looked down at the fey preventing me from leaving, unsure if I should feel relieved that it wasn't Thallirin or annoyed that the rest were starting to act like him.

"Stay inside," the fey said. "The humans are coming."

Shifting my gaze to the runners, I counted humans. They were all there. Ryan's dad, Richard, was the first to arrive and climbed into the driver's seat of my truck. This was the first time he'd gone on a supply run with us.

"Looks like you'll be my co-pilot for this," he said calmly.

"What's going on?"

"A herd of infected were spotted six blocks away. Smart ones trying to sneak up on us. Not the first time they've tried that, though. We typically pull two trucks back, using them as decoys as we hightail it out of there. The fey will bring the supplies and thin the herd." Someone banged on his door twice, and he shifted into gear.

"We'll meet up with the rest of the fey and the trucks a few miles out. Your job is to keep an eye on your side of the road. Let me know if you see anything."

"Got it."

Adrenaline pumped through me as I watched the roadside for any sign of infected or traps. A number of fey ran ahead of us as a front guard. Tense minutes passed in the cab before Richard let off the gas and came to a gentle stop near a farm.

"We haven't checked this one. Might as well have a look around while we wait."

I turned to look at him.

"That's it? We're in the clear?"

He chuckled.

"We're as clear as it's going to get. Come on. I love checking farm basements. Never know what we'll find."

Following his lead, I jumped out of the truck. A few of the humans from the back of the truck were getting out, too.

"Brenna and I are going to check the house," Richard said.

Ryan glanced at me and grinned. "Don't let him talk you into trying anything out of a jar."

Richard waved a hand at his son and looked at me.

"Don't listen to him. It was a bad seal. The rest were fine."

I smiled at their easy banter and followed Richard across the snow toward the house. It wasn't until we were almost there that I realized Thallirin hadn't tried to stop me. I looked back and found him a step behind me, his expression grim.

"What's something you're craving?" Richard asked.

"At the moment, nothing really. Mom made biscuits last night with the supplies from our first haul."

"Biscuits are good." He groaned. "Biscuits and gravy would be better. I hope we find some sausage."

He stopped outside the house and looked back at the fey following us. Without a word, they went inside while Richard and I waited with Thallirin.

"Julie wants me to find some fresh food. Not an easy task," Richard said. "If the stores have heat, the produce inside is rotten by now. If there's no heat, then the slow freeze turned most of it to mush. We've had some luck with these farmhouses, though. See over there?" he asked, pointing to a row of gnarled, old trees. "Apple trees. I'm betting we'll find a bushel or two of apples worth saving."

The door opened, and the fey carried out two bodies to lay on the snow. Their legs were covered in human bite marks.

"It's clear," one of the fey said.

Richard held the door open for me. I stepped inside and leaned my bow against the wall, drawing the knife I carried from the sheath.

"You're not new to this," Richard said as my gaze swept the room, lingering on the couch and chair.

"No. Did you check under the couch?" I asked. "The smaller infected like hiding there." I couldn't say kids because they weren't kids anymore.

"Yes," one of the fey said. "A small one was there. We took him out the back."

I nodded and stepped farther into the room, sticking close to Richard.

We searched through the kitchen, placing what food there was on the table, then went down to the basement. Richard's prediction proved correct, and we found some apples in a cool, back corner that I wouldn't go near. Neither did he. We both had too much experience with infected to do something that risky when there was no need.

"Would any of you mind getting those apples?" he asked the fey. "And all the jars from those shelves? We'll eventually need to start preserving our own food."

The whole excursion didn't take long, and I was outside with my mom's bow over my shoulder in no time.

Richard clapped me on the back in acknowledgment of a job well done and returned to the truck.

I looked at Thallirin, who hadn't been more than a yard from me the whole time.

"Why didn't you stop me this time?" I asked.

"Why didn't you get mad at Richard for telling you what to do?"

"Because I knew I had a choice the whole time. I could have said no, and he would have been okay with that. Your turn."

"He said it would help you."

"In what way?"

"To be less angry." He studied me for a moment. "You still look at me with anger."

"You still look at me like you own me."

He shared a look with one of the fey carrying something from the house. The fey grunted in their caveman communication way and kept walking.

"I know I do not own you, Brenna," Thallirin said.

"Right." I let a heavy and obvious amount of doubt lace that single word.

Rather than trying to point out where his actions failed to support his statement, I went back to the vehicles, glad the rest of the group had joined us and we could leave.

However, arriving at Tenacity only served to remind me that my day was far from over. The majority of the fey were once again covered in infected goo, and the clean ones were avoiding eye contact.

"Tor," Richard called. "Get Brenna home, will you? She can start sorting the supplies as they come in." And just like that, Richard was my hero because one of the fey came jogging over.

I hurriedly removed my bow so I didn't break another one, but the precaution proved unnecessary. The new-to-me fey smiled good-naturedly and asked if he could carry me before he bent to pick me up and settled me against his bare chest. That he didn't act like I was an infected two seconds from biting him or cast continuous longing glances my way was a nice change. Not nice enough to strike up a conversation, but still nice.

Safely in his arms, I made the journey home in minutes and was at the storage shed as the supplies started trickling in. I wasn't alone, though. Julie was there, teaching me the ropes and chatting away.

She was easy to like and kept me distracted from Thallirin's quiet presence just inside the doorway.

“That’s the last of it,” she said with her hands on her hips. We looked at the shelves. Over half of them held items again.

“Go ahead and fill up two totes with whatever your family needs.”

I shook my head.

“We’re good for now. But, I really like knowing I can come in here at any time and grab something if we need it.”

She smiled at me.

“The door’s never locked. Thank you for going out today and for everything you do. You and your family help make Tolerance a better place.”

With those words, everything about today clicked.

“Mya told you.”

Julie’s smile softened.

“Of course she did, sweetie. She’s my daughter and is worried that you hate her. But that’s her problem, not yours. You were right to speak up for yourself. Don’t ever stop.”

She gave my arm a comforting squeeze then turned me toward the door, which was now empty.

“Go on. I’m sure your mom’s waiting.”

I left the supply shed with a positive attitude, sure that my day couldn’t possibly get any better. Well, getting through to Thallirin would make it better, but I was content with the wins so far.

That changed the minute I walked into my house and the scent of pepperoni pizza punched me in the face.

“No fucking way,” I yelled.

Mom laughed from the kitchen.

"Yes, fucking way," she said. "And watch your mouth. The last pepperoni pizza on the face of the planet is no reason to swear."

I tore out of my clothes and bolted for the kitchen. Not one, but three pizzas waited on the table. Both mom and Zach were grinning at my expression.

I looked at Zach.

"Was this you?"

"Who else? If I'm going into those houses, I'm taking what I want out."

I sat down with a smile and glanced at Uan, who remained quiet.

"This is the best," I said. "You're going to love it."

He looked at the pizza, his gaze doubtful.

Zach and I reached for a piece at the same time. I was the first one to take a bite and groaned. Never in a million years did I think I'd taste cheese and pepperoni again. Uan took a slice after Mom took two. From the corner of my eye, I watched him take a bite, chew it slowly, and set the pizza back on his plate. I could tell from his expression he wanted to spit it out.

Grinning, I swallowed quickly and stole his piece.

"You know what? If you don't like it, that's okay. It just means more pizza for us. Help yourself to whatever you want in the cupboard."

He grunted and did as I suggested, returning to the table with a can of dog food.

"This is my favorite," he said. "I will find many more for us."

Zach and I snorted, and Uan looked at us in question.

"That's dog food, Uan," Zach said. "It's what our pets eat."

Uan glanced at the can and then at Mom. She smiled at him.

"Sweetie, if that's what you want, you go ahead and eat it. No one's going to judge you. It's pure protein."

With that assurance, he dug his spoon into the can.

"Would either of you mind if Uan spent the night?" Mom asked casually.

"Like I'd say no to anything after pizza," I said.

"Agreed," Zach said, stuffing half a piece into his mouth.

"Great."

I WOKE up to the scent of pancakes and frying meat. Stomach rumbling, I crawled out of bed and went straight to the kitchen.

"Morning," Mom said with unusual good cheer.

The likely reason for her cheer was at the stove, shirtless and flipping pancakes. I grinned and took my seat at the table.

"Get a goodnight's sleep, Mom?"

She tore her gaze from Uan's extremely muscled back, which I couldn't deny was a sight, and gave me a sheepish look.

"The best in a long while."

"That's good, Mom. Really good."

She nodded, and I watched her shoulders lift and drop with a quiet exhale. She was still struggling. I knew she missed Dad and would always love him, just like she knew it was practical to look to the future instead of dwelling in the past. However, the heart often wanted what the head knew we couldn't have.

Zach joined us after Uan already had a decent stack on the table. The meat I'd smelled was more dog food. He put patties of it on a plate next to the pancakes.

"Your mom said it isn't something you like," he said. "You don't need to eat it, but it's protein."

I smiled and took a patty. It didn't look half bad fried.

"Since I plan to go out again today, I'll take the protein."

Mom smiled at me, then we all dug in. It felt weirdly normal eating together. Like I could rinse my plate and go turn on the TV to watch the news kind of normal. I liked it and knew Mom and Zach did, too.

"Thanks for breakfast, Uan," I said when I finished. "Pan-fried dog food patties will never be my favorite, but it's way better than dog food soup."

Uan grunted in acknowledgment, and I cleaned up my dishes before getting ready for the day. Zach was waiting for me by the front door when I emerged from my room.

"Be safe out there," Mom said, watching us add our warm layers.

"Always," I said. "We'll bring back something good for dinner."

We both kissed her cheek, waved to Uan, and left.

"Is it wrong of me to be looking forward to this?" Zach asked.

"Depends on why."

He thought about it for a minute.

"Mostly because I'm doing something useful. But eating better is up there, too. And it's crazy how much faster it goes with the fey's help."

"Is it safer, though?" I asked.

He shrugged.

"They don't let humans go into the houses first. We mostly go in after everything's been cleared. Ryan says they sometimes miss an infected, though. So, we can't let our guard down, just like when we would go out for supplies before."

It sounded like when I'd helped Richard with the farmhouse.

"Basically, we start gathering everything, and the fey pack it up and run it out," Zach said. "It's like we're on teams. One human to about six fey. That's how we get through so many houses so quickly."

I was glad Zach had found his stride on the supply runs, but I couldn't help feeling a little bitter that Thallirin was holding me back from being just as useful.

"Are we in trouble?" Zach asked quietly.

I looked up to see a fey standing in the middle of the road, waiting for us. In the dim pre-dawn light, I couldn't see the face, but knew by the stance it was Drav.

"Morning, Drav," I said when we drew close. "Something wrong?"

"Nothing is wrong. We rotate who goes on supply runs to ensure everyone rests. You will stay here today."

His gaze didn't once shift to Zach.

"Both of us or just me?" I asked.

"Just you."

"What a bunch of—"

Zach grabbed my arm.

"How long does she need to rest?" he asked.

Drav frowned, and his gaze shifted to the right. I followed it and saw Thallirin lurking in the shadows. My temper flared, and if he'd been standing close, I would have broken another bow. As it was, I raged in silence for several long seconds before looking at Drav.

"I've lost all respect for you. Hope this bullshit move is worth it." I turned to Zach. "You go ahead. Get as much as you can. We'll need it in Tenacity."

Zach nodded slowly and looked at Drav, then Thallirin, before jogging toward the wall.

I turned on my heel and marched back the way I'd come, seething that Drav and Mya would pull this after yesterday.

"You will not leave," Thallirin said from just behind me, making me jump a little.

I stopped and glared up at him. "What in the hell do you think is so great about this situation that I'd ever want to stay?"

"Uan wouldn't be accepted in Tenacity. He makes your mother happy."

His words were like a knife to the gut, and for several long minutes, I could say nothing. He thought he had me. He thought he'd manipulated me right where he wanted me.

"You're just like him," I said, trying to fight down the panic of Van's weight pressing down on me once more. My bow was off my shoulder and in my hand before I'd even thought about it. The nocked arrow shook as I aimed it right at Thallirin's throat. He didn't move.

"You're making me a prisoner. Telling me I'm safe. Telling me you'll never hurt me. Telling me I'll like it." My throat closed, and my eyes stung.

"I won't do it again. I'm not going to lie still while you use me, you fucking son of a bitch." I was shaking so hard, my fingers slipped. He moved quickly, his palm grazing the shaft as it released, knocking it off course.

"I am not using you, Brenna," he said, his words slow and deep.

"I'm not stupid, Thallirin. Van didn't use me the first night, either. He waited until I was hungry and desperate and had no choice but to agree." I stepped closer to him, looking him in the eyes. "But rape is rape, Thallirin. You can lie to yourself and say I want it, but I don't. I won't. Ever."

CHAPTER SEVEN

MOM KNOCKED ON MY BEDROOM DOOR AGAIN.

"I'll talk when I'm ready, and I'm not ready," I said, struggling to control my emotions.

I was a hot mess. Panic clawed at me.

As I sat on my bed, I felt more trapped than ever and hated Drav for his order to stay inside Tolerance's wall. It didn't take a genius to know the mandate had nothing to do with me resting. He wanted me to stay here so I'd mingle with the fey lingering. Specifically, Thallirin. And, I didn't know what to do about any of it. If I told Mom what Drav was doing, she'd agree we needed to leave and, without hesitation, would throw away her chance for a possible fresh start with Uan and immunity. I couldn't do that to her.

The knock came again.

"It's Eden. We need to talk. I'm coming in, so don't shoot me."

The door opened a moment later. Eden slipped in and quickly closed the door behind her.

"I'm sorry I'm barging in," she said, looking truly apologetic as she sat beside me on the bed.

"Let me guess, Thallirin came to your house again because his chosen vagina is being difficult."

Eden cringed at that.

"He did show up, but not because you're being difficult. He's freaking out because you told him you were raped and hinted that you think he's going to do the same thing. That, on top of the pedophile comment, has him an emotional mess."

I looked at her.

"What exactly does Thallirin's freak out expression look like? Is it this or this?" My serious expression never changed.

"Definitely the second one," she said.

I snorted.

"I don't care what he's feeling. I'm barely holding my shit together. He's doing everything the same. I'm suffocating. It's like the weight..." I placed a hand on my chest and just breathed.

"Talk to me," she said softly. "I'm probably the only person here who will understand."

"How can I feel so broken and so whole at the same time? I should be over it. It wasn't that bad."

Eden's sniffle was the only warning I got before I was being hugged hard by her.

"I'm so sorry."

Her hold and sincerity fractured me. For the first time

since the bunker, I let the hurt out. I cried, and it was so bad. I shook and sobbed and snotted all over her. I broke into so many pieces that I knew the old me would never come back.

I wasn't sure how long we stayed like that, but piece by piece, I slid back together, and a numbness blanketed my emotions enough that the tears dried so I could talk.

"Van and his dad wanted women to have babies. When Van's group saw me out gathering supplies with my family, they shot my Dad and took Zach and me. Mom was left behind because Van thought she'd be useless.

"That first day, Zach and I were too scared to notice we didn't eat. The second day, though... We noticed. Van said only those who worked their share got fed. He said he'd give me his food ration if I let him fuck me."

I pulled out of Eden's hold and stared blankly out the window.

"He said it was my choice. That I could say no. But, they never gave Zach or me a chance to work. There was no choice. It was rape or starvation. That's when I figured out why Zach had been taken, too. Leverage. I could starve myself, but not him."

I exhaled shakily and continued.

"The fey let us stay here and promised we'd be safe. But the truth is that we're here because they want females and babies, just like Van and his men. I've said no to the fey, repeatedly, and now the noose is tightening. How long before we don't get fed? How long before I'm on my back again so I don't have to listen to Zach's stomach growl in his sleep?"

Tears made slow trails down my cheeks. I wiped them away, wondering if I was really put back together at all.

"And you wanted to escape that fate by going to live at Tenacity. Then Thallirin made you feel trapped again by pointing out you'd be breaking up Uan and your mom. Just a new form of leverage, am I right?"

I nodded then paused.

"He told you what he said?"

She gave me a small smile.

"I overheard him talking to Ghua. He really didn't understand." She stood and went to the door. "Now, I think he does."

She opened the door, revealing Thallirin. With his head bowed, he gripped the jamb of the door, his grey fingers almost white.

The sound of his harsh breathing filled the room and stirred my memory of the other time I'd seen a fey look like that. The morning I'd been rescued from the bunker, the fey had helped carry one of their own out. That fey had been attacked by a hellhound and was in so much pain that, even unconscious, he'd made noise. Thallirin was acting the same.

Slowly, Thallirin straightened. My pulse jumped. He didn't look at me but turned around and left.

"If you want to go," Eden said quietly, "no one will stop you now. I'll stab anyone who tries."

She gave me a weak, sad smile then left.

The house remained quiet after the door closed behind her, and I just sat there and breathed. I should have been angry that Eden had brought Thallirin to listen in, but it seemed that she'd been right all along. Telling him the truth had finally gotten through to him.

The light in the room gradually changed, brightening to midday. My stomach growled, but I ignored it. It was the need for water that finally motivated me to move.

My legs felt weak, and my head hurt when I stood. I shuffled to the bathroom, drank from the sink, and took something for the pain from our meager supply of home medications. Moving in a fashion reminiscent of one of the infected, I made my way to the kitchen.

Uan held Mom in his lap in the living room. Both watched me closely as I went to the cupboards.

"How much did you hear, Uan?" I asked without looking at him.

"All of it."

With their hearing, I'd figured as much.

"I'd kill for a bag of chips right now." I sighed and closed the cupboard to face them both. "I'm hurt and grieving, but I refuse to be broken. So, don't treat me like I am."

"We won't," Mom said. But, I could see the pain and pity in her eyes.

I sighed again and looked around.

"I think I'm going to go take a shift on the wall." I went to the entry and started putting on my layers. When I had everything, I called that I would see them at dinner then left.

The brisk air felt good on my face. Clean and new, in a way. I breathed in deeply and let it out. The ache inside of me eased a little. I knew it wouldn't just disappear, though. It never truly did, not since what Van and Oscar had done to me and my family.

The fey at my usual spot on the wall nodded to me and moved farther down. While it felt good to do something, I wished I wasn't in Tolerance. I wished I was with Zach, gathering supplies. No, I wished I was shoving my face full of cheesy, powder-coated tortilla chips of some kind. I wouldn't have even cared what brand at that point. I just wanted to lick my wounds and eat junk food.

I wasted away several hours on the wall, until the sky started to darken, then waved to the nearest fey and headed down the ladder.

The yeasty smell of fresh bread and garlic greeted me when I opened the door.

"Please tell me it's spaghetti night," I said, hurrying to strip out of my boots.

I entered the kitchen, scanning for any sign of garlic bread, and noted Mom stirring something at the stove and Zach at the table with a serious expression on his face.

"What's wrong with you?" I asked.

He shook his head.

"Mom told me. Sorry your day was shitty. I should have stayed."

"The spectator count to my meltdown was high enough. Speaking of spectators, where's Uan?"

"I thought we should have dinner alone tonight," Mom said, wheeling to the table.

"Why?" I drew out the word. "Don't tell me he doesn't like spaghetti, either."

"I don't know. But I do know that we need to talk, as a family, about our future. When I said I wanted to find a fey so I could be immune and you would have someone to look after you both if something happened to me, I hope it went without saying that I would never put that as a priority over either of you."

"We know that," I said, looking at Zach.

"Then why in the hell didn't you tell me what was happening?" she asked angrily. "I would have done something about it."

I stayed quiet because we *had* talked about things as they'd happened. Neither of us had understood how big of a deal it was for me until today, though.

"I think we should give moving to Tenacity some serious consideration," Mom said calmly. "I'm not saying that we have to live there forever, but what would it hurt if we tried to stay there for a while? Uan is willing to help us carry over our food and promised to start going out on supply runs with you."

She was giving me the out I'd so desperately needed. Yet, as much as I wanted to take it, I knew we couldn't.

"Tenacity won't be any better than here, and we all know it. Despite the new rule that anyone who steals would get kicked out, Matt admitted that he's worried people with a cache of supplies will be targeted, just like they were here. And if Zach, Uan, and I are out getting supplies, that leaves you home alone."

"I'm not helpless," she said irritably.

"I'm not suggesting that you are. Me? You? Zach? It wouldn't matter who was home alone. The same thing would likely happen to all of us. We're safer here. And better fed.

"What happened today was a perfect storm. The fey were trying to manipulate me into liking Thallirin, and it backfired in the worst way possible. I'm sure every fey here now knows what happened to me. If I'm lucky, they'll look at me like damaged goods and leave me alone. If I'm not lucky, they might still try to manipulate me. But, I punched Drav in the throat for breaking my bow, and he didn't lift a finger against me. And I almost shot Thallirin with an arrow, and he didn't even bat an eye at it. They're not going to hurt me. They'll probably just keep annoying the hell out of me."

Mom gave me a long look.

"You're not damaged goods," she said firmly.

"You and I know that, but they don't need to," I said with a small smile.

"If someone even hints that you need to be with anyone—"

"You will be the first one to know," I promised.

"No. I will," said Zach. "I'm not leaving your side."

"Yes, you are. I refuse to be chained to my little brother forever. This is our life now. Our home. We need to make it work for us, not the other way around."

A NEW LAYER of snow crunched under our feet as we walked toward the wall.

"Is it just me, or is it quieter than usual?" Zach asked.

"Way quieter. Think Drav will mind if I shoot him in the thigh if he tries to stop me this time?"

Zach looked less than amused with my attempt at a joke. However, Drav didn't stand in the street, blocking our way. We made it to the wall without a single fey sighting, which was weird even this early in the morning.

The regular group of humans waited along with a very healthy number of fey, including Thallirin, who stood apart from the rest. For a change, the big grey fey wasn't watching me. He was staring at the ground like he wanted to fight it.

Ryan saw us and jogged our way.

"Glad you could make it. We're just about to leave." He lowered his voice. "I don't think you'll have any problems anymore."

The fact that even Ryan knew made my insides churn sickeningly.

"Great," I managed.

He nodded and called out to the group that we could head out. Zach walked with me to the fey. They were strangely quiet and quick to avoid eye contact with me. It reminded me of how students behaved when not wanting to get picked by the teacher.

"Would you mind carrying me?" I asked one at random.

He grunted and held out his arms like I was supposed to jump into them.

"Dude, don't be a dick," Zach said irritably. "Just pick her up and carry her."

The fey gently picked me up, said a quick apology, and started over the wall. He ran like I was on fire. I'd been kidding about hoping they'd treat me like damaged goods. Actually being treated like that hurt my feelings more than a little by the time we reached Tenacity. The fey didn't drop me or anything, but I'd never been placed on my feet faster. With a last apology, he backed away, his gaze averted.

Zach came over to stand by me.

"They're acting weird," I said.

"Um...don't they always?"

I rolled my eyes at Zach, glad that at least he wasn't making a big deal out of it, and waited for Ryan and Matt to do their usual meet and greet to find out how many others would be joining us. Matt called out three names. That was it.

"You're letting fear starve you," I called. "My family had pizza the other night and spaghetti with garlic bread last night. The food is out there for those brave enough to find it for themselves."

Someone said, "Fuck it," then several more people stepped forward.

"I hope this is worth it," a man said, looking at me.

"Me, too. I really want some chips this time."

I used the ladders along with the rest of the humans to get out to the trucks and took my usual spot as co-pilot for Garrett.

"Morning," he said. "Hope you brought your hand warmers. It feels colder today."

"I have four," I said, patting my pocket. "Enough to keep my toes nice and toasty. It'll be a sad day when I run out."

"We'll find more."

He started the truck and rolled along behind Ryan's vehicle. When I glanced out the window, I caught a fey watching me, but he quickly looked away. I sighed and leaned back into the seat.

"How does it work? You living at Tolerance?" I asked.

"What do you mean?"

"Well, the fey want all the girls for themselves. I would have thought they would see you as competition and kick you out."

"They see me like another Ryan. They accept him because he's Mya's family. They accept me because Angel claimed me as her family. Shax very briefly thought I was making moves on Angel, and let's just say I will never horn in on any woman a fey has his heart set on. Truly terrifying," he said with a chuckle.

"So, what does that mean for you? You're supposed to just resign yourself to a life alone?"

He grew serious.

"I hope not. But thinking of that possibility always helps me understand how the fey probably feel. And there's a lot more prejudice against them than me."

I looked out at the fey running alongside the trucks and immediately spotted Thallirin. As always, he was a bit apart from the rest. Was the thought of a life alone why he'd been so overbearingly stalkerish? On the tail of that thought, I couldn't help but wonder, "Why me out of all the other women in the two safe zones?" What about me had made him think I would be the solution to a lifetime of loneliness?

The ride to Harrisonville took a lot longer because we needed to go around to the west side. My butt was numb by the time Garrett pulled to a stop behind Ryan's truck.

"About time," I grumbled.

"We're not there yet," he said. "Watch this." He cut the engine and slipped the gear into neutral.

Fey lined up behind the truck in front of us and started pushing it forward.

"Stealth mode," Garrett said before our truck started moving, too. "Pulling the trucks up to the houses after we've been spotted is dangerous. Driving in right away is dangerous. Both make too much noise. This is a hell of a lot quieter, gets the trucks closer for immediate loading, and gets us out faster when we're done."

"Hey, no justification needed on my end. It's a smart idea."

I kind of felt bad for the fey who had to push the huge trucks, though. My gaze went to Thallirin, who was in front of us. Unlike the other fey, whose strain was visible because they wore no shirt, or wore something that barely fit, Thallirin was covered by a large jacket that went to his hips. Though he was probably working just as hard as the rest, there was no view of rippling muscles to show it off. I briefly wondered why.

We rolled right up to the first house, turning so that the passenger truck would be the first one out and the soft-sided supply trucks would be closest to the houses.

An infected came around the side of a house at a run. One of the fey intercepted it and pulled its head clean off. I'd never get used to the ease with which the fey decapitated infected.

"Be careful out there," Garrett said softly before easing his door open.

I did the same and lightly jumped down. Zach jogged past me with a nod and joined six fey who broke off toward one of the houses. I moved to the grille of the truck then climbed my way to the roof for a better view.

It was weird being in the trenches and seeing the scavenging as it happened. Fey and humans alike worked in tandem, going from house to house, clearing the supplies and bringing them back to the trucks. It wasn't completely noiseless, but there was nothing that I thought would draw attention.

Soon the immediate street was clear, and the groups moved deeper into the neighborhood.

I glanced at Thallirin and the five other fey who remained with me. They watched the houses and the yards, keeping their backs to the trucks as they continually moved.

Several streets away, I watched a fey jump from a low roof to one of the two-story buildings. A lookout.

Knowing he would spot anything coming at us from straight ahead, I focused on the houses to our right and left. Everything was quiet, and supplies continued to trickle our way as the teams cleared more houses. I was pretty sure I even spotted a bag of potato chips in one of the bins. A small and very quiet happy dance may have occurred at the sight.

From the corner of my eye, I thought I caught the reflection of a face in an upstairs window. When I looked, there was nothing there.

I didn't doubt what I'd seen, though, and made a small "hst" sound to catch the fey's attention.

"Brenna?" Thallirin said softly.

"Second story. Window on the end. Maybe nothing," I said, trying to be as brief and as quiet as possible.

He looked at one of the other fey, who went into the house. Knowing the fey would deal with whatever he found, I refocused and studied the other homes around us. Farther down, something moved in another second story window as well. I wasn't the only one to see it, though. A fey went running off.

I frowned and glanced at the remaining four fey. Why did I feel like the infected were thinning the herd?

A thump of noise came from the original house, and I looked over to see the fey holding up a head in the window. Making a face, I turned away.

My gaze caught on the bay door of the garage next to us. The twelve-inch gap wasn't a big deal. People did that all the time for cats to come and go as they pleased. It could have been like that when we pulled up, and I just hadn't noticed. Yet, the undisturbed snow line in front of the door said otherwise.

As I stared, a hand appeared, its pale fingers grasping the edge of the door.

"Infected," I said softly.

Another hand appeared then another.

I lifted my bow. That's when I noticed that the garage door two houses down started to lift. I swung my head and saw the same on the other side.

"Stay on the roof, Brenna," Thallirin said.

The doors flew upward all at once, and infected poured out. I fired arrow after arrow, aiming for the eyes. Some shots killed. Some blinded. Both worked, but not quickly enough. Infected swarmed the fey and rushed the truck. Giving up on protecting the fey, I focused on protecting myself as the infected started to climb the sides and the hood of the truck.

With growing fear, I fought to keep up with their advance. There were too many infected. I couldn't shoot fast enough.

A roar shattered the silence. Deep and raw, it stopped all movement for half a second. I didn't look to see who was making the sound. Deep down, I knew.

Thallirin.

From the corner of my eye, I caught an eruption of bodies and blood to my right. I barely registered the devastation or its source as I nocked, drew, aimed, and released again and again. As my arrows found their marks, my targets would fall back from the truck, only to make room for the next ones. As a whole, they climbed higher, clearing the hood and reaching for me.

The truck lurched under my feet at the same time I heard the squeal and crunch of metal. The front bumper swung through the infected on the hood, knocking half of them back to the ground. The infected it missed didn't look to see what was happening but rushed for me. I never stopped firing as I stepped back from the cab, trying to give myself room. The canvas of the soft-sided truck slightly gave under my foot but held.

I stepped back and up again, onto the first support, relentless in my determination to live. I retreated onto the soft canvas again.

One second, the roof was holding; the next, it ripped. My right foot went through. Hands closed around it. I screamed, struggling to pull free as the canvas ripped further. The bow slipped from my hands.

Thallirin roared.

The truck tilted and started to fall to the side, taking me with it as teeth bit down on my calf. I cried out and watched the blood-soaked pavement rush toward me.

CHAPTER EIGHT

THALLIRIN APPEARED BEFORE I HIT THE GROUND, PULLING ME free and taking off at a run. He jumped onto the roof of a car, the metal buckling under his weight, launched us onto the roof of a ranch house, then landed on top of a two-story home.

The moment he set me down, we both clawed at my leg. The first layer of clothing was torn and bloody. A choked sob escaped me, and I started shaking violently as Thallirin continued to peel back layers of material. It was hard to see anything until he exposed my reddened and unbroken skin.

I stared at the two crescent-shaped indents for several long moments then fell back against the shingles and looked up at the pale blue sky.

I'd been bitten.

"Holy fuck," I said shakily.

If not for my layers, I would be changing already.

Morphing into a mindless meat-sack. No. I'd be headless. Dead.

Sitting up, I looked at the skin again, disbelief and relief making the marks seem surreal.

A tremor underneath me drew my attention from the bite to Thallirin, who knelt in the same spot, still looking at my leg. He was shaking hard enough to send snow sliding down the roof.

There was a torn bit of earlobe on top of his head—it wasn't his because it wasn't grey—and a general coating of gore covering him. I remembered the explosion of bodies and bloody bits and then the bumper. He'd been trying to get to me, I realized.

He lifted his gaze from my leg to my face.

If I'd thought him cold and angry looking before, I'd been wrong. He was dark with rage and barely keeping his shit together. But was that rage directed at me for being bitten or at the infected?

Before I could decide, he grabbed the back of my head, his steel fingers holding me in place, and set his forehead to mine. For a heartbeat, I thought he was going to try to kiss me and that I'd need to throat punch him. But, he didn't. Instead, his shuddering exhale warmed my face before he closed his eyes.

It took a moment to realize that he wasn't mad at me or trying to make a move. He was scared and probably just as relieved as I was that the bite hadn't broken the skin.

Below us, the fighting continued, infected calling out to

one another as they tried to overcome the few fey guarding the precious trucks, our only escape route.

"They need you," I said.

"You need me."

His words were barely more than a rasp, and in them, I heard a pain so deep I wanted to cringe away. Yet, at the same time, I wanted to comfort him. Him. Thallirin, my stalker. The guy who obsessively watched over me and just saved my life because of that deep obsession. The same guy who was acting like losing me would have been the end of his world.

I couldn't wrap my head around any of it, and I knew we didn't have time for me to try.

"I swear I'm not leaving this roof," I said. "There's too many infected down there and not enough fey."

He pulled away and stared at me for a very long moment as groans and squishy noises continued to assault us.

"Take the snow and wash your face. Now."

The calm, slow way he said it tripped my panic switch. I looked down at myself, noting the goo on my clothes. I was covered with transferred goo from being carried, a risk we both knew he'd needed to take to keep me alive. And, looking at the mess on his face, I realized what I probably had on my forehead, too.

I grabbed a wad of snow and rubbed it over my face.

"Did I get it all?" I asked with my eyes closed.

"Again," he said.

I repeated the process twice more before he said I was clean.

"They can use ladders," he said, standing. "Yell for me." Then he jumped off the roof into the mess of infected and started thinning the herd.

A weird feeling settled in my stomach, and I wasn't sure what to think. The depth of his infatuation was scary in its intensity because I had no doubt that he'd abandon his fellow fey to get to me again if I called out for him.

I watched him fight, viciously ripping off head after head. He was a machine. A monster. But, the kind I'd want with me in just this situation. He kept the infected from reaching the house and helped his brothers determinedly fight the horde.

I couldn't say how many infected there were. The creatures were smart, though. They kept trying to get to the truck engines now that I was out of reach. The one I'd fallen through lay on its side with the hood open and fluids spilling onto the ground.

The infected not trying to gut the trucks were swarming the fey, who worked tirelessly, ripping off heads. I lost sight of Thallirin twice under their numbers and felt a twinge of worry, mostly for my fate if something happened to him.

Abruptly, the infected started to flee like someone had called a retreat. One minute, the street was filled with a writhing mass of bodies; the next, it was empty.

The fey looked around and at each other.

"What do you see, Brenna?" Thallirin asked.

I stood carefully and looked around. The infected were gone, leaving only trampled snow in their wake.

"Nothing."

He looked at one of the other fey.

"Use the roofs and find the others."

The fey hopped up onto a building and took off at a run, jumping from house to house, following the path that our group had left. Below me, the fey started moving the infected bodies to the side, clearing the road. They righted the truck, and I wondered if it could be fixed.

Thallirin jumped to another roof and used the snow to clean off what he could. The rest of the fey took turns doing the same.

I stayed where I was, face stinging with cold, safely freezing my ass off on the roof. I could feel Thallirin's gaze on me as we waited.

It didn't take long for everyone to show up. Most of the fey were carrying totes of supplies. The ones who weren't loaded down with totes carried the humans.

"What happened?" Ryan asked.

"Infected trap," Thallirin said. "Brenna's on the roof."

The fey carrying Ryan set him down and jumped up by me.

"Can I help you?" he asked.

"Yes, please."

Under Thallirin's sharp eye, the fey held me gently as he delivered me to the blood-soaked ground and left me beside Garrett. Around us, the fey loaded the trucks in a flurry while Ryan and another fey checked the engine the infected had tried to destroy.

Someone gave me a new, clean jacket to switch into, as well.

"How did they spring the trap?" Garrett asked.

"They were hiding in the garages. On this street and on other streets, I think. They all came out at once. It was crazy. How did they know to be here? And why wait so long to come out?"

"They're getting smarter. They saw our pattern and set a trap. Disable the vehicles and our means of escape, and we'd be easier targets."

The idea that the infected were getting that much smarter made me a little sick.

Zach came over and stood on the other side of me.

"Was there any trouble where you were?" I asked.

"None," Zach said. "It was creepy how quiet it was."

"We'll need to be smarter next time," Garrett said.

DREAMS OF BECOMING infected and of lying in wait to eat Zach and kill my mom plagued me all night. I gave up trying to sleep and rose well before dawn to make breakfast. Steaks and biscuits were ready by the time Zach emerged.

"Couldn't sleep?" he asked.

"Not well. I think I killed you twice."

"Good to know I'll be one of your targets if you turn."

I gave him a look just as Mom rolled into the kitchen with Uan not far behind.

"Stop teasing your sister, Zachy," Mom said.

He grinned and took a big bite of his steak. Mom looked at me with concern.

"You okay?" she asked.

She'd freaked out when I told her what happened and showed her the bite bruise. But, she didn't try to tell me I shouldn't go out again or try to keep Zach home. Supplies were necessary to live.

"I'm fine," I said, lying.

The idea of going out again made my hands shake. I knew it would just be easier to let the fey do everything for us, but that was setting us up for failure. My family and I were adapting with the world as it changed. Hiding away would just make it harder when we had to gather for ourselves. And, we would at some point. I'd already seen a few other fey pairing up with single women and gathering just for them. Eventually, it would be every family for itself.

Zach and I hurried to finish breakfast so we could arrive at the wall just before first light. The same number of humans were there despite what happened yesterday. Since they hadn't been bitten, it made sense.

Zach stopped me in the middle of the street before we reached the group.

"You're not fine, and you know it," he said quietly. "I can feel you shaking. If you go, your fear will put us all at risk. Give yourself today."

"And let you go out alone?"

"I won't be alone," he said, tilting his head toward the group.

Ryan noticed us then.

"Morning," he called. "You two ready?"

Zach and I closed the distance to the group.

"I'm staying back today," I said.

"You okay?" he asked.

"Just a little bruised. Nothing that will keep me benched for too long."

He nodded and glanced at Zach. "We'll stick together."

"Thanks," I said.

I watched everyone leave, not noticing Thallirin by the wall until it was just us.

"Not going today?" I asked, walking toward him.

"There's no need."

I glanced away uncomfortably, knowing it was because I hadn't gone. My discomfort and annoyance didn't remove my need to say what needed to be said, though.

"Thank you," I said, looking at him again. "I know I've been rude in my rejections, but that didn't stop you from helping me. If not for you, I'd be dead. The headless kind of dead."

He turned his head, looking away from me for a moment. Before I could wonder why, I saw an oozing bite on his neck.

I hissed out a sympathetic breath.

"I'm sorry, Thallirin. I was so caught up in what happened to me I never thought to ask if you were okay. You should really go to Cassie's to get that bite cleaned up."

His steady gaze claimed mine, making me nervous as he continued to say nothing. I hated when he just watched. Feeling nervous was as bad as feeling fear.

"Well, um. Just...thanks. I'll see you around."

I hightailed it out of there.

Briefly, I considered going to the wall to guard, but Zach was right about giving myself time. I needed to think of something else besides survival for today. Before the quakes, when I'd wanted a break from life, I would binge watch some TV. TV was out, but we had a whole stack of movies.

My steps quickened as I neared the house. I wondered if Uan had ever watched *Pretty Woman*.

I opened the door and took one step into the house before freezing. The faint sounds coming from Mom's bedroom made my mouth drop. Her gasping squeals and Uan's echoing grunts and groans had me backing up and carefully shutting the door again.

I stared at the dark panel in shock.

My mom was having sex. With Uan. Vigorously.

"You knew it was going to happen," I said to myself.

But I hadn't considered that I'd hear it. Ever.

Having the option of a day watching movies shockingly ripped away from me, I turned and wandered away from the house. Briefly, I wondered if my close call yesterday pushed Mom to rush into having sex with Uan. Just as quickly as the thought occurred, I brushed it away. Based on the sounds she'd been making, she was having a good time. A really good time. There wasn't a lot of pleasure to be had in this world anymore, and I was glad she'd grabbed some for herself, no matter what the reason.

When was the last time I'd had that level of a good time? I struggled to remember. I'd had two boyfriends where the relationship had progressed far enough for sex, and I'd liked it well enough. Then Van had happened. Right now, the idea of sleeping with anyone didn't spark any interest in me, and I doubted it ever would again.

I walked for several minutes before it dawned on me that I had nowhere to go. Stopping in the center of the street, I looked around at the houses, lost.

A crunch of snow behind me had me pivoting.

Thallirin was there, watching me. I studied his expression, wondering what was going through his head, and decided to ask.

"I can never tell what you're thinking. Your expression doesn't seem to change. Are you mad?"

"No."

"So what are you thinking?"

"You look worried. Why?"

I found it kind of funny we were both speculating about each other's thoughts. Since I sure as hell wasn't going to tell him I just busted my mom and Uan having sex or that I was debating if I would ever have nice sex again, I settled for a safer topic.

"I...uh...how's your bite? Did Cassie clean it up?"

"No. She is with her children."

"You should really get it looked at. It could get infected. At least go home and take a shower?"

I tried to say it nicely so he didn't feel like I was trying to get rid of him. But, I kind of was. As much as I appreciated what he'd done yesterday, I did not want to spend my day with him trailing behind me.

"I do not have a home."

That brought my errant thoughts to a halt.

"Where do you sleep?"

"Outside."

"Are you kidding me?"

"No."

"Are you always this serious and literal?"

"Yes."

I shook my head and knew what I needed to do even if I didn't like it.

"Come on. Let's find you a house where you can at least shower and wash that bite."

I looked around at the houses, wondering who would be willing to let a fey in. Probably another fey.

"This way," Thallirin said, taking charge before I could decide a direction.

I followed him to Hannah and Emily's house. It was a choice that surprised me until I saw Merdon standing outside, leaning against a tree in Hannah's front yard.

"Hey, Merdon," I said. "Do you—"

The door opened.

"Brenna!" Hannah called. "Come in here. You can help me."

I tore my gaze from Merdon's scowl and looked at Hannah as she swayed on her feet.

"What do you need help with?" I asked.

"Finishing this." She held up a bottle of tequila, and I smiled.

"That's perfect. Thanks, Hannah." I looked at Thallirin. "Come on."

He followed me to the house, and Hannah frowned at him.

"Are you going to poop on my party?" she asked, blocking the door.

"He won't," I said. "But he does need to use your shower. Is that okay?"

She shrugged.

"Sure. Come on in."

She swept her arm aside and gestured for us to enter. The house felt toasty warm as I stepped in. Taking off my shoes, I looked around the space. There was a dining room table set up in the middle of the room with a chair pushed aside near the TV, which was playing a movie.

"How much do you want?" Hannah asked, holding up the bottle.

"At least a half a glass," I said, smiling at her. "Thanks so much for inviting us in. Where's the bathroom?"

She waved a hand down the hall then wandered in the direction of the kitchen.

"Go ahead and shower," I said. "Call me when you're done and dressed again. I'll help you disinfect the bite."

He glanced at me, then Hannah. I could see his shoulders rise and fall in a deep breath.

"Go ahead and say what you want to say," I said.

"It is nothing."

He walked away from me, and I stared after him. I didn't like it when people hedged around what they wanted to say. Blunt honesty might hurt a little, but it took a lot of guesswork out of trying to figure out what people really meant by their long looks or sullen silences.

"Well, damn," Hannah said. "How'd you get him to not be bossy? Because Merdon needs a lesson in shutting his mouth."

I looked at Hannah as she wove her way toward me, a half-filled glass in one hand and the bottle in the other.

"That's a pretty dress," I said.

She looked down at her dress, and I gently removed the bottle from her grip while she was distracted.

"I haven't worn anything pretty in ages," I continued, fibbing. "Here, take a seat. I want to feel like a real person for a while. Do you mind if I pour myself a glass?"

"Go for it," she said with a wave of her hand, the half-glass she was still holding for me already forgotten.

Hannah wasn't the first drunk I'd manipulated. Before the quakes, Mom had occasionally gotten down on herself. It hadn't happened since the quakes, but I figured it was more due to the scarcity of booze than an improvement in circumstances.

I went to Hannah's kitchen and checked the cupboards for glasses. I found a cache of tequila bottles and a decent store of food.

"You have chips," I called. "Wanna break them out?" They were the plain potato kind but better than nothing.

"Sure," she said.

I poured myself half of a glass of tequila and grabbed a clean kitchen towel and the chips. Her eyes were closed when I returned to the table.

"Here's the chips. Looks like you need a refresher. Let me add a little more to your glass."

She opened her eyes to look at me as I took her drink and returned to the kitchen.

"So, where's your roommate?" I asked, covering the noise of the running faucet as I filled a new glass with water. I set the alcohol aside, not wanting to waste it.

"Emily's visiting James and Mary. The old people."

"Yeah, I've heard of James and Mary. Haven't seen them much."

"Nah, it's too cold for them. And they're too old to go out for supplies. The fey are good about getting stuff for them, though. James likes his scotch, but the fey can't read. So, I trade him for whatever he doesn't want." Hannah let out a small snort, like she found that funny, before continuing. "Mya doesn't know what the fey are bringing James and Mary. Even if she did, I doubt the fey would stop. Mary likes cooking for them. They always have a handful of fey over for dinner."

"That sounds nice." I came back to the table and set her

drink down. "Try that with the chips. The chips will be saltier."

I opened the bag and handed her a chip. She ate it and took a drink of her water and nodded.

"It's good."

"Have some more." I took out a handful and munched happily while considering Hannah's setup. She and Emily had it made. They had to be around my age and had a place of their own.

"What did you have to do to get your own house?" I asked.

"Watch my family die." She ate another chip slowly and stared at the table. I wasn't sure what to say to her, so I let the silence grow.

A door opened down the hall, and I looked up at Thallirin with relief. His dark, wet hair was pulled back from his neck, exposing the bite. It was hard to focus on the wound, though, when he wore no shirt. I took in the enormous breadth of his shoulders and chest. He'd always seemed too large and intimidating to me. Shirtless, he was more so. And I would have been freaking out about his motivation for the shirtlessness if I couldn't see the reason for it with my own eyes. His torso was covered in bites, too.

"Damn," Hannah said, looking at Thallirin. "You have more scars than Mary has wrinkles."

Thallirin looked away, the tips of his ears darkening. The way his hand tightened on his shirt and how he shifted his weight spoke volumes. He was nervous, embarrassed, and considering running. The idea that the guy, who never seemed to experience any emotion other than anger, was feeling the same things I often felt around him was weird. It also tripped my guilt a little.

"Eat your chips, Hannah," I said.

I stood, turned the chair, and gestured to the seat while looking at Thallirin.

"Unlike the infected, I won't bite."

He moved toward me, his steps measured like he was debating the wisdom of his decision.

"I think receiving the bites was the worst part," I said, setting a consoling hand on his shoulder.

The skin under my palm radiated an insane amount of heat. So much that I slid my hand over his shoulder in awe.

He turned his head ever so slowly to look at me. A shiver ran through him. Too late, I understood the significance of what I'd done. While the fey willingly carried humans for supply runs, very rarely were the fey willingly touched by a human. And a woman's touch was something they all dreamed of.

Removing my hand, I mumbled an apology and grabbed the cloth and alcohol.

"Disinfecting them with this should be enough." I added, "I hope," under my breath.

He held still as I dabbed the tequila-soaked towel against each bite. I counted seventeen wounds by the time I reached the one on his neck.

"Does it hurt?" I asked. "The alcohol?"

"It stings."

I wouldn't have guessed it because he hadn't moved a muscle the entire time.

"Why do you wear a jacket? The rest of the fey seem fine with shirts or nothing at all. And you seem pretty warm to me. Do you get colder than the rest of the fey?"

"No. My scars scare people."

He was covering up to be less scary? That just made me a little sad for him because it wasn't the scars that made him scary. It was him. All of him. His largeness. The intensity of his observant gaze. The way a person never knew what he was thinking. But, all of that seemed a whole lot less scary seeing the way he still nervously gripped his shirt.

Finished, I stepped back.

"You're all set."

Picking up the cup I'd used, I saw Hannah had her head on the table, out cold.

"We should put her in bed. She's probably going to sleep all day."

Thallirin put on his shirt while I got rid of the towel and cup since I didn't think either should be reused. He picked Hannah up carefully when I returned and followed me upstairs. I picked a bedroom at random and stepped aside for him. The way he set Hannah down gently, even taking the time to adjust the pillow under her head and brush her hair back from her face, seemed so out of character for a man who tried to boss me around at every turn. Then, again, I hadn't ever seen him interact with any other woman. It was always just me.

"Why me?" I asked when he turned. "Why not Hannah or some other girl?"

He straightened away from Hannah and looked at me. The beat of silence stretched to the point where I thought he wouldn't answer. When he did, it was low and almost angry.

"Many lifetimes ago, Merdon and I were banished, sent to live alone in the caves apart from our brothers. They would not look at us or speak to us. We were dead to them.

"We existed in silence. Always alert, hunted by the hellhounds. Always alone."

He slowly crossed the room, stalking me. I retreated into the hall, thinking he meant to leave. Instead, he backed me against the wall. Just like on the ladder, he set his hands on the wall on each side of my head. He didn't touch me, but I still felt boxed in. Trapped. I fought to focus on what he was saying and not my growing panic.

"Coming to the surface was a chance to end our isolation. A chance for redemption in the eyes of our brothers. Merdon and I thought the humans we found were pathetic in their weakness."

He tilted his head, studying my face.

"You are not pathetic, Brenna, and have more power than you know. It wasn't until we learned Drav had discovered a female that we thought to want something more than redemption. But I learned quickly I would not have a female of my own. Women look at me with fear and turn away in disgust."

The way he continued to study me made me nervous.

"The first time you saw me, you didn't look away. You met my gaze. There was no fear in your eyes.

"You gave me hope." He looked away from me then. "I have heard your words, Brenna. I know you do not want me as I want you. When you look at me without fear, I tell myself your gaze means nothing and try to kill the hope that you might someday change your mind. But, like a hellhound, the hope refuses to die."

With a last look at me, he walked down the hall, and the front door opened and closed.

I stood there, trying to process what had just happened. His admission made me feel cruel. He'd been shunned and feared by all the other women he'd laid eyes on before me.

I might not have looked at him with fear in my eyes, but I'd still felt it. How many times had I told him to leave me alone because of it?

My guilt grew stronger at the realization that he was as desperate for me to notice him as something more than a big, scarred, scary fey as I'd been to have him stop noticing me.

What was I supposed to do now?

From the bedroom, Hannah said, "Don't worry, Brenna. Everything dies."

CHAPTER NINE

SWEARING SOFTLY, I RUSHED TO PUT ON MY JACKET AND BOOTS and yanked the front door open. However, I didn't see Thallirin anywhere. Tolerance was big, but not that big.

Closing the door behind me, I hurriedly started down Hannah's front walk.

"Brenna!"

I looked at the figure approaching from the left. Angel waved and picked up her pace. I scanned the area to my right again, searching for any sign of Thallirin before moving toward her.

"I thought you were going to run away from me for a minute there," she said with a smile when I reached her.

"No. I was looking for someone."

"Oh?"

"Did you need something?" I asked, ignoring her hint that I should tell her who.

"I wanted to invite you to lunch."

"Why?" I didn't mean to say it like I had, but I couldn't help feeling her invitation was a little strange since we didn't really know each other.

"For something to do. Now, I'm not complaining," she said, holding up her hands. "I appreciate the relative safety here. But, it does get a little boring. Spontaneous infected breaks-ins aside." She tucked her hands into her big jacket pockets and shrugged. "I figured being stuck in here for the day was probably driving you crazy after all the exciting supply runs."

"Going on supply runs isn't exciting. It's a terrifying necessity."

"Necessity?" she asked, looking truly confused.

"Yeah, how else are we going to keep feeding ourselves?"

"You could ask one of the fey to bring you supplies."

I shook my head.

"That's not a long-term solution. Eventually, some girl is going to give in, and that fey will be gathering supplies exclusively for her. Like you and Shax."

She smiled.

"You have a point. All I have to do is mention a craving, and he's out the door to look for it. I have a case of snack cakes in the kitchen because of it."

"Snack cakes?" My mouth watered at the thought of one. I'd been so busy craving anything not dog food that I'd forgotten how amazing dessert could be.

"Come on. I'll share." She turned and started walking but only made it two steps before pausing.

"Do you need to find someone first?" she asked.

"That can wait," I said, catching up to her. Thallirin had left in a rush for a reason. Maybe giving him a little time was for the best. I knew that was my stomach talking and not my conscience, though.

Angel and I walked in silence for a moment.

"Garrett mentioned you've been his partner in the truck the last few days. He makes it sound boringly harmless being out there, but I know better. I heard that yesterday was far from safe for you."

"Heard from who?" I asked, preferring not to dwell on what had happened.

"The fey talk. If you ever want to know something, just ask one of them. They don't know the meaning of privacy or secrets. Which is the second reason I thought you might want to have lunch with me. I heard that Uan's spending the day with your mom."

"Yeah, I could have used that heads up earlier."

Angel laughed.

"Have you been traumatized for life?" she asked.

"Not for life, but dinner's sure going to be awkward."

"Only if you let it," she said. "I swear, the fey don't care. My understanding is that they didn't wear much in the caves. Shirtless is their preference, even up here in the snow. I can't say I mind the views. Their muscles have muscles." A wistful smile curled her lips.

"Are we trying to unscar me or make some more?"

She chuckled.

"You've had to notice. I mean, you're not blind."

"Yeah, I've noticed. I've just been smart enough to keep that notice to myself."

"Why? These guys would love the ego boost. I accidentally flashed one. I think it was the best day of his life."

I snorted. Angel had no boundaries, it seemed.

"So, who's caught your attention?" she asked. "Any fey I know?"

"It wasn't anyone specific," I said quickly. "Just general observation."

"Oh, that's too bad. Liking one of them would fix your problem."

"Problem?"

"Having to go on supply runs. You said you didn't want to ask a fey because you might lose him to a girl. Ever think that maybe you could be that girl?"

She turned up the sidewalk of one of the houses and opened the door for me. I stepped inside before answering.

"Not really," I said. "Although I suppose now that Uan's with Mom, he'll probably get supplies, too." I kicked off my boots. "I'm not sure I'd want to stop going on supply runs, though."

"Why's that?" Angel asked, removing her jacket.

"Going outside the wall is scary. The infected are changing. Getting smarter. If I stop going out there, then something happens to force me out again, I'm not sure I'd have the skills or knowledge to survive. Going out as I am now is forcing me to adapt with the changes."

She nodded, hung my jacket by the door, and motioned for me to follow.

"Makes sense. But what about the other benefits of having a fey of your own?"

"Like what?"

She went to a kitchen cupboard and pulled out a whole box of snack cakes, which she tossed to me.

"Like not ever having to worry about turning because of a bite to the leg," she said as I caught the box.

"What kind of relationship would it be if I'm just there for the food and the sex?"

"A really good one?" She grinned. "There are a million reasons to be with a fey, not just food and sex. They're attentive, caring, funny, affectionate, great at backrubs, loyal, trustworthy—not with secrets, though—and kind, even in the face of extreme prejudice. Should I go on?"

"Kind might be a bit of a stretch," I said. "It's definitely circumstantial for those not of the fairer sex."

I opened the box and ripped into a snack cake.

"You're right, there. Shax would have tossed Garrett over the wall if I hadn't stopped him. But that was jealousy."

She opened her own box of cakes and sat at the table.

"Seriously, you've never considered taking up with a fey just for the sake of safety from infection?"

I sat and toyed with my cake.

"That's what my mom's doing. I mean, she really does like Uan. But, that's why she considered hooking up with one of them in the first place so soon after..."

It hurt to think that we'd lost Dad just over a month ago. Yet, it felt like a lifetime. So much had happened. So much had changed and kept changing.

"I'm sorry about your dad," Angel said softly.

"Me too." I took a large bite to soothe the ache in my heart.

"Thallirin would give up both testicles to be your grey someone."

I choked on my cake so hard that I teared up.

"You think I'm kidding, but I'm not," she said.

I managed to swallow and shook my head at her.

"I know you're not kidding. However, Thallirin's complicated."

"How so?"

"He wants to control everything. It's beyond stifling. It's the kind of control where you stop being who you are."

She tilted her head at me.

"Are you sure about that? I thought Shax wanted me just for the baby. That I was going to be a passing fling. That once the baby was born, he'd go back to wanting Hannah or some other girl. But he proves that theory wrong every day. Instead of assuming something, ask. The fey are incredibly honest. Like run and hide from the embarrassing moments kind of honest. You might find he doesn't want to control you at all. He probably just doesn't know how to behave around you. You're the first girl he's ever been interested in."

Thallirin's words echoed in my mind as I swallowed my last bite of cake. All the other women he'd met had been too terrified of his scars to ever give him a chance. While his scars didn't scare me, what I'd thought he wanted from me had. And because of my fear, I'd treated him just as horribly as all the rest of the assholes from Whiteman. I was better than that.

With the food in my stomach and Angel's well-meaning advice, my conscience grew so loud I could no longer ignore it.

"I think I need to take a raincheck on lunch."

"Oh, no. Why? I swear I can make us just about anything." She opened a cupboard to show her stock of food. It was downright enviable.

"It's not that. I appreciate the snack cake a lot. But, I need to go talk to Thallirin. He's the one I was trying to find," I admitted.

She grinned at me.

"That's easy. The best way to find a fey is to just shout his name. Shax can make it to the house in less than a minute, no matter where he is in Tolerance."

"I'm not going to go out there and yell Thallirin's name."

She shrugged.

"Suit yourself. It's pretty rewarding seeing one run to you."

"Like a trained dog?"

"No, like a man in love, desperate to keep you safe, fed, and happy."

I sighed. That was the last thing I wanted to see.

"I think walking to look for him will do me good. I have a lot to think about."

She nodded and followed me to the door.

"Come back anytime," she said as I slipped my boots on. "If we don't answer right away, give us a few minutes." She winked to make it clear why a few minutes might be needed, then opened the door for me.

"Thanks for the talk," I said.

"Thanks for listening."

I walked away from Angel's house with a lot on my mind.

Every single attribute that Angel had listed about the fey was true. They were decent. Never once had any of the fey done anything to justify the hate the survivors from Whiteman unleashed on them. The idea that I'd been treating Thallirin just as poorly as the Whiteman asshats had treated him didn't sit well with me. Sure, I could try to justify my bad behavior as the only means to get him to leave me alone, but I knew that wasn't true. Eden had proven that her suggestion to just tell Thallirin the truth had been the right one.

My fear had blinded me, and I cringed at the thought of what other decisions my emotions might be negatively influencing. Angel's comment about me being some fey's girl echoed in my mind.

While I knew women, including my mom, were hooking up with fey for food and immunity, I just couldn't see it as an option for myself. It felt too much like the decision I'd been forced into back at the bunker. Yet, was I being a fool for ignoring the most obvious answer for safety? The fey, for all their bigness and muscle, were nothing like Van. They were completely naïve about women and many other things, just as Angel had pointed out. And just as I'd pointed out to my mom, neither Drav nor Thallirin had threatened me or even gotten angry when I'd struck out at them.

I sighed heavily.

The bite yesterday had been terrifying. The idea that I could turn and become infected obviously weighed on me, given how much I'd dreamt about it.

Was it foolish to dismiss Thallirin's interest?

While I wasn't ready to make the decision Mom made, maybe I should talk to Thallirin and ask some questions about what exactly he wanted from me. Oh, I knew his long-term goal was to get me to be his girl in every way. But what about short-term? He was determined to protect me and had already been providing supplies for us without expecting sex from me. In fact, he'd done all of that while I was being angry and rude. Was it wrong to try to be nice to him in return?

While the answer would be 'no' for most people, it wasn't for me. It felt like all the things he'd done had been to create an obligation for me to be nice.

I sighed in frustration, hating the mental loop I was in.

Even if he continued to do as he'd done, watching out for me and my family, it seemed wrong to decide to just stay home and let the fey take all the risks when I was able-bodied. While it made sense for Angel, given her condition, and Mom, given her limitations, I couldn't see it ever making sense for me. And I couldn't imagine a life where I was safely tucked away in a house.

Yet, everyone here seemed okay with the tradeoff. Sex for safety. Although Thallirin had never said anything about sex, I hated that it felt as though everyone was pushing me toward him like he was my prearranged marriage or something.

My steps slowed, and I considered the conversation with Angel in a new light. Had she been doing the same thing?

I shook my head and kept walking. Whether she was or wasn't didn't matter because she'd said something that was completely true. Something I'd already determined for myself. I didn't know Thallirin, and if I wanted to fully understand why he had acted the way he had, then I needed to ask him.

I slowed for a fey walking toward me.

"Have you seen Thallirin?" I asked.

He shook his head but looked around us.

"He should be close," he said.

"Thanks."

I stopped a few more fey before giving up. I was starting to think that Angel was right and I'd need to yell his name to find him. My cheeks flushed at the thought. Everyone would think things that weren't true. While I didn't care what they thought in theory, I did care in reality because I didn't want them to go back to treating me like I belonged to Thallirin.

"Brenna."

I whirled around at the sound of Thallirin's voice and found him just behind me.

"You're hard to find," I said.

"Why are you looking for me?"

"Because you left before we were done talking."

He studied me in silence, and I glanced around us. The neighborhood seemed quiet, but I knew better. The fey were out there with their sharp eyes and keen ears.

"Is there somewhere we can go to continue our conversation in private?" I asked.

He nodded and started walking in the direction I'd been headed. I hurried to catch up, glancing at his face, trying to read him.

"Are you okay with talking to me?"

"Yes."

"I can't tell. It's hard to read how you're feeling based on your expression. What does your angry face look like?"

He glanced at me.

"I don't know."

"Are you angry now?"

"No."

That answer made me nervous. If that wasn't his angry face, I really didn't want to see him when he was angry. I recalled his cold expression on the roof when he'd thought I'd been bitten. It was just a flash memory because I'd been so terrified myself at the time, but I could remember the worry I'd felt.

"How often do you get angry?" I asked.

"Rarely."

"Good to know."

His steps slowed.

"You wanted to talk about my temper?"

"Not really."

He grunted and kept going. We wove our way toward the center of "town," and I followed him to a house that matched all the other homes in that section. Opening the front door, he let himself in and turned to wait for me. I hesitated to go inside.

"I thought you said you didn't have a house."

"I don't. This is Uan's. He's with your mom."

"He's not going to mind if we use it?"

"No, he's not using it now." He said it as if it was completely obvious that Uan's lack of current occupancy meant the house was free to use.

Hoping Uan truly wouldn't mind, I stepped inside. Thallirin closed the door and then stayed there, standing really close to me. I tipped my head up to look at him then started taking off my jacket.

"What are you thinking?" I asked as he watched me.

"I'm wondering what you want to say to me."

I hung my jacket in the coat closet and held out my hand.

"Can I have your jacket?"

He shrugged out of it, his chest rippling with the move. The image of him shirtless flashed in my mind. It wasn't his scars or bites that stood out in the memory but the hard ridges of his abs and the slight dip above his navel. Was I noticing because of Angel's talk or just because?

I hung the jacket up and kicked off my shoes.

"I guess it's not just one thing I want to talk about. Let's go sit in the living room."

He followed me and waited until I sat on the couch before taking the nearby chair. It creaked under his weight, and I wondered if I looked as dwarfed by him as the chair did.

"I've been very vocal about not wanting anything to do

with you. Yet, you've continued to watch out for me and bring supplies to our house. Why? Is it because of the hope you have that I'll change my mind?"

"The hope I feel is my burden, not yours. Choose no one. Choose another fey. It won't matter. I will still keep you safe and see you fed. I want nothing from you."

"That's not true. You do want something from me even if you're trying not to want it. You said you wanted a female for companionship. But we both know that's not all you want. What about sex?"

"I will not have sex with you."

The abrupt way he said it surprised me.

"Ever?"

His gaze shifted, searching the room as if he was seeking a quick escape. It was more annoying than funny. He'd already run from me once. I didn't want that happening again.

"You and I are having problems because we don't understand each other, and we never will if we keep running away from the conversations we need to have.

"We have a rule in my family. If you're thinking something, say it. Miscommunication is the number one problem in relationships."

His gaze locked onto mine at that last word.

Damn hope.

"Any kind of relationship," I said, clarifying. "Since you're always around, I'm hoping we can put aside our differences and try to be friends. To get to know one another. I was mean and rude to you because I was afraid you'd take anything else as encouragement to pursue me. I don't want to keep going as we have. But I need to know what your long-term hope is because if it's something I don't think I can give, I want to be upfront about it. I don't want to lead you on."

His ears darkened, something I'd noticed happens with the fey.

"Are you embarrassed?"

He grunted, and I felt a small amount of pity for the guy. Like Angel had pointed out, I was probably the first girl he ever liked.

"Don't be embarrassed. Just be honest. Do you want to have sex with me?"

"We shouldn't be talking about this," he said, his face getting even darker.

Realization hit me.

"Because I'm not eighteen yet?"

"Yes."

"Okay. Thank you for clarifying. I thought talking about sex was embarrassing you."

"No."

"Once I'm eighteen, do you hope to have sex with me?"

His gaze met mine. The intensity there was more than a little intimidating.

"I don't want to scare you."

"I'm not afraid of sex."

"You think I'll rape you."

I exhaled heavily and considered him for a moment.

"I was angry and afraid because you were trying to control

my options and taking away my freedom of choice. I need to choose who I'm with as much as the other person has the right to choose me. Do you understand?"

"Yes."

"If you want sex, and I tell you I don't want sex, would you force me to have sex anyway?"

"No."

"Would you try to bribe me with food or manipulate me into having sex?"

"Never."

"What about forcing me to do other things? Like staying home instead of going on supply runs? Or sitting inside a house when I don't want to?"

He leaned forward in his chair, bracing his hands on his legs.

"I don't want to take your choices from you ever, Brenna. But I will not hesitate to do so if you are in danger. I didn't ask to hold you in my arms when the infected were attacking. I did it anyway. I didn't ask to look at your leg. I needed to be sure you were safe. I will not take your choices, but I will not sacrifice your safety for your pride."

I blinked at him for a moment, trying to decide if I needed to be offended or properly reassured. I went for reassured.

"It's not pride, Thallirin. It's fear. You say you don't see it in my eyes, but it's here inside of me. I'm afraid of you, not because of your scars but because of the power you could have over me if you wanted."

He looked down, and a small smile tugged at his lips. It

was the first expression outside of his normal, cold detachment I'd ever seen on him.

"What's funny about that?" I asked.

"That you think I have any power over you. You control me, Brenna. Not the other way around."

I considered him for a long moment, liking the idea of holding power over someone like him. It made me feel safer. But was it true? He'd just admitted there were times he would override my choices. But when it came to sex, I didn't think he would. In that one instance, I truly believed that I would have the power and freedom of choice.

Elation, almost to the point of tears, filled me as I studied him. For the first time, I saw him for what he was. My protector, whether I wanted him or not.

The sound of a plane flying low over the houses had me looking at the window. When I glanced back at Thallirin, he was watching me again.

"What's your favorite food since coming to the surface?" I asked, trying to make good on my vow to get to know him.

"Meat."

"What food do you miss from back home?"

"None."

"Really? Nothing." He shook his head. "Okay. What do you do to relax and have fun?"

"I do nothing."

"You mean you literally just sit and do nothing to relax, or you haven't found anything fun and relaxing yet?"

“I haven’t found anything. Why are you asking these questions?”

“I meant what I said. I want to get to know you and to try to be friends, but I don’t want you to read more into that than there is. It’s just friends.”

He nodded once.

“Do you want to watch a movie with me?” I asked.

He grunted, and I smiled. I could deal with his short-term goal of companionship, and as long as he understood my stance on his long-term goal, which he’d aptly said was his burden, not mine, we’d be fine. He’d given me enough information to feel more comfortable around him and to think that Angel was probably right. He was bossy and just didn’t know how to act around me. And, that was something that would change the more time we spent together.

I got up and picked a movie from Uan’s selection and settled in for some TV time like I’d planned hours ago.

Thallirin barely moved throughout the movie. I knew that because I glanced at him often, trying to gauge if he was having a good time or not. He didn’t laugh at any funny scenes; he just sat there. When the credits rolled, I stood and put the movie away.

It was far too early to go home without potentially catching mom in a compromising situation, again.

“Do you think Uan would mind if we raided his kitchen for some food?” I asked.

“He will not mind.”

Thallirin followed me to the kitchen. I started opening doors at random while Thallirin shadowed me.

"Check those cupboards over there," I said, pointing. "If it's in a bag, I'm interested. If it's in a can, keep looking."

Since we were raiding Uan's supply, I felt no guilt about eating the good stuff. He owed me after what I heard earlier.

"There are bags here," Thallirin said.

I closed the door to the cupboard full of canned meats and glanced at Thallirin's find. The shelf was full of junk food.

With a squeal, I crossed the room and reached around him to snag a bag of cheesy curls. I wasn't thinking beyond my next junk food fix. That my chest had rubbed against Thallirin's arm didn't register until I was already two steps away from him and tearing into the bag.

He stood where he'd been, in front of the cupboard, the tips of his ears darkened.

The move hadn't been intentional, and the contact brief at best, but the way he continued to stand there like I'd stabbed him made me wonder what the contact really meant to him. I knew the fey craved female attention. Just talking to them made their day. Touching them could put them over the moon. Until recently, Thallirin hadn't spent much time in Tolerance. Was this the first time anyone had ever casually touched him?

"Are you okay?" I asked.

He grunted but stayed where he was, his hand gripping the cabinet door.

"I can't decide if that grunt means 'run for your life' or 'everything's fine.'"

“Everything is fine,” he rasped, his voice rougher than usual.

“We both know that’s not the truth based on how you’re gripping that handle. Are you upset because I brushed up against you? Embarrassed?”

“No.”

“Did my boob touching you freak you out because I’m not eighteen?”

“No.”

I munched on a cheese curl while considering him, then took another one and offered it to him.

“I’m not good at guessing. It’d be easier if you just told me what you’re thinking.”

He turned his head, meeting my gaze, then bit the little snack from my fingers, somehow managing to use his tongue in the process. It was warm against my fingers, and I felt it all the way to my toes.

I stared at him, guessing where his thoughts were because of the accidental brush, and I was no longer sure everything was okay. Not because of him, but because of the way my stomach had somersaulted at the feel of his tongue against the pad of my finger.

“We should watch another movie,” I said.

“Yes.”

The cupboard knob was deformed when he released it.

CHAPTER TEN

Thallirin's hand closed over my arm, halting my hasty retreat to the living room.

"Why are you afraid?" he asked.

"Why would you think I'm afraid?"

In the reflection of the television screen, I watched him tilt his head at me.

"I can hear your heart. It beats almost as quickly as when we were on the roof."

"When I was afraid I'd been bitten."

He grunted, and this time, I knew it was in agreement. Reluctantly, I turned and looked up at him.

"You liked it when I brushed up against you."

"I did."

"How much?"

"I would give anything to have you do it again...when you're old enough."

I took a deep, slow breath, considering what that meant. He was being clear and honest with me about his feelings. He wanted me as a man wants a woman, but he had also told me his wants weren't my problem. Over eighteen or under eighteen, he wasn't going to force me in any way. All of that reassured me immeasurably. What didn't reassure me was the way my pulse was now racing and the way my gaze dipped to his mouth. Was my age protecting me or hindering me?

I wasn't sure I was ready to consider that question in depth.

"If you're worried that I'm afraid of you because of what happened in the kitchen, I'm not. And I'd rather not talk about why my heart isn't behaving as it should right now. Let's just focus on spending some non-hostile time together."

He released me to take the snack that I handed him, and I moved to find another movie. Looking at the titles didn't distract me from the cause of my racing pulse.

Like a switch had been turned on, I couldn't stop feeling his tongue against my finger. It was messing with my head. After what had happened at the bunker, I'd thought any sexual type of feelings had been killed. But, apparently, I'd been wrong. Why Thallirin, though? Was it because he was the first one to touch me like that since I'd been rescued?

When I turned back to him, he was standing where I'd left him.

"Do you want to sit next to me?" I asked.

He tilted his head and studied me for a moment.

"What do you want?" he asked.

Another strong surge of relief swept through me. He'd truly understood all my talk about choices.

"I'd like to try sitting next to you if that's okay."

"Yes."

He sat on the couch, and I put in another movie then joined him. A full couch cushion separated us, and I was okay with that. Yet, instead of watching the opening scene, I studied him, noticing more than I ever had before.

Scars crisscrossed his face. Some lighter and smaller, some darker and bigger. They continued down his neck, and I knew from seeing him shirtless that he had them elsewhere, too. I wanted to ask why he was so marked when fey supposedly healed miraculously but knew he was sensitive about them.

Seeing beyond the scars, I studied his features. He was handsome with his dark grey skin, arched brows, strong chin, and sculpted nose. The pointed ears were a little distracting, but I was growing more used to the sight of them by the day.

"Thallirin?"

He looked at me.

"Never mind," I said, having glimpsed the color of his eyes. Dark green edged the deep yellow of his irises.

Why was I paying attention to all of these details now? I turned toward the TV and tried to forget my weird reaction to him when he'd licked my finger.

We watched the second movie together with no other conversation. When it finished, I set the half-eaten bag of junk food aside and swiveled on the couch so I faced him again.

"I don't know about you, but I could go for some real food. Would you like to come over for dinner?"

"Yes."

"Please don't read into this invitation and go back to acting like you own me."

He looked down, that rueful smile reappearing.

"What?" I asked.

His smile vanished as he met my gaze.

"I will never own you, Brenna. You own me."

Uncomfortable, I stood and went to the kitchen. I didn't want to own Thallirin.

I reached for the damaged knob, my fingers tracing the evidence of how much Thallirin wanted me. My stomach did a weird, twisting flip, and my heart joined in. What was wrong with me?

I opened the cupboard and put the snack food away. When I turned, Thallirin was only a few steps behind me.

"I think it should be safe enough to head back to my house now."

We left Uan's and walked side by side down the street. The long stares our companionable stroll drew from the meandering fey had me shaking my head. By the end of the day, Thallirin would be inundated with questions about how he'd changed my mind.

It took a few minutes to reach home since I wasn't in any rush. And when we got there, I rang the doorbell instead of just letting myself in. Uan answered the door almost immediately.

"Hey, Uan," I said. "Zach back yet?"

"Yes," he said, moving aside so we could enter.

I put away my things and went to the kitchen. My eyes widened at the sight of the boxes spread all over the place. Mom and Zach were sorting through all the food the boxes contained.

"I take it today went well," I said, looking at Zach.

"For me. Do you know you have a shadow?"

I glanced at Thallirin, who stood back, watching us.

"Yeah. Mom, this is Thallirin. Thallirin, this is my mom, Nancy. I hope it's okay I invited him to dinner."

"Of course," Mom said, studying me. "Is that why you rang the doorbell?"

I slowly shook my head.

"As you probably already know, I didn't go on the supply run today."

"Oh." I could see by her face that she knew exactly what had happened and why I'd used the doorbell.

"I'm sorry about that, sweetie. Had I known..."

I waved my hand at her.

"Don't worry about it. Thallirin and I hung out at Uan's and watched some movies. It was good."

She smiled and glanced at Thallirin again.

"We're having roast tonight. I think you'll like it." She looked at Zach. "Let's put all of this in the living room for now. I'm not sure what we'll do with a case of adult diapers, but maybe someone can use them."

"Adult diapers?" I asked, looking at Zach.

"There was so much stuff that Uan and I just some grabbed boxes and came home."

"Where did you go?" I went to the cupboard for dishes while Uan, Zach, and Thallirin began to move boxes.

"Harrisonville again. There was a distribution center south of town, way off the highway. A fey spotted it last night, but Ryan figured there would be too many infected. However, given the trap they set for us in town, he decided we should try it. There were only a handful of infected in the place. Slower ones. There was so much stuff we filled the supply trucks in less than an hour. One of the guys from Tenacity knew how to drive a semi-truck. So, we filled up the trailer of one by the loading dock and brought back as much as we could."

Mom set the table, and I brought over the food. When the guys were finished moving everything to the living room, they joined us.

"And get this," Zach said, taking the lid off the slow cooker to fork himself a hunk of roast. "Matt would only take thirty percent from what we fit in the three trucks we borrowed." He passed the meat fork to Uan. "Granted, we crammed as many of us as we could in the cab of every vehicle in order to pack supplies in the truck the humans rode in, but still. A full semi-trailer's worth of supplies came here. There wasn't enough room on the shelves of the supply shed for everything we brought back."

"That's great," I said, helping myself to some carrots and potatoes. "About the supplies, not about Matt. Why did he refuse more?"

"I think he's keeping to the rules so people know not to expect handouts instead of working."

It made sense.

I took a bite, enjoying the vegetables. I'd eaten too many cheese curls.

"I hope you don't mind, but I ate some of your food today, Uan," I said after swallowing. "I didn't want to come back and bug you guys."

"You are welcome to any food I have," he said. "It will be my turn to go on supply runs soon, and I will bring more." He glanced at Mom. "In a few days."

She blushed, and Zach and I shared a look.

"So, Thallirin and I heard the plane fly overhead today," I said, changing the subject.

"We did, too," Mom said.

"Oh, yeah. Matt said they spotted some signs of survivors to the southeast," Zach said. "They want a group to go out tomorrow to look for them instead of going on a supply run."

One day without me, and Zach had all the interesting news.

"Are they looking for volunteers for that?" I asked.

Zach shook his head.

"They're keeping it small. Just Ryan, Richard, and Garrett to represent the humans. Looks like tomorrow's another day off."

I ROLLED over in bed and tacoed the pillow around my head. It didn't muffle the sounds coming from the room next door, though.

I regretted not leaving with Thallirin right after dinner. I should have offered to take a shift at the wall or something. Anything would have been better than listening to Mom and Uan have "quiet" sex all night.

Giving up on sleep, I tossed my pillow aside and slipped a pair of jeans on over my sleep shorts. My door opened soundlessly, and the noises continued as I crept down the hall. In the dim kitchen light, I wrote a quick note that I'd gone to Uan's for the night. I wasn't doing it to guilt Mom. She'd understand the note was so she wouldn't worry that I'd just disappeared.

Making as little noise as possible, I tossed my jacket over my tank top and slid my bare feet into my boots, not planning on being in the cold for long. I slipped outside and jogged down the road that led to Uan's place. I read the house numbers as I moved, counting them down until I found the right one. The neighborhood was quiet as I let myself inside.

In the dark, I kicked off my boots and tossed my jacket in the direction of the hooks. Then, I felt around for a light switch. I'd only explored the living room and kitchen and had no idea where the bedrooms were. I really hoped Uan had a decent bed.

Finding the switch, I flicked it on and saw a person standing less than a foot away.

I screamed. The sound was cut short by a hand over my mouth.

"Brenna, you are safe," Thallirin said, his expression showing his shock.

Dragging in a breath, I pulled his hand from my mouth.

"Shit, Thallirin. I think you almost gave me a heart attack. What are you doing here?"

Even as I asked it, his current wardrobe gave me my answer. He wore a pair of athletic shorts. That was it. The broad expanse of his scarred chest distracted me from my question. Yes, I'd seen him shirtless while at Hannah's, but I hadn't truly noticed just how muscled the man was. It was impressive and very drool-worthy. I didn't blink until his hand came up and nervously swiped over his scars.

I focused on his face, guilty I'd made him uncomfortable.

"Uan told me I could have his house," Thallirin said in his low rumble, answering the question I'd already forgotten I'd asked. "He will live with your mom now."

"Oh." I looked around awkwardly. "I'm so sorry I just barged in. I thought it would be empty."

"Why are you here, Brenna?"

I could feel a flush creeping into my cheeks as I looked up at him.

"My mom and Uan are having sex. A lot of it, and very loudly. I can't fall asleep there. I figured since Uan wasn't using his house, I could sleep here. I didn't know he'd given it to you."

I turned to reach for my jacket.

"You can sleep here if you wish," Thallirin said behind me. "There are three bedrooms to choose from. I can sleep outside."

My initial "hell, nah!" reaction to sleeping in the same house with him was killed with that last addition. It struck me right in my still sprinting, treacherous chest organ that he would endure another cold night outside just to put me at ease.

I dropped my jacket back on the floor.

"There's no way I'm kicking you out to sleep in the cold. But if there's three bedrooms and you don't mind me taking one by myself, I'll gratefully stay."

He grunted and stepped aside.

I turned down the hall opposite the kitchen and peeked into all the rooms. The master was obviously used by Uan, and more recently, Thallirin. The other two rooms were neatly made up, ready for me to claim.

"I'll take this one," I said. "See you in the morning."

I closed the door behind me, took off my jeans, and climbed into bed.

My level of trust with Thallirin was higher than I realized because I immediately fell asleep and remained comatose until early morning light shined through the bedroom's window.

Stretching, I listened to my knees pop and yawned loudly before frowning and lifting my head to look at the open door. I'd definitely closed it last night.

Frowning, I got out of bed, more worried about the hint of

char I smelled in the air than why Thallirin had opened my door. My nose led me to the kitchen. Still dressed in athletic shorts, Thallirin stood in front of the stove, staring down at the smoking pan.

I waved my hand in front of my face and coughed lightly.

"I don't know what you're cooking, but if it starts smoking, it's usually done."

"Something isn't right. It's still gooey," he said, glancing back at me.

His gaze swept over me, and the plastic spatula in his hand snapped in half. I looked down at myself. Nothing was hanging out of my top, and my shorts covered my bits. All I was showing was legs and arms.

Shaking my head at his reaction, I crossed the room and reached around him to turn off the burner.

"You have the heat too high for pancakes," I said, looking at the mess in the pan. "Lower is better for those. And a cover." I reached up and turned on the hood vent. "This thing vents the smoke outside. I can't believe the smoke detectors aren't going off."

He continued to hold completely still in front of the stove, watching me.

"So, you like pancakes?"

"No," he rasped. "I was making them for you."

"You didn't need to do that."

"I wanted to do something for you. Something that was given freely." The words were sweet as was the way his eyes kept flicking to my pajamas.

"Does what I'm wearing make you uncomfortable?" I asked. "I can go put my jeans—"

"No," he said quickly.

His gaze dipped to my chest, and I watched in fascination as the tips of his ears darkened. My pulse jumped a little.

Trying to ignore both our reactions, I reached up and gently set my fingers on his chin, turning his head so I could look at his neck.

"The bite looks better," I said. I carefully ran my finger over the skin just around the scab. "It's not overly warm, which is good." I leaned closer, frowning. "In fact, it looks mostly healed. That's amazing."

He closed his eyes, and a full-body shudder shook him, obviously too much touching for him to handle while I was still wearing pajamas.

"Sorry."

I went to take my hand away, but his closed over mine. He didn't force it back, but he held it like he wanted to. Like he was trying so hard not to.

"I didn't mean to upset you," I said.

"I'm not upset."

"You look like you are."

He exhaled slowly.

"I'm desperate and confused and trying to be neither."

His honesty had me willingly returning my hand to his skin just below the bite. He didn't try to stop me, but a small noise did escape him. For the first time, I really considered what this moment might mean to him.

While my experience at the bunker previously had me writing off sexual contact for the rest of my life, I'd never once wanted to give up physical contact. Mom and Zach hugging me was a balm to my soul. Even the smallest touch or gesture from them, when I was feeling down and alone, helped. I couldn't imagine going through a lifetime without that kind of contact, let alone several lifetimes. That Thallirin had endured just that only to come to the surface and feel like I—the girl who the rules said he couldn't yet be with—was the one for him had to be torture.

"You want to be touched just as much as you don't want to be touched. Am I right?"

He closed his eyes and gave a small nod.

"I understand," I said. I trailed my fingers down his throat to his chest, tracing over the scars. He shuddered again.

"Will you tell me to stop if something bothers you?"

"Yes." The word was a rasp of a whisper.

I could lie to myself and say that I was trying to comfort him with my touch, but I wasn't. I was touching him for me, too. Because with each scar I traced, my heart beat just a little faster. My breathing became just a little shallower. I was touching him to test me. To try to figure out why I was reacting the way I was. Was it real? Why him? Those two questions quietly whispered into my mind until they wouldn't leave me alone.

"Do you want to touch me?" I asked, smoothing my palms over his shoulders.

"Yes."

The word was filled with enough need that I should have been running for the door. But I didn't. I stood my ground and asked the most terrifying question I had ever asked.

"How do you want to touch me?"

I braced myself for a boob grab or a southern grope but received neither. He opened his eyes, his gaze feathering over my face as he reached up, his hand trembling, and gently stroked a finger down my hair. Another tremor ran through him, and he dropped his hand to his side again.

That was it. He'd wanted to touch my hair.

I took his hand and lifted it to my cheek. His breathing grew ragged. Knowing I'd pushed us both far enough, I turned my head and pressed my lips to his palm to comfort and thank him.

He jerked back from me as if scalded, and an angry growl echoed from his chest.

"I'm sorry," I said, inching back. "I didn't mean to upset you."

He fisted his hand at his side, and I looked down at it, wondering what he meant to do. My gaze didn't stay there, though. It shifted to his waist, where all thought of an enraged fey evaporated at the sight of the massive tent he was sporting. No, tent was the wrong word for it. The shorts weren't that loose. His meat-mallet was trying to rip its way free of the pathetic material.

He wasn't angry. He was raging the biggest boner I'd ever witnessed. I'd never be able to unsee it.

As I stared, it twitched.

His fingers touched the bottom of my chin and forced my gaze up to his eyes.

"You're too young, Brenna. Eat. I will return."

He left the kitchen, and I stared after him in amazement. He didn't just have restraint; he had an iron will. And probably a set of blue balls from hell.

Why did that make me want to grin like an idiot?

I scraped the burnt pancake mess from the pan and started over on the breakfast he'd been trying to make me. I knew pancakes weren't the fey's first choice in breakfast food. It was meat. It was always meat. That Thallirin had been up trying to cook something specifically for me only made me smile more. Even with the promise of nothing, he was still doing what he'd said he would do.

My smile fell, and I felt a little cruel. Oh, guilt wasn't going to get me to hop into bed with him, but I sure was going to try to be a lot nicer and more understanding.

By the time Thallirin returned, showered and dressed, I had a nice stack of pancakes made and the table set.

We had a quiet breakfast together where he kept glancing at me.

"What are your plans for today?" I asked finally.

"I have no plans."

"Me either. Want to spend some more time together?"

"Yes."

"Great. I'm going to head back to my house to shower and change. Should I meet you back here in an hour?"

He grunted, and I went to the bedroom to put on my jeans.

They weren't on the floor where I'd left them, but on the bed, neatly folded. The bed was made, too.

"You don't have to clean up after me," I called. "You're already doing me a favor by letting me stay here." I tugged on my pants and buttoned them.

Turning, I squeaked at the sight of him standing in the doorway. I was beginning to recognize when I'd done something he'd really liked by the color of his ears. Watching me put jeans on over my sleep shorts was about a six in his book. The palm kiss had been a seven. I wondered how he would react when I did something that ranked higher. The thought didn't upset me. In fact, I kind of wanted to find out.

Dangerous territory.

"I'll see you in a bit," I said, edging past him. "Don't give my room away while I'm gone. I might need it again tonight."

Outside, I took a deep breath and smiled. Maybe it was the good night's sleep. Maybe it was knowing I had another day where I didn't need to leave the safety of Tolerance. Or maybe it was Thallirin's now flattering attention and my resolution to be nicer to him. Whatever it was, I felt alive and happy.

Smiling even bigger, I started home. I'd only made it a block when I spotted Zach coming my way.

"If you're headed home, don't," he said.

I took in the dark circles under his eyes.

"They didn't stop?"

"Not yet. Next time you have a bright idea in the middle of the night, come get me, too," he said.

"I thought you were sleeping."

"Like anyone could sleep through that. Uan's a machine. There were like fifteen-minute breaks, at most."

"Have they come out of the room yet? Did you make sure Mom was okay?"

He gave me a disgruntled look.

"Yeah, Uan came out to make me breakfast because Mom was sleeping. He was bare-assed while making me waffles. Like I was going to eat his pube waffles."

I was laughing so hard I snorted.

"He made enough for you, too. You should go check on Mom."

"I'm good," I said between giggles. "What are you going to do today? Want to come back to Uan's? Well, not Uan's. He gave it to Thallirin because Uan's officially moving in, I guess."

Zach's expression vacillated between horror and confusion.

"I'm not sure what's getting me more. The idea of listening to Uan and Mom go at it like rabbits every night or the idea of you willingly hanging with Thallirin."

"Har-har. Thallirin didn't understand what was going on before or why what he was doing was so abrasive. Now that we understand each other a little better and he's not trying to boss me around, he's pretty nice. He tried making me pancakes this morning."

"You know what? I think I'm going to go see what Garrett's up to today. He has a house to himself. Maybe I'll crash there tonight, too."

I cringed at what he was hinting at.

"You think Mom and Uan will be at it the same way tonight?"

"I don't see it changing any time soon. Not the way they look at each other." His humor fled, and he looked down at the ground. I knew where his head had gone, and I gave his arm a comforting squeeze.

"She'll always be our mom," I said. "But she needs this, Zach."

He nodded.

"It just feels like the family is falling apart."

"No. It's going through an awkward growth phase. Enjoy your freedom at Garrett's while you can because Mom's going to put her foot down and demand you come home as soon as she figures out what you're doing."

"What about you? Are you going to risk staying at Thallirin's again tonight?"

Staying at Thallirin's didn't feel like a risk at all. In fact, the idea of waking up and seeing him again tomorrow morning appealed to me far too much.

CHAPTER ELEVEN

"I'M GOING TO ENJOY MY FREEDOM, TOO, WHILE I HAVE IT, AND I'm eating all of Uan's junk food while I'm there." I shivered and looked in the direction of our house. "I'd planned to go home to shower and change, but I'm not sure I want an eyeful of Uan. Let me know if there's anything going on today. Two days in a row watching movies is going to get a little boring."

"Will do. You do the same."

"I will."

He walked off toward Garrett's, and I turned around to head back to Thallirin's. If I was lucky, I'd find something else to wear at his house. The fey were known to collect women's clothes in hopes that they'd catch a female for themselves as if we were wild rabbits just running around waiting for their snares and cuddles.

Thallirin opened the door for me before I even reached it.

"Hey," I said. "Hope you don't mind I'm back so soon." I

stepped inside and removed my jacket. "Turns out Mom and Uan are still having sex. You wouldn't happen to have any spare clothes here, would you? I was hoping for a shower and a clean change of clothes when I went home."

"Go shower. I will find you something and put it in your room."

"Really? Thanks."

I closed myself into the guest bathroom and stripped down. Because of the supply runs, I didn't usually shower in the morning. It was too cold to have wet hair while guarding the trucks. And I'd skipped my shower last night because I'd assumed I'd have one this morning—it being a no-supply-run day. After going for days at a time without bathing post-quakes, I ensured I got my daily showers when I could.

Testing the water, I ducked under the spray with a sigh and washed my hair. I didn't linger long. Just long enough for my skin to turn pink and my fingers to prune. Okay, I took my sweet-ass time and loved it.

When I finally got out of the shower, I dried off then wrapped the damp towel around my torso to cross the hall. A set of clothes waited on my bed as promised.

"Thank you," I called as I dropped the towel and picked up the underwear he'd set out for me. They were mine.

Frowning, I looked in the bag on the chair and found that everything in it was mine.

I turned toward the bed again and froze at the sight of Thallirin in the doorway. He was gripping the frame, and his head hung low like he'd been punched in the balls. He wasn't looking at the ground, though. He was looking at me with tormented eyes.

As I watched, the darkness consuming the tips of his ears spread to his face and down his neck.

"Are you okay?" I said softly.

"Forgive me."

He straightened and stepped into the room.

My pulse skyrocketed, and I retreated a pace.

He didn't follow, though. He reached for the knob and pulled the door closed so I could dress in private. I exhaled slowly and wondered how I felt about what had just happened. Sure, my pulse was pounding in fear, but there was something else there, too. Something terrifyingly unexpected. Disappointment. But was it because he hadn't chased me or because I'd retreated from him and likely hurt his feelings?

I hurried to dress then left my room to look for Thallirin, unsure if I needed to apologize or thank him. He wasn't anywhere in the house, though. Figuring he might need some time to cool off, I went to the snack cupboard to look for something new then put on another movie.

It took Thallirin an hour to return, and he wasn't alone.

"Bundle up, Brenna," Zach said, in greeting. "Garrett and I had an idea."

I turned off the TV and tossed Zach what was left of the snack mix I'd opened.

"Oooh. This stuff's good."

I watched in amusement as he scooped a handful into his mouth and chewed.

"Maybe you better explain what's going on," I said.

Given Zach's mouthful, I looked to Thallirin for an explanation. For the first time ever, the big guy wasn't studying me. Thallirin's attention remained on Zach as he answered, and I knew it wasn't because Zach was horking down the snacks.

"Zach wants to take the supplies you don't need and trade at Tenacity."

Instead of asking if he was all right, I decided to let Thallirin's weirdness slide until we were alone and could talk about what had happened.

Zach finished chewing and rolled up what was left of the bag to put into his pocket.

"Garrett's in the same boat as we are. He has a surplus of stuff and is hoping he can trade for more diversity. While we could just swap out supplies with what's in the shed, we figured trading with Tenacity might open up more goodwill. And, with new survivors hopefully coming their way, maybe we can help Matt out without making it look like a freebie."

"And seeing the fey willing to trade would be a good impression on the new people," I added.

Zach grinned.

"So, you in?" he asked.

"I'm in." I hurriedly layered my outerwear then followed the pair to our house, where other fey were coming out with boxes of stuff.

"How much are we trading?" I asked.

"Mom's inside sorting. It's up to her."

"She's up and dressed?"

"Yeah, Uan came looking for me after this guy woke Mom up to get some clothes for you," he said, nodding toward Thallirin, who walked in front of us for a change.

I went inside and found Mom in the living room, directing fey.

"Morning, sweetie," she said with a smile. I went to give her a kiss, and she caught me in a hard hug.

"You, Zach, and I will need to talk tonight. Okay?"

I nodded and hugged her back.

She released me and explained what she was trying to do. We had a surplus of toiletries. She was sending most of that, except for the toilet paper, and some tomato-based canned goods that the fey didn't really care for.

"I don't expect to get much food for the soaps, but maybe people would be willing to part with some clothes big enough to fit the fey." She paused. "You know, so they don't have to walk around in the buff. And, any canned vegetables that they're willing to swap for pasta sauce would be good."

I grinned.

"I'll do my best. But I don't think you need to worry so much about clothes for the fey. They always seem to find something to wear when they want it."

She frowned at Uan, who was watching us.

"We're an open family, Mom. Remember? It's no big deal."

"You weren't here listening to your brother gag."

"According to Zach, you were still sleeping."

Mom flushed.

"Chicken," I said softly.

She swatted me.

"Go trade and come home for dinner. Both of you."

"Yes, Ma'am," I said playfully.

Zach, Thallirin, and I followed the fey to the wall, where we met up with Garrett and a few other fey.

"I'm swapping some stuff out for food, too," Garrett said, inspecting our boxes. "I think there should be enough interest. Ready?"

One of the fey stepped up to carry me. I looked at Thallirin, who conveniently had a box in his arms.

"Would you mind taking the box so Thallirin can carry me?"

Thallirin flinched a little.

"Unless you don't want to carry me?"

All the fey around us looked at him, waiting for an answer.

"I want to carry you," he said gruffly.

"Good."

The fey beside me took Thallirin's box, and I stood before him, waiting. He picked me up gently as if I were made of glass. I looked up at him, noting the dark flush in his face as he continued to look anywhere but at me. The slight tremble in his arms melted me a little, and I laid my head against his chest. His flinch at the contact was thoroughly confusing, though. In Uan's kitchen, Thallirin had been pretty clear that he'd liked me touching him. I'd seen the resulting tent. He'd definitely liked touching me. Why was carrying me different? Wasn't that what he'd wanted all along? Did seeing me naked turn him off? The idea that it might have hurt more than a little.

"Did I do something wrong?" I asked quietly.

His arms tightened around me ever so slightly.

"No."

Then he jumped the wall and was running before I could say more. I turned my head into his chest to escape the wind. He smelled nice. Like soap and him. I inhaled more deeply, and he trembled again.

"Sorry," I mumbled.

We arrived at Tenacity before my legs got too cold from the wind. The people who witnessed a swarm of fey coming over the wall were less than welcoming until they saw the supplies in the fey's arms.

Comments like "take your grey asses back home" were quickly replaced with "I can take that from here."

"The fey aren't bringing you supplies," Garrett said. "This is some of the stuff that Zach and I got on the last run. We have too much of some things and are hoping to trade."

Some of the bystanders left. One said he'd get Matt for us. The rest grumbled because they weren't getting the handouts they'd thought they were getting.

Ignoring them, I looked up at Thallirin.

"You going to let me stand?"

The muscle in his jaw flexed as I waited for some kind of answer. Slowly, he lowered me. He still wouldn't meet my eyes, though, when he straightened.

"Thank you, Thallirin," I said instead. "Will you carry me home, too?"

He grunted.

Staying by him, I waited for Matt with Garrett and Zach. If Matt was surprised to see us with a bunch of fey and supplies, he didn't let on.

"Welcome back," he said with a handshake for each of us. "I hear you want to trade."

"If you think anyone would be interested," Garrett said.

"Oh, I think there might be interest. What are you looking to trade for?"

"Anything we don't currently have," Garrett said. "We'll consider each offer."

Matt waved us over to their supply shed. "Set up in here. It'll keep you out of the wind. And keep things orderly." He turned to the crowd.

"Spread the word that some of the humans from Tolerance are here to trade. Everyone's welcome to see what they have and to make offers."

People came in droves to look at what we had and left again to check their homes for anything we might want. I spent most of my day negotiating for things I thought any of us might use. There wasn't much to be had. I let four jars of sauce go in exchange for a can of tuna fish because the woman had seemed a little desperate. Zach started doing the same, taking two new movies in exchange for another jar of pasta sauce.

Near noon, one woman came with a hot portion of stew for Garrett, Zach, and myself in exchange for two cans of diced tomatoes, each. Since my stomach was growling, I readily agreed. We took a small break while the fey watched over our things. I took a bite of potatoes and peas then stabbed a piece of meat and held it out to Thallirin.

"Do you want some?"

He ate it off my fork without reply. I shared at least half the meat with Thallirin before I licked the gravy from the bowl with my finger. When I looked up, I caught Thallirin staring before he quickly averted his gaze.

Returning to my spot, I started up the trading once more. Our supplies slowly dwindled, and our eclectic collection of items grew.

We only had a few boxes left when we heard the engines approach from outside the wall. Matt, who'd been monitoring the trading from a distance, came over.

"The new survivors are here," he said. "I've sent word to Mya. She and Drav are coming over to talk to them. You're welcome to stay, but I think we should shut down the trading for now."

"Sure thing," Garrett said. "Mind if we do this again sometime?"

"Anytime. You were more than fair with your trading." He lowered his voice. "This will go a long way to keep relations between the two camps hospitable, too."

Garrett nodded.

"That's what we were thinking."

We packed up quickly.

"Want to stay and listen to Mya's speech?" Zach asked.

"No, thanks. I've heard it once before. I think I'm ready to head home instead of gawk at scared, starved people."

By silent agreement, Zach and I left what remained of the supplies we'd originally brought with us and took back only what we'd traded for. Matt would need the supplies for the new mouths.

I looked up at Thallirin.

"Ready to take me home?" He immediately scooped me up, cradling me gently once more, and strode from the storage shed.

I didn't say anything until we crossed over Tolerance's walls.

"We need to talk," I said. "In private."

He grunted and jogged to Uan's house. No. Thallirin's house. My feet finally touched ground again on Thallirin's front step. He reached around me to open the door. Heat enveloped me as I took off my boots and jacket.

"I know Mom said we're having dinner there, but I'm hungry now." I went to the kitchen and dug around for the open bag of cheese curls. While I hadn't been kidding about my hunger, I mostly needed a moment to collect my thoughts.

Turning, I found Thallirin watching me from the other side of the table. He averted his gaze.

"I'm sorry about this morning," I said. "I know I'm safe with you, and I shouldn't have backed away when you saw me in the bedroom."

He grunted but still didn't look at me.

"Are you mad at me?"

That got his attention, and he looked up as he spoke.

"Never."

His gaze slid back to the table, and I considered him for a long, silent moment.

"Then, I'm guessing this whole not looking at me thing is because of seeing me naked. I am sorry if it took you by surprise. I'll try to be more conscious of closing the door. But, nudity is nothing to be ashamed of, and I would be really grateful if you stopped acting like I did something wrong."

His gaze slowly lifted.

"You did nothing wrong. The only shame this morning was mine."

"Why?"

He exhaled slowly, still watching me.

"I did not think of you as a child when I saw you."

"Ah." I considered him for a moment, more than a little relieved he hadn't been turned off at the sight of me. "Since I have the body of a woman, I think it's understandable. I'm not a child anymore, Thallirin. I haven't been for a while."

"You're eighteen?"

"No. Not yet. But, that doesn't make me a child."

His brow twitched slightly, and I knew I'd confused him.

"How about we watch a movie for a while and stop overthinking this, okay?"

He grunted and went to the living room. I followed.

"What are you in the mood for?" I asked, bending to inspect the movies. "Action? Comedy?" I glanced back and caught him staring at my butt. When he saw I'd noticed, he immediately averted his gaze.

"Okay. You win," I said, crossing my arms and facing him. There was safety in him thinking of me as a child, but it wasn't fair to him. Feeling what he was feeling for me, and all the things I'd said to him about being a pedophile, was tearing him apart. And, it was making him act weirder than the fey-norm.

"I'm not a child, Thallirin," I said. "Go on. Say it."

"You are still a child, Brenna."

"By how many days?" He blinked at me. "You don't know. Me, either. My birthday is in March. Sometimes the snow is gone by then, sometimes it's not. It really just depends on the year.

"It was Thanksgiving before the quakes. It's been months since then. Christmas and New Year's have passed. But by how much? I've lost track of the days, and there's no calendar to know. So, am I turning eighteen tomorrow or in two months? And if it's in two short months, how does that still make me a child? Do you think there's some magical change that occurs on the stroke of midnight on my birthday?"

"I'm not trying to be mean, Thallirin. All I want is for you to realize that turning the big one-eight isn't going to change who I am. My body will look the same. Well, maybe a little fuller if I keep eating all the junk food in this house, but I'll still be this same person I am now. I'll still be me."

"I know."

"Then stop trying to not look at me. If you want to look,

look. It doesn't make you a pedophile because I'm not a child. I should have never said that to you. If having you look at me upsets me, I will tell you. But, right now, it's more upsetting having you act all weird around me. I was starting to like the you before you saw my boobs."

He grunted.

"Does that mean we're good and you're going to stop pretending like I don't exist?"

"I know you exist."

"Good." I went back to the movies and picked something fun.

When I turned, Thallirin was watching me. This time, he didn't look away. I smiled and sat beside him. He handed me my snacks, and I spent the next little while happily crunching away. When it started to get dark out, I paused the movie.

"We better head over to Mom's for dinner," I said, standing.

He stood slowly, crowding into my space when I didn't back up. I tilted my head to look at him.

"Do you want to come to dinner with me?"

"Yes."

"Do you mind if I sleep here, again, afterward?"

"No."

I smiled my thanks but didn't move, my pulse hammering in my chest again. I didn't know what I wanted from him. But, I wanted something. A touch? Some affectionate words? None of it felt right yet, but thinking of walking away felt wrong, too.

He seemed to be in the same place because he didn't move

either. His gaze dipped to my lips, and my heart stuttered for a moment.

"Go get your jacket, Brenna," he said.

I quickly stepped around him and put my stuff on.

The walk to Mom's was quiet, each of us lost in our own thoughts. Like the evening before, I rang the doorbell. Uan answered it with a grim expression.

"No more doorbells," he said.

"Um...okay. Why?"

"Because this is your damn house," Mom said from the kitchen as I took off my jacket.

She was scowling when I entered the kitchen. Ignoring it, I went to her and kissed her cheek.

"I know this is my house. I also know that you two love birds are in a new phase, and I'm trying to respectfully give you some time and space."

She looked only slightly appeased.

"Have you seen Zachy?"

"He'll be here. He's hanging out at Garrett's, I think."

"Do you want me to find him?" Uan asked, coming to stand by Mom. He rested his hand on her shoulder, and she reached up to cover it with her own. When she looked up at Uan, her expression softened. She might be afraid that her kids were pulling away, but it was very clear she was happy with her choice.

I glanced at Thallirin and found him watching me. This time, I was the one to flush because I was wondering if I would be as happy if I did someday give in to Thallirin.

We didn't need to wait long for Zach. He showed up with Garrett in tow.

"I brought a friend," he said. "Mom, this is Garrett. Garrett, this is my mom, Nancy."

Garrett said hello.

"Garrett has a game console and some multi-player games to go with it. Can I stay over at his place tonight?" Zach asked as they hung up their jackets and joined us at the table.

"Just for tonight," Mom said. "This is still your house." She passed the veggies to me, and I helped myself to a large portion.

"I know," Zach said. "But this might be the last working game console on Earth. My teen-boy blood can't turn its back on that."

Mom rolled her eyes.

Knowing that Thallirin and Uan wouldn't care for the veggies, I half-stood and passed them over to Garrett. Because seating was a little squished, my boob brushed against Thallirin's arm again. I pretended not to notice his bent fork or his slight shiver.

Dinner progressed nicely, and it was fun to have a full table. When we were done, Mom suggested the guys go outside while she and I cleaned up. As soon as the door shut behind them, she arched a brow at me.

"Next time pound on the wall and tell us to stop," she said. "The last thing I meant to do was to drive my children out of their home. Or make you stay with someone who makes you uncomfortable."

I snorted.

"I am not pounding on the walls. And staying with Thallirin doesn't make me uncomfortable. After he overheard what happened to me, he and I talked. As usual, communication cleared up any misunderstandings, and he's been good. No bossing me around, talking to me openly about his concerns...I think I actually like being around him now."

She studied me for a minute.

"Right cupboard above the stove," she said.

Curious, I looked and found a stack of birth control packets.

"Uan spread the word that it's dangerous for someone my age to have a baby, so all the birth control they find has been coming here. Cassie said to pick one kind and stick with it. Help yourself."

"Whoa. I said I liked being around him, not that I wanted to have sex."

"I know. And I'm not suggesting you should. I'm suggesting you start taking the pill so, if you ever want to change your mind, you're ready. We aren't living in the same world we used to live in, Brenna. The old rules don't apply. Don't let anything hold you back from what you want, you hear me?"

CHAPTER TWELVE

I ROLLED OVER AND HEARD SOMETHING IN THE HALL. LIFTING MY head, I saw Thallirin's familiar shape in the doorway.

"Is it time to get up?" I asked groggily.

After dinner last night, I'd promised Zach that I would go on today's supply run with him.

"No. Not yet."

I rubbed my eyes to look at Thallirin again, trying to figure out why he was just standing there.

"Were you watching me sleep?"

"Yes."

"Have you slept at all?"

"When I close my eyes, I see you leaving."

That got me right in the feels.

Pushing off the covers, I climbed out of bed. He didn't move as I approached.

"I'm not leaving in the middle of the night, Thallirin," I said, taking his hand and leading him to his bedroom.

"You left your house in the middle of the night."

"That's because Uan was having noisy sex with my mom. No one's having sex here, right?" I turned him and pushed him back onto his bed.

The bedframe groaned in protest.

"Lay down," I said tiredly.

He'd barely done as I asked before I climbed over him and crawled under the covers. He flinched as I snuggled against his side, but I didn't pay it any attention.

"Go to sleep, Thallirin. I need you alert tomorrow."

I closed my eyes and drifted off to sleep.

THE BED WAS SHAKING like crazy. My eyes popped open, and I looked around wildly, certain we were having another earthquake. It wasn't a quake, though. Thallirin hovered over me, his arms bracing his weight as he shielded me with his body.

"What's wrong?" I asked. My gaze darted around the room. "Infected?"

But if it was infected, wouldn't he be running with me, not hovering protectively? Confused, I looked up at him. His gaze was riveted on my face. He didn't speak, and the shaking continued.

"You're scaring me, Thallirin."

He made a sound between a growl and groan and slowly set his forehead against mine. I didn't understand what was going on.

I reached up to touch his face, wondering if he'd had another dream about me leaving. Just as my fingers touched his scarred cheek, I felt a weird tug on my chest. My shirt had twisted in my sleep, and my meager offerings were spilling out from the low neckline and the armpit.

A hint of panic swept through me. How could it not? He was acting like a crazy man. Not a man, I reminded myself. A fey.

Ignoring my racing pulse, I pushed his head back enough so I could focus on him.

"Am I safe?" I whispered.

His expression became more pained.

"Always."

I removed my hand from his cheek and slowly tugged my shirt back into place. Wiggling around while trapped in the cage of his arms meant a few accidental bumps. His eyes didn't waver from mine for a moment. I wasn't sure if I should feel reassured by that or terrified.

When I finished, he touched his forehead to mine again.

"Don't leave me," he whispered.

I wrapped my arms around his torso and gave him a half-hug. I wasn't sure pressing up against him completely would be a wise choice at the moment.

"I'm not," I said. "But I'd feel a lot better if you could explain why you're on top of me like this."

He shuddered harder.

"The curtains are open."

Harsh pounding started on the door, evoking a growl from Thallirin as he jerked his head from mine.

"Shit. We have to go," I said even as I heard Zach call my name.

I looked back up at Thallirin and saw his hesitation.

"Thallirin?"

He lifted an arm so I could slide out from under him.

"Go," he said softly.

I bolted from the bed to the bathroom then to my bedroom and hurriedly yanked on my clothes. When I emerged, I could hear the low murmur of voices in the kitchen.

"You sure you're okay? You look a little mad. Did Brenna keep you up all night with her snoring?"

Before I could yell at Zach to cut it out, Thallirin answered.

"Brenna does not snore."

I walked into the kitchen and saw Thallirin was already dressed and scowling at Zach. I did a double-take and wondered why I thought it was a scowl when his expression really wasn't any different from his normal one.

Passing Zach, I reached into the cupboard for a granola bar. It wouldn't taste too good on top of toothpaste, but I couldn't afford to be picky.

"Sorry we're late," I said. "We didn't set an alarm."

"No problem. Ryan's waiting. He said we're not likely to get much help from Tenacity, anyway, because we're going back to Harrisonville. I think those people are stupid if they don't come with us. We're hitting that distribution center again. There's enough to feed us for months in just that warehouse alone. It was untouched."

He headed for the door.

"They're not stupid," I said, following him outside. "It's dangerous any time we go out. You know that. Don't get full of yourself and let your guard down."

He rolled his eyes at me.

"I'm not letting my guard down, and I'm not saying it's going to be easy. All I'm saying is there's a lot of food there for a group that's desperate for it."

He was right, of course. But the people in Tenacity didn't understand their short-term choice wasn't much different than their long-term one. Stay inside the safety of the walls and potentially slowly starve or leave the walls and potentially be bitten. Each option had an equal potential for death.

"Come on." He started jogging. I didn't mind. It warmed me up and got the blood flowing. Cleared my head, too, until we stopped by the group and another fey walked up to offer me a ride.

"That's okay. Thallirin, can—"

"He already left," the fey said.

I looked behind me and didn't see my shadow. Confused, I agreed to the fey's offer. Maybe Thallirin was still worked up over this morning and thought it would be a bad idea to carry me. I'd just lectured Zach about not being distracted, so it made sense Thallirin wouldn't want to carry me. However, it didn't stop me from feeling a tinge of hurt.

Thanking the fey, I gripped my bow and nodded that I was ready. He carefully picked me up but didn't hold me like I was fragile and would shatter at the slightest jarring like Thallirin did.

When my fey cleared the wall and started running, I looked for Thallirin. He was running ahead of us. I caught myself wondering what was going on with him before putting it aside. I could worry about Thallirin and his sudden change of heart about carrying me tonight when I was safely back inside Tolerance's wall. Until then, I needed to focus.

My eyes went to the trees, watching for signs of infected. Everything was quiet the entire trip.

Matt and a few others waited for us outside the wall by the trucks.

"Thirty percent of what the trucks bring back belongs to Tenacity," he said.

"Agreed," Ryan said. "As long as you'll take an additional week's worth of supplies for each new household so they see what supplies can be found when they venture outside the wall with the fey."

Matt and Ryan shook on it as the fey delivered me to Garrett's truck.

"Morning, Brenna. Ready for some easy pickings?" he asked.

"Don't jinx it," I warned, getting in and taking the granola bar from my pocket.

I ate while we waited. It didn't take long for the volunteers to load up and for the fey to get into position. Our truck rumbled forward, and I got comfortable. During the drive, Garrett explained the distribution center's layout and our plan for today.

"The infected probably heard the trucks yesterday, so there's a chance they set a trap for us. But more than likely, because we haven't hit the same area twice, they'll be waiting for us somewhere else."

"And if they're not waiting somewhere else?"

"The fey are going in first to check while we back the trucks up to the dock. When they give the all-clear, we work together to load as much as we can as quickly as we can, picking up where we left off. You'll be watching the trucks again, but there will be fey on the roof as well. The place is huge."

Instead of taking Highway 2 all the way west, Garrett took a back road south and met up with Highway 7. There didn't look like much around. Only a gas station that was probably well-picked over and a fireworks store once we crossed the overpass.

"How did the fey even find this distribution place?" I asked.

"Not sure. A few of them always scout while we're out."

We turned off onto a backroad that looked like it led to nothing. After a few minutes, I saw a huge building ahead.

"That's it?" I asked.

"Yep."

We followed the road around to the side of the building where rows and rows of semi-trailers just sat there.

"It couldn't have been easy to park them like that," I said, looking at how only a few were turned so the hitch was toward the parking lot. "What's in them?"

"A few have pallets of supplies. Most are empty." He turned the truck around and backed toward one of the empty docks. "Now we sit tight until the fey check things out. It takes a while." He reached under his seat and pulled out a bag of trail mix.

We munched and watched for signs of infected. The temperature in the truck dropped quickly, and I used my first set of hand warmers to keep my toes toasty.

A knock on Garrett's door, a good deal later, startled me.

"It's time," the fey called.

We got out, and I immediately climbed up the hood of the truck to take my position up top. The volunteers cautiously exited their truck.

"Humans stay close to your fey," Ryan said softly. "Work quickly and quietly. The place is big, and there can be infected anywhere."

The groups slipped in through a bay door that one of the fey had pried open, and I started my watch, not that there was a lot to see. Across the wide expanse of snow-dusted blacktop, sat the long line of trailers. Behind them, barren trees. The trailers shielded me from the wind but obstructed my view of the trees and fields beyond.

I glanced at the fey who paced the roof, knowing with the extra height, they'd have no problem seeing anything that came our way. However, instead of looking at the trees and fields, the fey closest to me was looking down toward the trailers.

Turning, I saw the reason for his attention. Thallirin was inspecting one of the nearby trailers. He reached out, touching the unlatched lock, then looked at his finger. I couldn't see what he was seeing, but I was sure it had to be blood by the way he stared. And, only one thing would leave a bloody lock.

I drew an arrow from my quiver and nocked it, ready. Thallirin looked up at me, holding my gaze. Behind him, the door to the trailer moved.

My eyes widened.

Undeterred, he turned to the trailer and reached for the handle.

Was he stupid?

The twang of my bowstring gave him pause. He looked back at me just as the arrow whisked past his face and pinged off the lock. I shook my head at him.

"It's a trap," I said softly.

He nodded once then reached for the door, anyway. It opened with a whisper of noise, and a single infected fell out. It moved jerkily toward Thallirin, who gripped its head and tore it free. He tossed the infected's head aside and peered into the trailer before closing the door again.

I exhaled in relief.

Then the door of a trailer several bays down moved. Thallirin started walking toward it. Behind me, I heard the same noise and twisted to see a fey going to look at another trailer.

My stomach dropped to my toes. It was just like the last time. They were baiting the fey farther away.

The low creak of metal echoed off the skeletal trees as one of the trailer doors across the pavement eased open.

"Trap!" I yelled, nocking another arrow.

Everything slowed.

Fey came pouring out of the building, carrying humans. Infected spilled out of the trailers, swarming the pavement. The fey with the humans jumped to the nearest truck then the roof of the building to safely dump their passengers. But the infected were just as fast. They reached the trucks as the first fey jumped down.

"Brenna!" Zach's panic fed my own as I watched the infected scramble up the hood of the truck I was standing on.

I didn't release my nocked arrow. It wouldn't do any good. There were too many infected. The first one grabbed onto my leg and pulled. I started to go down and wondered how much of me they'd eat before I turned.

Something came flying at me from the right. It hit me hard, and I felt the roof buckle under my feet. Then I was tumbling through the air. Sounds collided. The thump of something hitting metal and a jarring impact that rattled my bones at the same instant. Then, the infected moaning. The humans yelling. Chaos reigned, and pain followed, shooting up my leg.

I hit metal again, and there were hands all over me.

"I smell her blood," Thallirin said.

I blinked at him and Zach, who leaned over me, and tried to make sense of the moment.

"My leg," I said, shaking uncontrollably.

"Zach, get back," Ryan said. "Thallirin, you're full of infected blood. Back up and let me. Just in case."

I looked up at all the human faces as they backed away and watched Ryan lift my pant leg.

My stomach twisted with the pain, and I choked back the trail mix that wanted to come up.

"I can't tell if it's a bite or not," Ryan said. "I'm sorry."

He stood and moved away. Thallirin fell to his knees beside me and took my hand. His was sticky with infected blood.

"You will not be alone," he said. "Ever."

That was it? I was done. I started to shake. I wasn't sure if it was from fear, adrenaline, or the change. I closed my eyes and waited to feel something other than pain. What I felt was Thallirin's fingers against mine, gently stroking my skin. His trembles. I gave his hand a small squeeze, feeling sorry for both of us.

Below, the fighting continued. Fey shouted out to one another. Someone took my quiver and bow.

The pain in my leg didn't grow any worse, but it didn't get any better, either.

"They're running again," someone yelled.

The sounds of fighting started to fade.

"How are you feeling?" Ryan asked.

"Like a truck hit me and ripped open my damn leg."

"Good."

I opened my eyes and gave him a what-the-fuck look. He grinned at me.

"It's been more than fifteen minutes. I have a first aid kit in the truck. Don't move. Don't touch anything. Thallirin, you might want to move away from her and clean up. She's at risk with an open wound."

I glanced at Thallirin, who didn't release his hold on me.

"You okay?" I asked.

"No."

"That's twice, now," I said.

"Yes."

"Still going to let me keep choosing?"

He exhaled shakily.

"I'm not sure."

"Thank you for the honesty. And the second save."

"Thank you for not shooting me." With that, he stood and left me so he could start scrubbing down with the snow from the roof. I frowned after him, wondering what the heck his comment meant.

Ryan returned with the first aid kit and tested my extensive knowledge of cuss words as he disinfected then bandaged the cut.

"I'm pretty sure you're going to need stitches. The bandage is only to keep it clean until we get home."

I sat up and used a bottle of water to wash my hands then some of the alcohol to disinfect.

"I'm fine for now. Please tell me we're going to keep loading."

"No," Thallirin said firmly.

"What if the humans stay on the roof and let the fey do all

the loading?" Ryan asked. "We can't pass up on the supplies in there."

Thallirin looked at the rest of the fey. There were grunts of agreement. A dozen fey were left on the roof with us to keep watch, and the rest went below, including Thallirin.

Zach sat by me so I could lean against him.

"Why does everything happen to you?" he asked.

"I'm willing to take turns."

He laughed.

"I have a feeling you might not be allowed to go on runs, anymore. If Thallirin doesn't keep you home, Mom will. Especially if we have the supplies to last us a while."

I sighed, knowing he was right. It wasn't like I really wanted to go on supply runs anyway. Too bad I liked eating so much, though.

I STARED at the back of Thallirin's head as he ran ahead of us in the fading light. We'd pushed the supply gathering to the limit, filling several trailers and bringing a caravan of goods back to Tenacity. The fey and Matt agreed we would unload the majority of it the next day.

Because of the noise the trucks made from Harrisonville to Tenacity, several of the fey stayed behind to watch the road and help guard against any extra infected who might follow our trail. After this last supply run, there was no doubt that the infected were getting smart enough to do that.

But none of that explained why I was in some other fey's arms or why Thallirin hadn't talked to me since the roof. My leg could be falling off for all he knew.

Crossing my arms, I waited impatiently for Tolerance to come into view. My ride wasn't done when we went over the wall, though. The fey holding me took me straight to Cassie's house.

Kerr opened the door with his usual stoic expression.

"Hey, Kerr, is Cassie around to stitch me up?" I asked from my princess position.

"Bring her in," Cassie called from somewhere inside. I was handed off to Kerr like a toddler and carried to the kitchen.

"What happened?" she asked, glancing at my bloody pants leg and quickly setting the pot of mac and cheese down.

"I'm pretty sure I was cut on a piece of metal. Not rusty. And yes, I'm good on my tetanus for a few years, yet."

"Good thing because I wouldn't be able to do anything about that. Stitches I can help with, though." She looked at Kerr. "Take her to the guest room."

He carried me down the hall to a room Cassie had set up to treat people.

"She'll want to get to the cut," Kerr said, setting me on the bed.

"So pants off?"

He grunted and left me to strip on my own. Cassie didn't make me wait in my underwear for long.

"Let's take a look."

She peeled back the bandage and made what I would

consider an uh-oh sound when coming from someone in the medical profession.

"What?" I asked.

"It does need stitches."

"I kind of figured. It hurts like hell."

"I only have one way to numb it."

I watched her walk across the room and open a cabinet.

"I have a stock of high proof rum, vodka, and whiskey. Name your flavor."

"Rum. I want to be a damn pirate!"

She laughed and took a bottle from the cupboard. "Rum, it is." She handed it over and promised to check in on me in a few minutes.

The first swallow burned, and I grimaced. There was no way I wanted to do stitches sober, though, so I kept at it. By the time Cassie returned, I was ready with my pirate-speak.

"Ay, Captain. The deck is good and scrubbed." Only what came out was... "Ay." Hiccup. "Dish deck be good shcrubbed." Hiccup.

"Oh, boy," she said before going back to the door. "Kerr, I'm going to need your help in here. Can you put a movie on for the kids?"

She returned and started taking things out of the cupboards.

"Shtill gunna hurt, inna it?" I looked at the bottle. "Shtuff inna working. I'm shtil not want schtitches."

I took another sip and watched the room spin a little.

"The stitches would have hurt more without it," she said, setting some packages on the bed. Kerr walked in then.

"I need you to hold her leg still."

"Nope," I said, pulling my leg out of his way. "No one holdsh me down again. Not even drunk."

Cassie considered me for a moment.

"Not even with me here? You know I won't let anything happen to you."

I looked at Kerr then Cassie. Pouting, I took another sip from the bottle and lowered my leg again.

"I doan like it."

"I'll go as fast as I can. Okay?"

I let out a large, aggrieved sigh.

"Fiiineee."

Kerr's hand closed over my leg, and I stared at him. He didn't look at me, though. He watched Cassie as she cleaned the wound and opened a package.

"I heard there are a lot of supplies coming our way because of today," Cassie said.

"Yep. Good shtuff an things."

Something stung my leg, and I tried to jerk back. Kerr's hold was firm. But, only on one leg. I lifted my other foot and stuck my big toe in his ear.

"How you like genn poked?"

He closed a hand over my ankle and brought it back to the bed. I pouted and took another sip.

"I think you can stop drinking," Cassie said just before a bee stung my leg again.

"Nah-ah. Imma pirate, and piratesh need rum."

"Next time, use a glass," Kerr said.

Cassie grinned.

"They're more relaxed when they can self-medicate. Besides, look at the bottle. She really didn't have much."

I peered at the bottle, trying to focus on the line. It kept sloshing around, though. Shrugging, I took another sip and almost spit it all over Cassie when I was stung again.

"Kill it already," I said, choking on my swallow. My windpipe burned more fiercely than the next two bee stings, though.

"And you're all set," Cassie said. "You'll need to keep it dry for a few days, but I'll be over to check on you first thing in the morning since I'm not sure you'll remember any of this." She tried to take the bottle from me, but I held tight.

"Pirates never give booty," I slurred.

Cassie sighed.

"Can you wrap her in a blanket and take her home?"

I peered at Kerr, who she was looking at, then shook my head at her.

"Ohhhh. My mom's going to be so mad at him."

Cassie glanced at me.

"Why?"

I waggled the rum bottle at her.

"Can't go home," I said.

"I'll take her to Thallirin's," Kerr said. "He can take her home."

I giggled.

"Right under the bush." Bush? I tried saying bus again but more bush came out. I stuck out my tongue to check that it was in the right spot.

Cassie used my distraction to steal my bottle.

"I'll see you tomorrow," she said while Kerr wrapped me up in a blanket burrito.

CHAPTER THIRTEEN

My legs were cold, and my world was swimming. Stars glittered overhead, occasionally blocked out by my foggy exhales.

Kerr stopped walking, and I lifted my head to watch him knock on the door.

Thallirin answered a moment later.

"You're in big trouble, mishter!" I said, scowling at him.

"She had alcohol to dull the pain of receiving stitches. She said her mom will be angry if she is returned home drunk."

Kerr shoved me at Thallirin, who had no choice but to take me.

"Thank you," Thallirin said before stepping back and kicking the door shut.

Then, finally, he looked at me.

"I shoulda shot you," I said with a scowl. "You leff me." My scowl turned to a sad mew. "Why you leave me?"

He set his forehead to mine, and I reached up to cup his face.

"I like you, Thall-ririn. You're supposed to like me, too."

"I like you very much, Brenna."

"Then shtop running away. Ish mean. I can't think here." I tapped his head then tilted mine to rub my nose against his and bring our lips closer. He held so still. For me. My captive.

"Do you want me or nah? I dunno with you noring me."

"I want you, Brenna. Always."

I liked how his exhale warmed my face and made my middle dance. My fingers drifted over his cheek scar then along the hard length of his clenched jaw.

"I feel things," I said just before my tongue darted out and lightly stroked over his lower lip.

He started shaking, and I grinned. I liked that reaction much better than when he ran.

"Did you eat?" he asked gruffly, distracting me from licking him again.

"No, bah I shure drank lots."

He carried me to the kitchen and set me on a chair. I watched him inspect the cupboards then return to the table with a bag of popcorn.

"I doan wan that," I said, nudging it away.

"What do you want?"

"More rum!"

He filled a glass of water and gave it to me.

"Drink this first."

"Brenna do this. Brenna do that." I chugged the water then

thunked the glass back down on the table. "I have choices," I said, standing. The room wobbled, and I put my hand out, steadying myself on Thallirin's chest.

Frowning, I stared at the grey skin under my fingers.

"Where'd your shirt go?"

I looked up at him.

"I didn't have one on."

I grunted like a fey and grinned at my cleverness. Then I started tracing my fingers down his sternum.

"I wunner where thish goesh..."

I GROANED as I became aware of the pounding in my skull.

"Why?" I moaned.

"Take this." I lifted my head to look at Thallirin. He held out two white pills. I took them along with the glass of water that he offered.

As I swallowed, bits of the night before filtered in.

Me going through all the cupboards and demanding Thallirin make cupcakes. Thallirin petting my hair as I heaved my guts out in the toilet. Thallirin putting paste on my toothbrush so I could brush. Thallirin trying to stop me from stripping out of my clothes before I crawled into his bed.

I lifted the covers, hoping I was remembering things wrong. Nope. Naked.

But before all of that, I remembered petting his chest and loving the way he shivered under my caresses. I'd really liked how it had made me feel. How he'd made me feel. I'd asked for friendship but realized I'd taken things a lot further than that. I wasn't ready for the end game, but I honestly didn't mind the evolution. Just so long as he didn't mind it, either. I remembered the way he'd gently dislodged my touch and tried to redirect my attention last night and mentally cringed.

"Cassie said you would feel sick today. She said no showers until she talks to you, herself."

I looked up at him, meeting his steady gaze.

"Did I wreck everything?"

"I cleaned the kitchen and the bathroom."

"Not that. I mean, I'm really sorry about all that. But, last night, did I wreck what was growing between us?"

"Are you asking if I still want to be with you?" he asked.

"Yeah. That."

"I've never wanted anything more."

Relief flooded through me before I frowned at him.

"What was up with ignoring me yesterday? I can understand the morning and wanting to keep your head in the game, but after I was hurt on the supply run? That's a dick move to have someone else take me to get stitches. What gives?"

He glanced away for a moment then sat on the bed next to me.

"I looked. I tried not to, but your skin is perfect. Pale. Smooth. Unmarked. I looked when I knew I shouldn't. And I couldn't bring myself to endure the hate and disgust I knew I would see in your eyes."

I stared at him for a minute, at first thinking he was telling me he'd snuck a peek last night. But it wasn't last night's strip tease he was talking about. He meant yesterday morning when I woke with my boobs hanging out of my shirt.

"You thought I'd get mad for something that wasn't your fault?"

"Looking is my fault," he said.

"Okay. Fine. Yes, you chose to look. But, it was just looking, Thallirin. I'm not ashamed of being naked. It's not that big of a deal. It hurts more to think that you don't like me after all the time you spent telling me you do."

"I did not give you a choice. You weren't awake."

The comment on the roof suddenly made sense. He was taking the choice-speech I'd given very seriously. While I appreciated it, I was also worried for him. He'd been torturing himself for nothing this time.

"You seriously thought I was trying to shoot you yesterday? I was trying to warn you not to go in that stupid trailer."

He grunted, and I exhaled heavily.

"We are so different," I said. "Not because you're fey and I'm human, but because you're a man and I'm a woman. We think completely different. If we want to avoid misunderstandings, we have to talk about stuff as it happens, Thallirin. Don't assume I'm thinking something because I'm probably not.

"I'm definitely not angry that you saw my boobs yesterday. And I don't think that you looking at them was taking a choice from me. It was something that just happened. How you reacted was a little scary at first because I didn't understand what was going on, but I wasn't mad."

He exhaled slowly.

"We're okay, then?" I asked.

"Yes."

"Good," I said with a smile. "How long do I have until Cassie comes back?"

"She didn't say."

I reached out and caught his hand.

"Thank you for helping me last night."

He turned my hand palm up and ran a finger over the sensitive skin, tracing the lines there.

"You're softer than I imagined," he said.

"My hands aren't soft," I said with a smile. "My fingers are almost as calloused as yours. Feel my stomach."

I pulled back the covers, exposing my middle as well as my top.

The air left him like I punched him in the gut.

"I told you before that nudity is nothing to be ashamed of, Thallirin." I took his hand and brought it to my navel. "This is softer skin here. No callouses."

His eyes held mine for a long moment before his gaze drifted down. He stared long and hard at my chest, and I could feel the heat creeping up into my cheeks as he went further south. I held still under his scrutiny, though.

The mattress underneath me started to tremble even though his fingers stayed right where I placed them.

"You have my permission to touch me, Thallirin."

His gaze flew to mine.

"No," he said.

"Why not?"

Instead of answering me, he got up and walked away. I wasn't offended. Annoyed that he wasn't talking to me, but not offended. Too hungover to push, I left him alone to sort through his feelings. Instead, I used the bathroom before returning to bed. His bed. The pain reliever and the hangover demanded a nap.

In a form of mild protest over his persistent hang-up with my birthday suit, I didn't bother putting on clothes.

Cassie woke me a while later with a gentle knock on the door.

"How are you feeling?" she asked when I turned from my stomach to my back.

"Better. The hangover is way worse than the stitches."

She grinned.

"Your mom was a little worried when she heard you came here, but Uan reassured her that everything was proper." She lifted her brow and nodded at the bare shoulders exposed above the covers.

"Is everything proper?" she asked.

I snorted.

"Thallirin accidentally saw my boobs and acted like he wanted to gouge his own eyes out. I don't think it can get any more proper."

"Fair enough. Any pain where I stitched?"

"Not really." I stuck my leg out so she could inspect it and listened to her instructions to take it easy.

"The cut wasn't very deep, and you're young. You'll be up and moving around soon."

"Yeah, it's not the leg that's keeping me in bed. It's the damn headache."

She grinned.

"Sorry about that."

"You don't look too sorry about it, but that's okay. I can't imagine what it would have been like to get those stitches without a little bit of liquid help."

She patted my hip and left me alone.

So did Thallirin. It gave me time to think. Two close calls were enough for me. I didn't ever again want to relive the terror of wondering if I would turn. There were two options to ensure that didn't happen. Stay locked in this house or gain immunity. Unfortunately, the only way to immunity was hiding somewhere in this house.

Thallirin had more than grown on me. But was I comfortable enough with him to have sex? My pulse started to race in a good way just at the thought of it.

Then I snorted to myself.

Did my comfort even matter, given his refusal of a simple touch to my stomach? I frowned, thinking of his likely answer to any actual advance I might make. He was resisting what was growing between us more than I was. Well, maybe just the physical piece. Yet, that resistance was what was helping to propel me forward. Thallirin wasn't like Van. I was starting to really see that the big grey guy wouldn't take what I wasn't willing to give.

I got out of bed and took one of the birth control pills my mom had given me. Only the third dose. She'd warned me not to do anything for a week after starting them. But that was fine. Thallirin and I weren't quite there yet, anyway. Thankfully, the wait would give me a few days to work up to being ready. Given Thallirin's repeated reactions to me, we would both need that time.

First, we needed to get him over the nudity thing. Since the day of my mom's return home after her accident, that had been one of the rules in the house. Probably a weird one for some people, but I'd seen what it'd done for Mom. Dad couldn't be there all the time. Zach and I had had to help with things most kids never had to deal with at our ages. Bathroom duty, especially bathing, hadn't been easy on her or us. No one wanted to see their mom naked because it was weird...until we made it not weird. Removing the stigma and boundaries of nudity had freed us all from awkwardness and had helped start the process of emotional healing for Mom.

I hoped removing the stigma here would help Thallirin become more comfortable around me.

Tossing the pills back in my bag, I went out to the kitchen. Thallirin's eyes nearly popped out of his head when he saw me.

"Might want to close the curtains," I said. "There are people out there with binoculars."

He moved with insane speed and had every window in my vicinity covered in seconds.

"Did we ever make those cupcakes last night?" I asked, moving around the kitchen, looking for anything that resembled a cupcake.

"Brenna, go put clothes on."

I glanced at him. He stood in the entry, completely still, his gaze riveted on me. Only this time, he looked his fill.

"Please," he whispered harshly.

I went to him, placing my hands on his shirt just over his heart. It was beating crazy fast.

"There's nothing wrong with my body," I said. "I wasn't born with clothes. We use them to keep warm. I'm warm in here. Does looking at me like this offend you?"

"No."

"Good. I want you to look at me, Thallirin. I want you to see me for the woman, not child, that I am because I don't want to turn into one of them. The infected. I'm not saying I'm ready to have sex right this minute, but I'd like us both to be okay with the idea that it could happen. Maybe soon?"

He shook his head slowly.

"No." The word was more of a tormented plea.

"Your reaction is hurting my feelings. I'm trying not to let it, but I'm starting to feel like there's something wrong with me." I looked down at myself. "I know I'm a little underfed, but we have more supplies now, and I'll fill back in. My boobs were never really big." I shrugged and met his gaze again. "In that department, what you see is what you'll probably get for life. But I think I look pretty normal."

"You are perfect."

The way he said it heated my cheeks a little, but I pressed on.

"So, it's truly just the age thing again?"

He averted his gaze for a second, and I sighed.

"I thought we went over this already. A few days or weeks isn't going to miraculously change me. Eighteen is just a number."

He shook his head without looking at me.

"Fine. But remember that if I go out there in a few days with a stitched leg and move too slow and get bitten, you're the first one I'm going after."

Annoyed, I went back to his bedroom and crawled into bed. I spent most of the day there. Naked and sleeping. Once I woke to a bowl of soup next to me, which I promptly ate. Near dark, I felt well enough to venture out again. I used the bathroom, brushed my teeth, and combed my hair. I felt human.

Still shunning clothes, I went to look for Thallirin. He was sitting on the couch. No lights. No TV. Just sitting there.

I flicked on the nearest lamp.

"You okay?" I asked.

He glanced at me then went back to staring at the dark TV.

"Please dress, Brenna."

"I will if you can look at me and tell me that my nudity is offending."

He fisted his hands and remained quiet.

I moved closer to him, standing by his knees.

"Will you let me try something?" I asked.

He nodded, not even questioning what I wanted to try. I modestly sat on his lap, draping my legs to one side and hooking my arm around his shoulder. His back twitched under my fingers.

Heart thundering in my ears, I gently turned his head toward me. I vaguely recalled kissing—well, licking more than kissing—him last night and liking it. I needed to know if that had been a real emotion or a drunken one.

Slowly closing the distance between us, I brushed my lips against his. A jolt of pleasure darted through my stomach at the same time he stopped breathing. His lips were firm and warm as I brushed mine against them once more. Heat continued to spiral inside of me, and I daringly opened my mouth to graze his lower lip with my tongue. He groaned. I didn't stop. I nipped and nibbled until, with a growl, Thallirin's arms wrapped around me.

He opened his mouth, and his tongue met mine. All thought fled at the contact.

He leaned over me, taking control and claiming what he'd known was his since the beginning. My heart hammered against my ribs, and I made a small sound of satisfaction as I dug my fingers into his hair. He was gentle yet demanding. Ridiculously strong while also achingly tender with each subtle touch.

Just as quickly as it started, it stopped. I found myself alone on the couch with Thallirin sitting in the far chair.

"Will you dress now?" he asked, his voice a tormented rasp.

Numbly, I reached up and touched my lips. All of me felt tingly and on fire. I'd never been more turned on in my life. What I'd felt during last night's drunken kiss had only been a liquor-muted shadow of what I now felt.

I wasn't broken forever. With Thallirin, it seemed I was whole and, more importantly, very willing.

Panting, I studied him for a minute. His pupils were dilated and the tips of his ears were such a dark grey they looked black. His hungry gaze pinned me, and based on the way he leaned forward as if he wanted to launch himself across the room again, his white-knuckled grip on the chair was the only thing keeping him in place. Yet, despite all the desire I saw, he looked tormented, like I'd pushed him too far.

I went to my room and closed the door to do as he'd asked. However, after putting on my sleep shorts and top, I sat on the bed and stared at the dresser in growing concern. What was I doing? I'd been very plain in what I wanted, but what about what Thallirin wanted? He'd made that plain, too, and I'd ignored it. Had I just used that kiss as extortion to see me dressed again?

Standing, I changed out of my sleepwear and got fully dressed. I needed to apologize, then clear my head.

Thallirin was still in his chair when I returned.

"I'm sorry I pushed you," I said. "I'm going to go to Mom's for dinner. Is it okay if I come back here when I'm done?"

He stood and stalked toward me, looking a bit more angry than usual.

"You're leaving?"

"Yeah. I thought you might want a little quiet time without me."

His arms wrapped around me, holding me just a little too tightly.

"No," he rumbled. "Don't leave."

His arms felt so good around me as I hugged him back.

"I'm not leaving-leaving. Just going to Mom's for dinner. I should have put clothes on like you asked. It wasn't fair for me to push you or use getting dressed as a bribe for a kiss. It was manipulation, plain and simple, and I wouldn't have liked it if you'd done that to me. I'm truly sorry, Thallirin, and I swear I won't ever do that to you again."

His hand stroked over my hair.

"I liked the kiss," he said. "More than I should have."

Annoyance flared as I understood the way he'd acted wasn't because of the kiss but because of my damn age. However, I'd said all I could say to help him see it the way I saw it. I sighed and rubbed my cheek against his shirt.

"Do you want to come to dinner with me?"

He grunted and picked me up.

"I can walk," I protested. "It doesn't hurt."

He stopped in front of the door and looked down at me.

"Do you want me to stop?"

The way his gaze skimmed over my face and his hands

tightened ever so slightly around me told me he liked holding me just as much as I liked being held by him.

"No." I rested my head against his shoulder. "Don't you want a jacket?"

"No."

I smiled, knowing what that meant. He was comfortable with me. He knew I wasn't looking at his scars, but at him. He stepped out into the cold and started toward Mom's house. I pressed my nose against his chest for warmth but ended up inhaling deeply instead.

"I like the way you smell," I said.

His steps slowed before picking up speed once more.

I grinned and smoothed my hand over his chest.

"I like the way you feel, too."

He slowed again.

"Do you want me to stop?" I asked.

"No."

"Can we kiss again tonight? After dinner?"

He looked down at me and started to shake his head. I gave him my best sad face. He stopped walking completely, and I could see he was torn. He wanted to make me happy, to give me what I wanted, what we both wanted, but he also wanted to respect the rule about my age.

"I liked kissing you, too, Thallirin. I was so worried I'd never like touching anyone that way ever again. But kissing doesn't have to mean sex. It can be a way for people to show that they have affection for one another or a way to test how much they feel for one another. That's what I was doing.

Testing how you make me feel. Sometimes kisses are just nice. Just nice isn't enough for me to start a relationship. I want kisses that are exciting and make my heart race."

Putting what I was feeling into words was making my heart feel weird. How could an organ feel tight?

I focused on his shirt and toyed with the fabric.

"I liked our first kiss, and I want to do it again to help understand just where my feelings for you are going. But I don't want you to feel that you have—"

"Brenna."

I looked up at him.

"Our kiss made my heart race. My blood heat. My hands itch to touch you in ways I shouldn't. Kissing you is dangerous."

That just made me want to kiss him more. But, I'd said my piece. And, I'd damn near begged. If he wasn't ready, I needed to respect that.

"Okay."

He growled a second before his lips claimed mine. It wasn't soft or sweet or tentative. It was hard and consuming. And, over almost as quickly as it had begun.

I blinked up at him, dazed.

"Your heart is racing," he said softly.

"Yeah, I think you're right."

He took a deep breath and started walking. I relaxed against him with a soft smile, my decision made.

Mom's house was lit up like a Christmas tree when we got

there. Not sure what was going on, I rang the doorbell just in case.

Uan answered and quickly stepped aside for us.

"Brenna is here," he called.

"About time," Mom called back. She appeared in the entry and crossed her arms as she gave me a stern Mom look.

"I've been worried sick. Zach told me you were hurt. I had to hear from Cassie that she stitched you up then sent you to Thallirin's house—drunk—because you told Kerr I would be mad if he brought you here, where you belong. What were you thinking?"

I tapped Thallirin's shoulder to indicate I wanted down. When I was on my own two feet, I crossed over to Mom and knelt by her chair. It tugged at my stitches a bit, but I ignored the ache. Mom was close to losing her shit.

"I wasn't thinking. I was hurt and intoxicated. We both know that's a bad combination. I'm sorry what happened scared you. It scared me, too. Enough that I think I'm ready."

Her expression lost some of its anger, and she looked from me to Thallirin, then back again. I followed her look and found him watching me with an indiscernible expression that wasn't as angry looking as usual.

"Reacting out of fear is dangerous. Mistakes are always made," Mom said, reclaiming my attention.

"It's not out of fear, Mom. It's something else completely."

"Are you sure?"

"I am. And I don't want you to think that recent life

changes pushed any of the decisions I'm making," I said, hoping she'd understand I meant Uan's moving in with her.

Her hand covered mine.

"You're too smart to let my choices bully you."

I kissed her cheek then hugged her.

"I love you, Mom."

"I love you, too."

I pulled back and looked at her. Really looked at her. Her hair was clean, which meant someone had helped her with the shower or into a bath. And she looked happy. I glanced back at Uan, who was watching us closely. He had that possessive glint in his eye any time he looked at Mom.

"Thank you for taking care of her."

"I will always care for her," he said.

"Can we eat yet?" Zach called from the kitchen.

I grinned and straightened, following Mom into the room that smelled like a burger joint. I nearly drooled when I saw the stack of grilled patties in the center of the table.

"Real ground beef. Butter toasted buns, too," Zach said. "Garrett and I found the grilling stuff at his place after we ran supplies over today. You should see the shed. It's overflowing even after delivering stuff to all the houses here."

"That's great," I said, sitting. I helped myself to a burger and loaded it with grilled onions, pickles, and ketchup. "Sorry I wasn't there to help."

"There wasn't any need. Since it was local, we just needed a few of us in the trailer to sort some supplies for Tenacity's new people and send the rest home. It didn't take too long."

"How many people did they find?" Mom asked.

"It was a group traveling up from the south. Mostly men. A few women. One kid. I think Matt said something like thirty-four of them. I caught a glimpse of one guy." He shook his head. "He looked half-starved. We doubled the amount of supplies that we had planned to give. They need it."

Hearing that almost made me feel guilty about the burger I was eating. Almost. I hadn't been lying about my assessment of my scrawny self to Thallirin. I took another bite, eating with appreciation.

When we finished the meal, I helped Mom clean up while the guys went outside for target practice. I liked that they gave us some time to speak privately, even if it was over dishes.

"What's he like?" she asked.

"He's hard to read, but sweet. He doesn't push. In fact, I think I'm the one pushing now, and it feels weird. He's making a big deal about me being under eighteen. I woke up with my shirt twisted, and he freaked out that he saw my boobs." I handed her a plate to dry. "I don't know what to do. With two close calls, I don't want to wait for summer when he'll know for sure I'm eighteen. Waiting seems stupid to me."

"Do you want me to talk to him?" Mom asked.

"I'm not sure that would help. I'm sure he and I will work it out, eventually."

"Don't go back out there until you know you're safe."

I shook my head at her.

"I'd never leave, then, because even if I can't get infected, I'm smart enough to know I'm never truly safe outside these walls. The breach proved we're not really safe inside, either. If I let fear hold me back, I'm already dead."

She sighed.

"You're right. Just be as safe as you can be."

"I will." I finished the last dish and handed it to her. "I'm going to go pack my things."

"I'm going to miss you," she said, sounding close to tears.

"No, you won't. I'm going to come home for dinner every night, and Uan's going to keep you busy when I'm gone."

She smiled and glanced out the door at him.

"I didn't think I'd ever feel this way again."

I followed her gaze and found Thallirin watching me through the patio doors. Butterflies took flight in my stomach, and I smiled at him before his gaze returned to Uan.

Leaving Mom, I went to my room and started packing, wondering how Thallirin would react to the news that I was moving in with him.

CHAPTER FOURTEEN

WITH THE BAG THAT THALLIRIN HAD ALREADY COLLECTED FOR me, there hadn't been much left to pack. The bag in my arms held the last of my clothes. Thallirin hadn't commented on its presence when I'd told him I was ready to go, and I wondered if he understood what it meant. If he didn't, he soon would.

Once we were in the house, he let me move around on my own. Well, not on my own. He followed me as I grabbed the first bag, then he stood in the doorway while I placed my clothes next to his in the dresser.

He stayed where he was as I stripped out of my pants and changed into one of his oversized shirts. I spared him a full exposure by taking my bra off once I was covered. When I finished changing, I tucked the bags in the closet and looked at him.

"All moved in," I said.

He didn't say anything. Just continued to study me.

"Is that your happy face or your how-do-I-get-rid-of-her-now face?"

"Happy," he said. "Very happy."

"Good. Want to watch a movie?"

I took his grunt as a yes and went to the living room to select a movie. That he chose to sit in the same spot on the couch as before wasn't lost on me. I sat on his lap, and leaned my head against his shoulder. He wrapped his arms around me, holding me close. As much as I tried to watch what was happening on the screen, I couldn't stop thinking about our previous kisses.

I shifted in his lap, looping an arm around his shoulders to press closer. Something moved underneath me. I turned my head toward his neck to hide my smile and brushed my lips against his skin.

This time he shifted, reseating me so I wasn't right on top of the enormous bulge he was sporting. I took one of his hands and brought it to my cheek. His palm covered all of it. I marveled at how large he was while still being so gentle with me.

He shifted under me as I kissed his palm then made a pained sound when I licked it. Grinning, I looked up at him then lightly bit the tip of one finger.

"Brenna."

The word was full of warning, but I wasn't worried. With me, Thallirin was careful. Always so careful.

Before he could guess my intention, I drew his hand down

to my breast. He grunted when his palm covered me over my shirt.

"Too small?" I asked.

His fingers twitched, feeling me before he jerked his hand away.

Before he could ditch me like last time, I changed positions and straddled his lap. The moment my hips settled over his, he froze.

"If you tell me to get up, I will. But I'm doing this because I really don't want you to run away again. You make my heart thunder in my chest, too, Thallirin. Kissing you is dangerous. But in a good way. It's making me better. Less afraid of what you want someday. Can I stay like this?"

He was quiet for a long time, and I knew he was fighting with what he should say versus what he wanted to say. I leaned forward and lightly kissed the corner of his mouth. He trembled under me even though I was careful to avoid full hip to hip contact. This eighteen rule was killing him, and it needed to stop.

"Tomorrow, we should go say hi to Drav and Mya," I said, feathering my fingers over his cheek.

He made a sound. I thought it was supposed to be his usually non-committal grunt, but it didn't come out that way. It sounded more tortured. Poor guy.

I kissed the other corner of his mouth.

"We could get some supplies from the supply shed afterward. If you want."

I brushed my lips over his, and his shaking intensified.

"And maybe go trade at Tenacity to help out over there," I said, my lips hovering over his.

He still didn't move, and the beat of his heart under my palm began to worry me.

"Do you want me to stop?" I asked.

He didn't answer, and I started to get up. His hands gripped my hips, anchoring me in place just over him, not quite touching where he likely ached most. I really wanted to be the one to soothe him.

I kissed him gently, little reassuring brushes of my lips over his mouth, his cheeks, his jaw. I worked lower to his neck, kissing scars and the few patches of unmarked skin that he had. Since he was letting me explore, I found the edge of his shirt and pushed the material upward, smoothing my palms over his honed muscles.

"I didn't think I'd like touching you this much," I whispered. "If you think my softness is mesmerizing, I'm just as taken with your hardness." My fingers glided over his pectorals as I spoke.

A shudder ran through him, and I lifted my head.

"Want to get rid of your shirt?"

His glazed eyes shifted from my lips to the shirt of his that I currently wore.

I smiled.

"I didn't mean mine, but I'm willing if you're interested."

"No."

The word was a dry rasp. Pained and full of need. It made my heart hammer harder and my own need stronger.

Carefully, I lowered myself, letting my hips rest on his. He hissed out a breath as my weight settled on his hard length. His fingers twitched on my hips but nothing more.

I wished he'd do something.

"Tell me to stop," I whispered as I moved slightly, pressing my core against him ever so slightly.

Other than a very loud exhale, he remained silent. Not me.

My mouth had dropped open at the intense ache the friction had created. I was pretty sure I'd made a noise. A squeak? A mewl? I slid my hips forward again, rubbing against the erection that strained against the confinement of his pants. It was definitely a mewl that erupted from me.

I rotated my hips, riding him through the material, and closed my eyes against the pleasure.

Finally, he moved.

One moment, I was on top; the next, I was on the couch, lying underneath him. His lips claimed mine in a kiss so hungry and full of need that I forgot to breathe. I wrapped my arms around his neck, sliding my hands into his hair, and held on for dear life. I tried to press up against him, but he was too far away. Even in this moment, he still managed to hold himself back.

I tore my lips from him, panting, and looked up at him.

He was breathing just as hard and placed his forehead against mine.

"You are my air, my will, my life."

Then he was gone. The sound of the door closing told me he'd left the house. I blinked at the TV screen, and the reality of just how completely and desperately Thallirin wanted me hit.

A shiver ran through me at the thought of what he would be like once that rule was no longer an issue.

I WAS SO comfortable and warm that I didn't want to move. But, I did. Sliding my leg over Thallirin's hips, I snuggled closer. I wasn't sure what time it was or when he'd finally come home, but I was glad he'd decided to sleep next to me rather than continue to avoid me. Doubly glad that he only wore his athletic shorts.

I rubbed my face against his chest, inhaling the smell of him, and felt his fingers playing with my hair.

"This is a nice way to wake up," I said.

A sound of agreement rumbled through his chest.

"Where'd you go last night?"

"To find hellhounds with Merdon."

I jerked my head up to see if he was serious. His unblinking gaze met mine.

"Why would you do that?"

"There is much in this world that wants to take you from me. I will not force my will on you and ask you to stay here, to not risk yourself on supply runs anymore. To give you your freedom to choose, I will remove the things that seek to hurt you."

My heart squeezed in joy and in fear. He wanted to protect

me so badly he would willingly risk himself in the name of an impossible goal.

"Thallirin, you can't kill every infected and hellhound out there."

"Not in one night. In time, my brothers and I will make this world safe again."

"At the risk of your own safety?"

"My life has little value compared to yours."

"It has value to me." I brushed my hand over the expanse of his chest then pressed a kiss to his skin. "I like sleeping next to you," I said.

"I like it, too."

I kissed him again, close to his nipple, and watched the scarred skin pucker. My fingers trailed around it and dipped lower, tracing over his abs and teasing the bare skin just below his navel. He didn't try to stop me, but I could hear his heart hammering under my ear.

"Can we have sex now?" I asked, not looking at him.

"No, Brenna. You are not eighteen."

I grinned against his skin.

"Do you like that I keep teasing you with kisses, anyway?"

"Yes," he said after a long moment of silence.

"Will you tell me if I push too far?"

"You will never push too far," he said.

My grin widened, and I sat up.

"Good. Because I can shower today and need your help wrapping my leg."

He got out of bed and followed me to the kitchen. My skin

began to tingle in anticipation. While he'd been gone, I'd given this plan a lot of thought. Now that I knew it was only my age holding him back, I didn't feel quite as guilty over what I was about to do to him.

Teasing him was exhilarating. Kissing him, even more so. Last night, I'd imagined what it would be like to finally give him what he wanted, and I'd discovered it wasn't just about what he wanted.

In the kitchen, I pulled out the plastic wrap and medical tape I'd prepared ahead of time.

"I just need your help wrapping this around my leg and taping the edges. You might want to kneel. I'll put my foot on the chair."

He did as I suggested, completely unaware of what I would expose when I lifted my foot to the seat of the chair. My shirt slid back and revealed the fact that I wasn't wearing any underwear.

Finally, I got to see his anguished expression.

"The plastic can be tricky," I said as he stared.

He licked his lips, and his nostrils flared. Ever so slightly, he leaned in.

My pulse started to race, and I decided anticipation might end up getting me before an infected did because Thallirin didn't close the distance. He just continued to stare like he'd die if he blinked or looked away.

This was the one thing all fey wanted. I couldn't even count the number of times I'd heard them talk about "seeing pussy" in hushed tones. There was no doubt he was liking the view. But either he had a will of steel or I'd broken him.

I took the plastic wrap from him and started unrolling it. After a moment, he woodenly helped. His attention kept shifting between what he was trying to do and what I'd exposed by lifting my leg.

He managed to cover the stitches and tape the edges with his shaking hands then, finally, looked up at me with such need that I tingled with my own.

"I'm not sure I'll be steady without help," I said breathlessly. It wasn't a lie. I was lightheaded from the fast breathing and the need for him to touch me.

"I think you'll need to take me to the shower."

He scooped me up and carried me to the bathroom. He didn't look away as I removed the shirt I wore then started the water warming.

I reached in to test the water, then stepped into the glass enclosure. Hands trembling, I grabbed the shampoo and looked out at Thallirin.

"Would you mind coming in here just in case I start to slip? I would feel safer."

He hesitated then reached for the door.

"Do you want to take off your shorts so they don't get wet?"

"No."

"Okay."

I handed him the bottle of shampoo then wet my hair. When I looked at him again, he was watching the water run down my torso. I held out my hand.

"Shampoo, please."

He passed the bottle back to me and watched as I soaped my hair and rinsed.

"I'm not sure I got it all," I said. "Will you help me?"

He moved closer and ran his fingers through my hair. Water droplets gathered on his skin. I itched to lick him.

"My leg's starting to ache," I said, putting it up on the bench seat like I had in the kitchen. His gaze flicked from my hair to my face.

"And I'm feeling a little light-headed." I set my hand against the wall. "Would you mind soaping up the rest of me?"

"You need to stop this, Brenna. For both of us."

"Stop what? Wanting you as much as you want me?"

"I don't want you, Brenna. I need you. And your need will never match mine."

"Is that a 'No' to washing me?"

He reached around me to turn off the water. I thought that meant playtime was done until he grabbed the soap and lathered his hands. He smoothed his hands down my arms and over my stomach. Then bent low to wash my legs, carefully avoiding my taped off stitches.

I watched him, waiting for him to look at something other than the limbs he was washing, but he stayed completely focused on all my proper parts.

"I like the way you touch me," I said. "So carefully, like I'm fragile."

"You are fragile."

"Compared to you, I am. But I won't break because you're

washing me, Thallirin."

He stood and turned on the water again.

"Rinse," he said.

"But you didn't wash my chest."

"It's already clean."

"But that's not the point, is it?"

His gaze finally dipped, taking in my breasts. His hand trembled as he reached forward. The heat of his palm branded me. My nipple hardened under his touch.

"You're wrong," I breathed. "I've never needed anyone more."

He kissed me hard, his hand exploring the shape and feel of my breast. The water disappeared, and he stepped away from me, panting.

"Your stitches will get wet," he said, and I knew we were done.

He opened the door and handed me a towel before taking one for himself. I followed him closely, stepping out and watching him. He'd known what I was doing. And I knew he'd only asked me to stop because he was worried about me. I wasn't worried, though.

But, seriously, how many times did a girl need to flash her vagina to talk a guy into sex?

"When I came up with this idea last night, I imagined how everything would go," I said, putting my foot on the counter and drying my leg, fully exposed.

"I imagined you on your knees in the kitchen. Instead of just looking, you were licking. Then, we'd move to the bathroom, and I'd be the one on my knees licking. But, no. You're too stubborn for your own good. And where does that leave me? Horny and more than a little desperate."

I started to carefully remove the tape. Everything underneath looked dry.

"And the worst part is that you knew what I was trying to do and you didn't walk away or tell me no. You tried to get me to change my mind. After all it took to get me here, to the point where I'm finally seeing the real you and needing you just like you wanted, you want me to go back to ignoring you.

"Now, you can add frustration to the list. Horny, desperate, and frustrated."

I wadded up the plastic and tossed it in the garbage.

"Are you done?" he asked.

"Drying off? Yes. Venting? Probably not."

He picked me up and carried me out of the bathroom. I was still frowning at him when he put me on the bed.

"Get dressed, and we'll go see Mya and Drav like you wanted." He pressed his lips to my forehead and closed himself in the bathroom.

I threw my towel at the door in annoyance.

"Stubborn," I said under my breath.

It didn't matter. The shower had been plan A. It always paid to have a plan B, and Mya was it.

When Thallirin found me in the kitchen later, I was already dressed and eating cereal with almond milk.

"I'm still mad," I said. "Marshmallow cereal can only fix so much."

He grunted and took a can of dog food out of the cupboard for himself.

"You guys really like that stuff."

"It's not as good as fresh meat but is better than pizza," he said.

I scoffed but didn't argue. As soon as I was done, I put on my jacket and waited for him to pick me up.

"We can stay here and have sex instead," I said.

We left the house, and I shook my head at him. Stubborn. But, so was I.

Drav opened the door after the third knock.

"Morning," I said. "Is Mya around? I really need to talk to her."

Drav scowled at me.

"You don't get to look at me like that," I said. "I still remember how you bullied me into staying home from a supply run because you felt I should be with Thallirin. Well, look who's carrying me. You got your way. Now, it's my turn."

The violent sound of heaving filled the silence.

"Don't care," I said. "Everyone wants me to suck it up so Mya can, too."

Drav's scowl grew a bit harsher, and his gaze flicked to Thallirin.

"Mya is nicer," Drav said.

"Ha!" He obviously didn't know Mya had been trying to guilt me into hooking up with Thallirin. Or maybe he did and just didn't see anything wrong with it. Probably, the latter.

"Let them in, Drav," Mya said from behind him. "I'm done

for now."

He stepped aside, and I saw Mya shuffle toward the couch. She was wearing pajama pants and a tank top, and her hair was in a bun on the top of her head. Overall, she looked like she was a sick mess.

"Can I talk to her alone, please?" I asked once Thallirin entered with me.

Both the fey grunted, and a few moments later, Mya and I were alone.

"I need your help," I said without preamble. "I did like everyone wanted and moved in with Thallirin. But, he won't have sex with me because I'm seventeen and nine-tenths or some crap like that. You came up with this eighteen or older rule. You need to tell him it's okay."

She leaned back into the couch.

"I can't."

"What do you mean you can't? You were pushing for this."

"I know. But I wanted it to mean something for both of you. I never meant to push you into something you didn't want."

"Who says I don't want it?"

"It wasn't even a week ago that you were in here calling me—"

"No need to repeat it," I said. "I still think what you were trying to do was wrong. However, I'm with Thallirin on my own terms and not because of what someone else did or said. I chose. Well, I tried to, but he's stubborn."

"I'm really sorry, Brenna. If you're as close to eighteen as you say, what's a few more days or weeks?"

I snorted.

"Easy for you to say. If you're bitten, you don't turn. Me? I'm headless."

Mya considered me for a long moment.

"I can't," she repeated. "I have to think of everyone, not just you. One of the new survivors at Tenacity is only thirteen. I need to think of her, too. The rule keeps her safe."

"Then make a sub-rule. No one under sixteen ever and no one under eighteen without the consent of a guardian."

"And your mom would be okay with this?"

"Of course. She doesn't want me to die either."

"It doesn't have to be a choice between sex and death, Brenna. You're safe here."

I gave her the same look my mom often gave me when I said something stupid.

"We've only had that one breach," Mya said. "It was a fluke."

"No, it wasn't. It was a calculated move by the infected and was successful. They're not stupid anymore. They're getting smarter. We need to get smarter, too."

"And lifting the under eighteen sex ban makes us smarter?"

I shook my head at her blindness.

"Once again, my fate is on you, Mya. When are you going to get tired of controlling people's futures?"

I turned toward the door and let myself out.

"I already am," she said before I closed it behind me.

Drav and Thallirin were waiting on the front lawn. Both

looked equally grumpy, so I kept walking. The whole situation was frustrating the heck out of me, and I was starting to feel stifled again. I tried to tell myself that no one was taking choices from me, but it wasn't feeling that way. It felt like everyone was controlling the direction of my life but me.

Thallirin caught up to me when I was almost to Garrett's house.

"Are you angry?" he asked.

"Yep."

He didn't say anything else as I knocked on the door.

Zach answered a minute later.

"Hey! Come in. Want some pancakes?"

"No, we already ate. I was wondering if you and Garrett wanted to go trade with Tenacity again today?"

"You sure you're up for it?"

"It's not like there's anything else for me to do."

"Okay. There's a bunch of stuff that Julie set aside for us to take over. She heard that the survivors had some livestock with them and suggested we try to trade for that."

I followed him into the kitchen where Garrett was manning the stove.

"Morning," he said. "How's the leg?"

"Stitched up and ready for adventure."

He grinned at me, but his expression lost all humor when his gaze shifted to Thallirin, who I knew stood just behind me. I glanced back at him and found him glaring at Garrett.

"You don't get to glare," I said, nudging him. "If Garrett wants to be nice to me, he can."

Thallirin slowly looked down at me, his face darkening at an alarming rate.

"No Garrett."

"Oh, shit," Garrett said from behind me.

"What the hell does 'No Garrett' mean?" I asked. "Like no looking at him, no talking to him, or what?"

Thallirin picked me up, set me aside, and started for a very panicked looking Garrett.

"Touch him, and I'm never sleeping next to you again," I said, quickly.

Thallirin slowed.

"Touch him, and I'm moving back in with Mom and Uan."

Thallirin stopped just inches from Garrett.

"I swear, I have no intention to be anything but a brother to Brenna," Garrett said, retreating from Thallirin. "Ever."

I rolled my eyes in understanding.

"I'm not interested in having sex with Garrett, Thallirin."

That broke the spell, and Thallirin turned to study me.

"And I'm even madder at you now than I was before."

That took the remaining anger out of his eyes.

Ignoring him, I sat at the table and waited for Garrett and Zach to finish eating.

"Be thankful you're not yet eighteen, Zach," Garrett said. "After that, you're squashable competition."

"I'm so tired of all this eighteen bullshit," I said. "It's a damn number to designate the average age most people attain a reasonable measure of adult-like maturity. It's not a hard line."

"Something you want to talk about?" Zach asked warily.

I looked at my younger brother and shook my head, knowing it wasn't something he really wanted to hear. He was only asking to uphold the family rule to communicate.

"No. I'll spare you my life drama."

Fifteen minutes later, I was in Thallirin's arms as he carried me toward Tenacity. We weren't alone. Garrett, Zach, and I had run into Eden and Ghua at the shed. Eden had taken one look at my angry expression and volunteered to go on the trade run with us.

As soon as we arrived, the fey carrying the supplies went straight to Tolerance's storage shed and started unloading. Then, they left to fetch another load while we waited for Matt.

Eden tugged me aside as people started to gather to look at what we had for trade.

"What's going on? Are you okay?"

"Not really. I've been this far away," I pinched my fingers together so there was only a sliver of space between them, "from infection twice. Now, Mr. Brenna-is-mine over there decides it's all talk and no go, spouting nonsense about me needing to turn eighteen. Do you even know what day it is? I sure as hell don't."

She gave me a quick hug.

"I'm so glad it's not what I was thinking," she said. Then she pulled back to frown at me. "He's seriously turning you down? What have you tried?"

"Full frontal exposure with leg lift."

"Damn. He didn't budge?"

She looked to where Thallirin was standing, arms crossed to keep the humans from getting too close to us.

"He kissed me, but that's not going to keep me safe."

"Maybe he needs to be romanced," she said. "Soft light. Dinner. Music. See-through clothing." She shook her head. "Honestly, I'm at a loss here. All I have to do is look at Ghua, and he starts stripping. It doesn't matter where we are or who else is in the room."

"Maybe Thallirin's not as into me as Ghua's into you," I said, feeling more than upset at the idea.

I looked at Thallirin again, but a flash of white hair in the crowd beyond him distracted me.

Time stopped. I knew that hair. The crowd shifted, and the view was gone before I could see a face.

"You just got really pale," Eden said.

Not answering her, I rushed past Thallirin and into the crowd even as fear crawled up my spine. Eden called my name, but I didn't take my eyes from the spot where I'd seen the hair. I had to know if it was true.

When I reached where I thought I'd seen the man, I turned a slow circle, looking for him. For a moment, I thought he'd noticed me and run. Then, the crowd shifted again, and I spotted an older man with a shock of white hair, holding the arm of an older woman. They saw me watching and smiled.

I managed a weak smile in return and exhaled slowly.

My eyes had been wrong.

Oscar, Van's father, wasn't in Tenacity.

CHAPTER FIFTEEN

Hands locked around my arms, and the unexpected contact startled a yip out of me. I jerked my gaze up as I was lifted off my feet and carried out of the crowd. Thallirin's gaze swept over my face. He didn't say anything until I was on my own two feet near the supply shed.

Bracing his arms against the metal wall on each side of me, he leaned in. I didn't feel caged but protected. It didn't matter that Oscar wasn't here. Thinking I'd seen him was enough of a reminder that it wasn't just the infected I needed to worry about.

"What happened?" Thallirin asked.

"I thought I saw someone that I knew. But, it wasn't who I thought it was. It just scared me for a minute. I'm fine."

"You saw someone who scared you, and you went running toward them?" He scowled at me.

I crossed my arms and scowled back.

"You say you want me, but as soon as I started wanting you back, you ran away. Don't scold me for contrary choices when you do the same."

He sighed heavily and pressed his forehead against mine.

"You are my heart, Brenna. Even when your words kick me in the testicles."

I snorted out a laugh.

"It's a relief to know you understand what's going on."

"Everything okay here?" Eden asked from nearby. I peeked under Thallirin's arm to smile at her.

"Yeah, it's fine."

"Why'd you go running off?" she asked.

"I thought I saw someone."

"Someone who scared her," Thallirin said, still caging me in.

I set my hand on his chest, not to push him away but for the connection. Both of us seemed to need it.

"And you went running toward that person?" Eden asked.

"I thought it was Oscar. I needed to know."

She swore softly.

"It wasn't, though," I said quickly. "It was an old guy with his wife."

She didn't seem to hear me as she looked out over the crowd.

"Who is Oscar?" Thallirin asked.

"No one important," I said, patting his chest.

Eden and I shared a look. I wasn't trying to hide anything from him, but given his reaction to Garrett this morning, I didn't want Thallirin to go crazy in a crowd of newcomers. It would be a bad first impression of the fey for them.

I looked up at Thallirin.

"You going to let me go?"

He grunted and stepped away from me.

"No more running into the crowd," he said.

I grinned and joined Garrett and Zach. They did most of the trade negotiating while I spoke to people off to the side, who were too hesitant to approach because of the fey. I tried to reassure them that the fey were nice and their physical differences didn't mean they were bad, but only a few seemed to listen to me. Others continued to look at the fey with suspicion.

The people who had the livestock quickly approached the group when they heard what we wanted.

The owner of the single, pregnant cow that had made it to Tenacity wasn't willing to give her up. However, he was willing to trade for a map of where he'd found her. He claimed there were more at a farm a few days' walk from us. His price was steep for the information. Half of what we'd brought to trade and a box of food every week for a year. If we found livestock still living, though, it would be worth the supplies.

A woman approached us with two chickens. Her price, like the first man's, was a box of food delivered to her house each week until the chickens died. One of the fey quickly agreed to it then asked her to show him where she lived. She was young enough and had no man with her. I wondered if she understood what she'd actually traded.

The rest of our supplies went in random trades to those who needed them, and we were ready to head back before my stomach had a chance to rumble for lunch.

Thallirin carried me again; and I spent my time watching him instead of the trees. I couldn't help but wonder if what Eden had said would work. Did he need more than just a flash of skin? Did he need some kind of assurance, too, that I wasn't just using him for his body to become immune?

As soon as we crossed over Tolerance's wall, Eden called Thallirin's name and waved for us to follow. I didn't realize her intent until we were standing on Mya's front lawn. Had I known where Eden was leading us, I would have convinced Thallirin to take me home first.

"Why are we here?" I asked.

"We need to let Mya and Drav know about the map and the cows. The animals won't live on their own for long. If we want any chance at long-term survival, we need to move fast to rescue them."

"But why do Thallirin and I need to be here?"

She flashed me a grin.

"You have other plans?" she asked.

"Maybe," I said, then scowled at Thallirin when he quickly put me down.

"That's what I thought," she said. "Come on. It's good to socialize."

With anyone else but Mya and Drav, I thought to myself.

Eden knocked on the door, and Drav opened it a minute later.

"Hey, Drav. If Mya's up for it, we have some news from Tenacity."

He let us in, and I saw Mya in her usual spot on the couch.

"Feeling any better?" Eden asked, removing her coat. I reluctantly did the same and followed her into the living room.

"It comes and goes," she said with a look at Drav.

He grunted his agreement before shifting his gaze to me. There was a lot less scowl this time, which just annoyed me.

Ghua sat and pulled Eden into his lap, where she snuggled comfortably. I looked at Thallirin, and he just stared back at me. Stubborn fool. I turned back to Mya.

"We traded goods for a map that supposedly leads to livestock," I said, just wanting to get the conversation over with. "Garrett has the map. It's a three-day walk, but it should be less than a day to drive there."

"Pregnant cows," Eden said. "Oscar was as obsessed with animals and needing them to survive as he was with needing women."

Ghua growled, and Eden absently patted his arm.

"The man was right on both counts, just wrong about how he went about obtaining them. If there's still something living out there, we should move quickly to bring it back."

"What do you have in mind?" Mya asked.

"I think a group should leave today," Eden said. "They'd probably reach the farm just before nightfall."

"That's too dangerous," Mya said. "The hellhounds—"

"Need to be hunted," Thallirin said. "Humans cannot go with us."

"Go ask for volunteers," Drav said. "Will you come?"

Thallirin nodded. Ghua stood and set Eden in the chair and left with Thallirin and Drav.

"What in the hell just happened?" I asked.

"I think they decided they're going to get the cows," Mya said, leaning her head back on the couch. "I can finally puke in peace."

"That bad?" Eden asked.

"It seems worse when I'm stressed, which has been constant since the breach."

If she was looking for pity, I wasn't going to give it. I felt bad about the stress and the baby situation but held firm to my belief that she'd handled things wrong with me all around. And when she'd had the opportunity to make amends, she didn't even want to do that.

"How are things with Thallirin?" she asked.

"Fine." I stood and grabbed my jacket. "I think I'll go home and sleep before I grab a night shift on the wall."

I MOVED AROUND THE KITCHEN, making myself dinner. It wasn't the nice candlelit dinner for two that I'd hoped for, just a lonely dinner for one. I could have gone to Mom and Uan's, but I didn't feel like company. The reality was that I missed Thallirin. At what point had I grown so used to his presence? I'd resented his attention and now I resented his absence.

His image rose in my mind. I didn't see his scars, only his

steady gaze. His stoic expression. That lack of apparent emotion had frustrated me at first. However, I now realized that his stability had comforted me more often than not.

Was stability enough of a reason for me to feel what I was feeling? Anger that he'd left me? Missing him to the point that I'd barely slept after returning home? I sighed and stared out the kitchen window at the fading light, knowing I wouldn't have the answer until he returned.

Finishing my soup, I rinsed the bowl and got ready for my shift on the wall. The quiet, cold night enveloped me the minute I stepped outside. I paused and looked around. A fey moved silently in the shadows across the street and nodded to me. Relieved that I wasn't totally alone, I nodded back.

The walk to the wall didn't take long, and I saw Uan in my usual place when I arrived.

"Your mom missed you at dinner," he said in lieu of a greeting.

I shook my head as I climbed the ladder and joined him.

"I slept so I could take a shift tonight," I said. "I figured with so many fey gone, we'd need the extra eyes."

Uan grunted and looked out at the skeletal trees.

"I thought you were avoiding us because you are angry Thallirin left."

I studied him.

"Why would I be mad about that?"

Uan's gaze met mine.

"You are often angry about many things," he said with a shrug.

I frowned at him. My first thought was to say it wasn't true. However, he was right. As much as I'd tried to hide it, even from myself, I was angry. Angry at Mya for not helping me. Angry at Thallirin for even looking at me after what happened at the bunker. At Van, for forcing me to do something I didn't want to do to survive. Mostly, though, I was angry my father died so I could live, and I was angry at what happened to the world I once knew and everything that followed that I couldn't prevent. It had all made me feel so helpless.

Then, it hit me. None of that anger had helped anything. It hadn't changed the past or taken away the pain. In fact, I had only added to that buried ball of emotion by holding onto it. And holding onto that resentment because of my past was keeping me from fully embracing my future.

I looked at Uan.

"I'm sorry for all the angry things I've said to you in the past."

"I've watched Byllo with Timmy. He watched Jessie with Savvy. When children are hurt and angry, parents hug them. Can I hug you?"

The simple request opened the world for me. I wasn't the only one hurt by her past.

I nodded to Uan, and he wrapped me in a hug.

"We cannot change the past. What is done is done. But we can decide our future. I choose your mother and you and Zach. You will be my family, and I will be happy because I won't be lonely anymore. What do you choose, Brenna?"

I hugged him back. Every fey had experienced their world

change, not once but twice. First, when they were locked away and, again, when they were set free. They didn't hold onto anger, though. They held onto hope. Hope for a family. Hope for a better future.

"Thank you, Uan. You've helped me more than you know."

He gave me an awkward back pat and released me. I smiled at him.

A long, low howl distantly echoed. We both stared out into the darkness.

"You should go stay with your—"

"I'd rather stay here and watch your back when you jump down there to kill that thing. You're important to Mom. And me."

He grunted and looked over to one of the fey farther down the wall. That fey nodded.

"Was that a silent communication to keep an eye on me?" I asked.

Uan grinned widely, the white of his sharp teeth showing in the darkness.

"You're important to all of us."

"I know. Thank you."

I waited with him, listening to the howl growing closer and the second one that joined it. Then the third. More fey came to the walls or started to patrol the grounds just inside them.

Several of the fey on the wall jumped down to the other side. They moved quietly as they stalked farther out into the trees. I'd seen the hellhounds up close when I'd been trapped in the bunker with Van. They'd attacked with a focused determination to get to the humans there, somehow sensing we were the weaker prey. Their single-minded focus had enabled the fey to kill the pair. But at a cost. One of them had died. Another, Ghua, had almost died.

The howling stopped, and I knew the hellhounds were stalking closer.

"Be careful," I said to Uan as he stepped forward to jump.

"Don't shoot me," he said with another smile before he disappeared down into the darkness.

I watched for the twin, glowing red dots that would signal the hellhounds' presence. When I saw them, I nocked an arrow and waited.

The hellhounds crept forward from the barren trees, stealthy shadows among shadows. I couldn't see the fey; and no one moved to stop the beasts, but I felt little fear. I knew the fey were there and wouldn't let anything happen to me.

When the beasts were close enough, I let an arrow fly straight toward one glowing eye. Wind. Distance. Timing. It all influenced accuracy. And although I knew I was good, the hellhounds were made to live. I didn't expect my arrow to do more than bounce off the impenetrable hide of my target. However, it flew so true it pierced one glowing eye.

The hound roared and swiped at the arrow. A light flared to life, flooding the area as fey dropped from the trees. They speared the creature while it was distracted and ripped open its chest to dig for its crystallized heart, the only way to kill it. I nocked another arrow and watched a second group circle the next beast. It snarled and lunged. Between its movement and the fey's, there was no safe shot.

The fey had to use nearly every spear to pin the hellhound to the ground to remove its black heart. The dark energy pulsed from the corrupt organ even as the creature continued to thrash and howl. Undead. The source of the spread of the infection.

I didn't lower my bow until all the hearts were nothing but dust and the creatures were finally silent.

"You did well," Uan called from below.

I smiled as other fey nodded at me. They pulled the corpses away then returned to whatever they'd been doing before the hounds' arrival.

"Do you think the noise will draw more infected?" I asked when Uan rejoined me.

"Maybe."

"I don't like that the infected just disappeared."

He looked at me curiously.

"They did not disappear. You were almost bitten on a supply run."

"Right. I meant I don't like that they vanished from here."

"They did not vanish from here. We killed them."

I snorted at his literal answers.

"You didn't kill all of them in the world. We shine lights up into the sky at night, make noise during the day, and go on supply runs. They're getting smarter, Uan. Not dumber. They know we're here. Why aren't they trying to get us? What are they waiting for?"

He grunted and continued to watch the darkness with me until just before dawn. I yawned and moved toward the ladder, knowing someone would take my place.

"Will you come with me to Tenacity after we eat breakfast?" he asked, jumping from the wall, to land beside me. "I have supplies to trade, but I know the humans there will not want to talk to me."

"Of course I'll go with you. What are we trading?"

We started walking toward Mom's...their house.

"Nancy wants me to find more canned meat." He sighed slightly. "She thinks I am not eating enough and wants me to trade the corn."

"Are you eating enough?" I asked.

"Everything has a season. Even in the caves, there were times our bellies begged for more. These lean times will not last forever."

I liked how he thought, but I still felt terrible that he wasn't eating enough. With the recent supply run, there was plenty to be had, but not a lot of meat. It made me wonder how many of the fey weren't eating enough. Especially those trying to provide for someone else.

"Do you love her?" I asked. "Mom?"

"I do. Very much. She has a smart mind and a kind heart. And I like the way she touches me."

"Okay. That's enough. I get the idea."

"Do you think she loves me?" he asked.

"She hasn't said anything?"

"She is like you. Instead of anger, she carries much sadness. I know she misses Russ."

It was weird hearing him say my dad's name.

"Dad would have liked you, I think. He was a good judge of character and understood what it meant to do the right thing by someone. Even if that person didn't want help." I looked at the house I'd called home for a few short weeks. "Mom's not good with being soft. She might not have said the words yet, but she wouldn't be with you if she didn't care about you a great deal. Never doubt that."

He grunted and opened the door for me.

"Nancy, Brenna is home," he called.

"About damn time," Mom called back.

I appreciatively sniffed the air as I stepped inside and started stripping off my layers of clothing.

"Are you making cornbread?" I asked.

She appeared in the hall with a scowl.

"No. I'm making pancakes." She disappeared into the kitchen again.

"She hides vegetables in my food and thinks I don't know," Uan said softly. "I know."

I smothered my grin and followed him into the kitchen, where Mom had a large stack of pancakes waiting on his plate.

"I'll make up some more batter in a minute," Mom said.

"There's no need," Uan said. "Brenna can have some of mine. We must hurry to Tenacity to trade."

I was barely keeping it together as he placed three of the

pancakes on my plate then hesitated before quickly adding a fourth under Mom's watchful gaze.

"She needs energy," Uan said lamely. "She is still healing."

Mom looked at me and shook her head. She knew exactly what he was doing.

"Do whatever it takes to get more meat. We're out of dog food, and he's barely eating."

"Don't worry. We'll figure something out," I said.

Fifteen minutes later, I was licking the maple syrup off my fingers as I walked beside Uan in the pre-dawn light. He and a friend of his, Tor, carried two boxes each of veggies.

"I can't believe you don't like syrup," I said. "It makes the pancakes so much better."

"Having no vegetables in them makes them better."

"Have you considered swapping this for whatever meat's in the supply shed?" I asked.

"The meat is for the humans. We will find more for us."

Tor nodded in agreement, and I frowned at them.

"That makes no sense. We're going to Tenacity to trade with humans for meat."

Uan flashed his pointed teeth at me.

"Yes, but we will be helping them because they will want far more cans of vegetables for their cans of meat. More cans of food mean less growling bellies."

So this trade wasn't really about him then. He was finding a way to help the other humans without breaking Mya and Matt's rules. And Uan already had a girl. I shook my head at myself. I'd been so blind to the fey's truly helpful nature. Sure, they wanted a woman of their own. They were all pretty open about that. But they honestly wanted to help everyone else, too. Well, most everyone. Their willingness to help the men was tentative so long as it didn't get in the way of their first objective.

We met Ryan and his group by the wall. Since a number of fey were still on the livestock run, he planned to take a small supply group out into the rural areas to see what they could find. It was safer than trying another run to Harrisonville undermanned.

At Tenacity, we found a few volunteers waiting to join the supply-run group. I waved to them as they left and helped Uan and Tor set up in the supply shed. Not that there was much to set up.

Despite the early hour, we got rid of the vegetables in minutes, people already having caught on to the fact that the fey liked meat. The seven meager cans we'd received in return weren't much, but the two fey seemed happy.

Uan cracked one open right away and offered me a bite.

"I'm full from breakfast," I said. "You go ahead."

Matt came jogging up before Uan finished eating and spoke directly to both fey.

"I'm glad you're still here. One of the newcomers, a young girl about thirteen, went missing last night. None of the guards saw her leave, which means she has to be here somewhere. With your heightened senses, I was hoping you could help us look." Matt glanced at me. "Would you be willing to keep an eye on the fey from the top of the wall and yell if there's any trouble?"

"Sure."

Matt focused on Uan and Tor again.

"I think the girl's scared. If you find her, don't approach. I'm not sure what set her off that she'd want to hide."

"Maybe the hounds last night," I said. "Could you hear them from here?"

He nodded grimly.

"Is everyone in Tolerance okay?"

"Yeah, the fey took care of the hounds."

"Three less to spread the infection," Uan said.

"Good," Matt said. "Thank you for killing the hellhounds, and thank you for your help now. We need every person we have."

I hurriedly climbed the wall and watched Tor leave with Matt while Uan trekked through the neighborhood on his own. Keeping an eye on them wasn't easy. The place was large, and people were starting to leave their homes and walk around.

I lost Uan when he turned to go down the next street and had to jog along the wall to find him. As I did, a person caught my attention. He was walking away from me, so I only saw the back of his head, but something about his swagger made me freeze.

A memory rose. I blinked, watching the man, but he had his hood up so I couldn't see his face.

Uan turned the corner and nodded to the man as he

jogged by. The man paused and turned to watch Uan, who waved at me.

I didn't look at Uan or raise my arm. I couldn't. It felt like all the blood in my body rushed to my toes. Lightheaded, I struggled to stay upright.

Van's gaze shifted from Uan to me, and a slow smile parted his lips.

CHAPTER SIXTEEN

THE MAN WHO'D RAPED ME MORE THAN A MONTH AGO, NODDED, turned, then disappeared around the next corner. Van couldn't be here. This couldn't be real. I staggered sideways a step as if struck by an invisible fist.

"Brenna!" Uan called.

When I didn't answer, he did the typical fey jump-climb up the wall. His arms wrapped around me, and he held me close.

"Get a room, fey-lover," someone yelled.

"Was someone mean to you?" Uan asked. He lowered his voice. "I can hurt them for you."

I wrapped my arms around his waist and hugged Uan in return, still shaking but not feeling as terrifyingly alone.

"You might not have made me, but you're as real of a dad as my first one was. Thank you."

He grunted and continued to hold me.

"Why is your heart running in fear?"

"Because for a minute, I felt alone again. But I'm not." I pulled back and managed to smile up at him. "I have you. And the rest of the fey."

"And Thallirin," he said.

And I never missed him more.

"Any luck finding the girl?" I asked.

"Yes. She was in a closet, crying. Matt is talking to her now, but we can go."

It seemed like my body knew it was the time of day to wake up because, despite spending the night on the wall and going straight to Tenacity afterward, my eyes wouldn't stay closed in the darkened bedroom. I kept thinking of Van.

The last time I'd seen him, he'd been standing with his father and the other gunmen just outside their coveted bunker. I recalled the look of anger on their faces, especially Van's scowl despite his broken nose, as I was led to the back of a truck with the other people the fey had saved from a life of subjugation.

What Van and his group had done, murdering my father and kidnapping us, was inexcusable even with the world gone to shit. Mom had wanted him dead, but Eden had talked her out of it because she thought Mom wouldn't want that weight on her shoulders. Given all he'd done to me and my family, I'd wanted him dead, too. However, after listening to Eden talk to Mom, I'd kept quiet because I hadn't wanted to make that choice, either. A deep part of me wasn't so sure she would have regretted the group's death. And, that had worried me.

In the end, it had been the decision of Matt's emissary that they leave the group where they were and take half their supplies.

Just as I'd kept my silence then, I'd kept my silence again when we left Tenacity. I was no longer sure what was right.

In our old society, those men would have been tried, found guilty, and put in jail. But there were no jails now. There was just outside the wall. And, outside the wall was eventual death.

If I turned Van in, just so he'd be cast out again, would that make me just like him? A killer? While I'd killed plenty of infected, I didn't know if I could live with sending Van to his death. Actually, I knew I could live with it, but I wasn't sure if I wanted to be that person.

But doing nothing felt like pardoning him.

I was seriously conflicted and trying not to be angry about it. Especially after my talk with Uan.

Had taking their supplies been enough to force them out of the bunker? Or were they at Tenacity because they wanted something else? It was the second question that worried me more. What if my silence hurt someone else? Turning Van in would then be to protect others, not for revenge. Yet, it was that small spark of need to see him hurt that made me wonder if my thoughts were only empty justifications for getting what I wanted.

Rolling over in an attempt to get comfortable, I almost missed hearing the kitchen door close. I lifted my head from the pillow and watched the hallway. The moment Thallirin appeared, his gaze met mine and he froze.

"I'm really glad you're home," I said.

He started toward the hall again and stepped into the bedroom. He was shirtless, already wearing shorts, and had wet hair. That he'd bathed before coming home wasn't a good sign.

"How did it go? Any trouble?"

"There were infected. And a few hellhounds."

He sat on the bed and gently ran his fingers along my cheek. I leaned into the touch, needing him more than I'd thought possible.

"I am glad I am home, too," he said.

"Did you sleep at all?"

He shook his head, and I patted the bed. The mattress dipped as he lay down beside me, and he settled in with a long exhale. I liked that he wrapped an arm around me so I could snuggle closer. My hand rested on his bare chest, just over the steady beat of his heart. Idly, I touched a scar.

His fingers toyed with my hair.

"I heard stories about when you first came to the surface. That you didn't know what we were and killed a lot of us. Is that true?"

"It is."

"Now that you know what we are, does it bother you that you killed some of us?"

"We were naïve and uninformed when we came here.

Knowledge often creates guilt. Why are you asking? Are you angry that I killed?"

I wasn't stupid. He'd worded his answer to sound like he felt guilty, but that wasn't what he'd said. He wasn't remorseful that he'd killed, and I wasn't judging him for it. I rather wished I could be like that.

"From what I'd heard, you were killing people who were shooting at you. It was defense."

"Sometimes. Sometimes, it was not. Does that change your answer?"

"No. I know who you are now." I lifted my head to meet his gaze. "You're a good man."

He grunted.

Resting my head on his shoulder once more, I thought about who I wanted to be. I wanted to be a good person. I wasn't yet sure what I would do, but I knew that I would have Thallirin's support, no matter what. I turned my head and pressed my lips against his bare chest.

His fingers stilled in my hair. Looking up at him, I met his hungry gaze.

"Will you kiss me?"

His hand moved in my hair, and he rolled to his side, bringing our faces closer together.

"I have done nothing in my life to deserve you. But I will never let you go."

He closed the distance as he held my gaze. When his lips met mine, it was in the briefest of caresses. He didn't pull back, though. His thumb stroked my cheek, and he kissed my bottom lip. Then the corner of my mouth. Each touch was sweeter than the last and made my heart ache and my pulse start to race.

When our lips met once more, I opened to him. He made a low sound the moment my tongue touched his. I wrapped my arms around his shoulders, desperate to feel him holding me, and caressed his skin, silently pleading for him to come closer. And he did, shifting so he hovered just above me.

I loved the way he started to shake as he tried to hold himself back and did what I could to break that control by slowly hooking one leg around his hip.

He growled, claiming my lips with an intensity that left me breathless. I needed more. It only took a little pressure for him to settle his hips against mine. The hard length of him pressed against my sweet spot and sent a shiver of need through me. I locked my other leg around his hips and ground against him.

Thallirin tore his lips from mine with a groan and arched into me, making me gasp with pleasure. I slid my hands from his shoulders to his clenched jaw and lifted enough to kiss him again as I continued to move under him.

The moment my fingers accidentally brushed his ears, I lost him.

One minute, he was on top of me; the next, he was standing by the bathroom door, his chest heaving and his pupils dilated.

I touched my lips as I looked at him.

"I'm tired of being alone. Let me be with you."

He closed his eyes and exhaled shakily.

"Soon," he said roughly.

"You're stubbornly annoying with this. And I hope we never have a reason to regret your hesitation."

I patted the bed.

"Lay by me. I promise not to touch you."

He remained by the door, still shaking lightly.

"I don't think I'll be able to fall asleep alone." I hated admitting it, but it was true.

"Why?" he asked softly.

"Because I don't know who I'll be when I wake up."

"Be who you are now."

"I don't even know who that is anymore."

"You're a hunter. A warrior woman who helps kill hellhounds. Who protects and gathers for her family."

I smiled slightly at the fact that he'd already heard about what had happened while he was gone. Fey were terrible gossipmongers.

Thallirin returned to the bed and pulled me close to his chest.

"You're also like me. Lost in a new world, looking for something to anchor you. Something to make your life whole again. But you can stop looking and find peace, now. You are mine, Brenna, and I am yours."

The simple statements wrapped around my heart. I yawned hugely and closed my eyes. Thallirin made me feel safe even when what I'd feared was myself.

"Sleep, Brenna."

THE FAINT SOUND of knocking woke me enough that I felt Thallirin untangle himself from my hold. Making a small noise in protest, I loosely grabbed for my personal fey body pillow. He chuckled, kissed my brow, and left.

I pouted with my eyes closed, drifting in that in-between state of sleep and awake. A soft murmur of voices pulled me from that pleasant, hazy state of being. Forcing my eyes open, I crawled out of bed to see who was there.

Zach grinned at me the minute I shuffled my way into the entry.

"You look like hell," he said.

I squinted at his silhouette in the afternoon light.

"Since I only managed a few hours of sleep, I'm not surprised. What's up?"

"We're doing a cow run."

"A what?"

He shook his head at me.

"Get dressed and come see. You can sleep later like a normal person."

Thallirin looked at me, letting me decide what to do.

"Fine. I'll be ready in a minute."

I went back to the bedroom and started pulling on clothes.

"You can sleep more," Thallirin said behind me.

"Nah. He's right. If I keep sleeping now, I won't be able to sleep tonight."

"Damn straight, I'm right," Zach called from the kitchen.

I rolled my eyes and closed myself into the bathroom while Thallirin dressed.

After a quick breakfast bar, Thallirin and I followed Zach out of the house. The first cow I spotted was wandering down a street. It mooed at us as we approached.

"Can we eat it?" I asked, eyeing its large belly.

"Not yet. According to the fey, every cow still alive was pregnant."

"Really?" I glanced at Thallirin, who gave a brief nod.

"They were in a cement building away from the others. Someone had been caring for them. We think maybe one of the newcomers."

"We have about thirty head of cattle." Zach grinned at me. "I've always wanted to say that."

"Should I look for a cowboy hat for you next time we're out?"

"I'd be much obliged."

I rolled my eyes.

"Anyway, it's dangerous having them all in one place. Drav talked it over with Matt, and Matt agreed. Tenacity will look after half the herd. We won't be able to eat any until after they give birth. Richard and Matt were talking about a butchering plan. They want the cattle to sustain us long term, but we need to be sure we can sustain them. Not only are we going to need to raid towns for supplies, we're also going to need to start raiding farms for feed."

"Fun," I mumbled.

Near Richard and Julie's place, we found the majority of

the cows grazing in an empty lot. Many of the fey were watching the animals, too. It wasn't until I was staring at the walking hamburgers that I thought to question how the fey had even gotten them in here.

"It wasn't easy," Thallirin said. "The cows are heavy and don't hold still."

"The fey carried them over the wall," Zach clarified. "Richard and Ryan are at Tenacity, now, engineering doors to get in and out. Want to come with us and check it out?"

I didn't. Not really. Because if I went back to Tenacity, I couldn't keep putting off deciding what to do about Van. I would have to talk to Matt and face Van. However, my desire to continue to avoid the situation was what prompted me to agree.

Zach beamed at me.

"I knew you wouldn't want to miss out."

I forced myself to smile while my stomach churned.

Zach ran off to let Garrett know we'd be going along.

"Are you still wondering who you are?" Thallirin asked.

Glancing at him, I found him watching me intently. The steadiness of his gaze made me feel like he was looking straight into my soul.

"Yes," I said simply.

The fey started prodding the cows from their lot to the street, and Thallirin picked me up to follow. He placed a kiss on my brow as he walked.

"What's that for?" I asked.

"To remind you. You are mine, Brenna."

"I like that you say it as if that's enough. To belong to someone else. I need to be me, too. An individual."

The tips of his ears darkened slightly.

"What did I say wrong?" I asked, reaching up and gently touching a tip. He shuddered and turned his head to set his forehead against mine.

"You said nothing wrong. That was the first time you acknowledged you are mine."

I pulled back to look at him.

"Was it?"

He grunted, and I grinned, still playing with his ear.

"I am yours, Thallirin. I just wish you'd do something about it."

His steps slowed, and he looked at the cows and the other fey. I could feel his resistance weakening and leaned up for a kiss, which he quickly gave and, just as quickly, ended.

"Be good, Brenna."

I sighed and settled into his arms.

"I'm trying to be."

He didn't talk to me again until we reached Tenacity. According to Thallirin, getting twelve of the cows over Tolerance's walls had been a chore. Driving those cows through Tenacity's newly acquired, but only semi-completed, double gates was a breeze.

"This is going to make loading up for supply runs a lot easier," Matt said, watching as Merdon and two other fey moved a pickup into place. I didn't know where they got the heavy iron doors from, but they looked like they could keep out a hellhound. For a while, anyway.

Richard and Ryan were on top of the outer set of doors, rigging floodlights that were aimed directly toward the ground.

“Looks like it’s been a busy day,” I said.

“Very. In a good way, though. Seeing animals alive like this has people excited. It helps that a few of Tolerance’s people are here trading, too. Food in the cupboard and food walking around on four legs is a good reminder that things are getting better.”

He sighed, the sound contradicting his words.

“I should go check on the trading,” he said.

“Let me,” I offered. “I think you’ll probably be more needed here. You too, Thallirin. They’ll want this closed up before dark.”

Thallirin’s steady gaze held mine.

“We should stay together.”

I smiled.

“I’ll be back in a few minutes. I’ll be fine.”

He grunted, and I walked away.

The supply shed still had a few people lingering around it. As I approached, I heard the exchange between the guy behind the table and a man standing in front of it.

“I think she’s on a bathroom break or something,” one man said. “I’m sure she’ll be back soon.”

“Can’t you just trade for her? She brought this stuff here for a reason.”

"Sorry. I don't know what she was looking for."

I stepped in before it got any more heated.

"Who was here?" I asked.

"Hannah," the guy said.

I looked down at the box full of food, knowing too well what she'd probably come to trade for, but I wasn't about to help her get more alcohol.

"What do you have to trade?" I asked.

I traded for meat on Hannah's behalf, figuring she could always trade up later. When her box was empty, I asked the guy to watch over her newly acquired stock until she got back.

"Fine, but I'm telling her you're the one who traded."

I waved to show I didn't care and left the shed, heading away from the wall.

Before I told Matt who he harbored within his walls, I had to know how many of them were here. I'd seen Van for certain, and possibly Oscar, but what about the other men in their group?

Staying alert, I looked at every person I passed. I was ready with an explanation for my odd behavior if anyone asked. I'd say I was looking for Hannah. Hopefully, no one would point out that I wasn't looking at the women walking around as much as I was carefully watching the men.

In the end, none of my behavior mattered. No one questioned me, and I never spotted anyone from the bunker.

Until Van found me.

CHAPTER SEVENTEEN

I HAD BEEN STANDING BETWEEN TWO HOUSES, FOLLOWING A SET of footprints in the snow when a prickle of awareness raced along my spine. Snow crunched behind me.

I whirled around, facing Van. He'd dyed his hair almost black. Eyebrows, too. He almost didn't look like the same man, except for the eyes. Those were the same.

Fear clawed at my insides. Not caring how it looked, I drew my knife.

His pleased expression didn't falter a bit at the sight of the blade in my hand.

"You are a sight for sore eyes," he said, his gaze roving over me. "I never thought I'd see you again."

"I'd hoped that would be the case," I said.

His expression clouded slightly.

"That hurts, Brenna."

"You raped me, Van. Did you think I would forget that?

Why are you here?"

"Rape? You said yes. I didn't hold you down. And, you enjoyed it." He stepped closer, his brow furrowing. "I felt you tighten around me. I treated you like a damn princess and fed your brother, too."

I shook my head at him, unable to believe he honestly didn't see what he'd done was rape. Not only was there no guilt in his eyes, the hunger was still there.

"I want you back, Brenna. I'll keep you, and any children we have, safe."

I made a choked sound.

"In what world do you ever think I'd willingly hook up with you?"

"In this one. You wouldn't want me picking someone else, would you?"

Given everyone's desperations, it wouldn't be hard for him to find some other woman to use. Then, he'd have everything he wanted. The safety of these walls and someone to rape whenever he had the itch. The idea that the next girl might believe like I'd believed, that she'd made the choice she had to in order to survive, made my insides twist. Van was right about one thing; I didn't want him picking someone else. But, I also sure as hell didn't want him picking me.

"I don't think you deserve to pick anyone. Even me."

"Aw, now you don't mean that. We'll be good together, just you wait and see."

He was insane, talking as if me being with him was a

foregone conclusion. My grip on my knife tightened. I could already visualize it going through the soft underside of his jaw.

"Does what I want even matter?" I asked.

He smiled with a handsome tilt of his lips that made me sick.

"It does if you want me as much as I want you."

His gaze shifted ever so slightly just behind me. I had no chance to turn before something covered my head and a thick arm closed around my throat. I couldn't breathe. Instead of using the knife like I should have, I flailed in panic. Someone pinned my arms to my sides and took my knife while another grabbed my legs.

"Don't kill her. I need her."

The words barely registered as I continued to try to suck in air and the world grew dark.

My head throbbed like a bitch, and I groggily wondered if the doctor had gotten me drunk again. I moaned at my stupidity, and the sound came out oddly muffled. Frowning, I tried to sit up.

It took a moment for the fog in my head to clear enough to understand why I couldn't.

I lay on my side with my hands bound behind my back and a cloth filling my mouth. I tried to force it out with my tongue, but it wouldn't move. Gagging from my efforts, I stopped and just concentrated on breathing through my nose.

When I was under control again, I lifted my head from the mattress and looked around. Across the room, a girl lay on another bed. She was young. Barely a teen. Her eyes were wide with fear as she stared back. Like me, she was bound and gagged and lying on her side.

Seeing the terror in her eyes forced me to calm my own. I nodded at her and noticed another girl on the floor between our beds. Hannah's curls were unmistakable.

Relaxing my head on the mattress, I tried to move my feet. They were bound, too, but had more wriggle room than my hands. In my hurry this morning, I hadn't tied my boots tightly. If I could—

"You're awake," Van said.

I looked up as he entered the bedroom. He had a tray with three glasses of water, which he placed on the dresser. He didn't look at the girl or Hannah but studied me intently.

"Seeing you like that..." He shook his head, his gaze heating. "It's sexy as hell. When we get to where we're going, you and I need to play with some rope. Don't worry. I don't plan on tying you. You can tie me. It's only fair, right?"

The only rope I wanted to tie on Van was one around his neck.

"Now, I have something to help take the edge off," he said. "It's some good stuff. If you take it, without any noise, I'll leave the gag off. Deal?"

I nodded, desperate to get the rag out of my mouth.

Van helped me to sit and untied my gag, petting my hair repeatedly while doing so and telling me how good I was and how much he'd missed me. I endured it and cracked my jaw the moment I could close my mouth again. No matter how much I tried to swallow, I couldn't seem to get any spit to come back into my mouth.

"Here," he said, offering me three small pills. "I'll give you water once you have these in your mouth."

He watched me with growing satisfaction as I opened my mouth.

"Tied and mouth open," he said quietly. "You're a fucking wet dream."

I wanted to bite the hand he was holding out to me so badly as he drew near. Common sense was my only restraint. If I bit him now, he'd gag me again. Good behavior would keep the gag off and, if I played my cards right, maybe even my feet freed.

Bitterly, I held still as he placed the pills in my mouth, one at a time, then helped me drink. The water was divine, and I didn't regret swallowing down those pills to get some. Hopefully, whatever he'd given me wouldn't act fast.

When I'd drained the glass, he took it away and watched me expectantly.

"Are you going to untie me?" I asked, my voice scratchy. Whatever they'd done to me, it felt like they'd bruised my damn throat. Assholes.

"Soon. You be good, and let me help the little one first."

"Why did you take her?"

"Why do you think?"

My stomach twisted. They planned to have sex with her? Babies?

He reached out to pet my head again.

"Don't worry. You're mine."

He turned his back on me and looked at the girl. She was huddled back in the corner where her bed was wedged against the outer and the side wall. Thankfully, it appeared that Van had been honest in his interest in me over her because he untied her gag without any petting.

Good.

When he finished with her, he tilted Hannah's head back by her hair. She was out cold without a gag. I could smell the alcohol on her from where I lay. She'd been in Tenacity long enough to set up a table and had gone missing shortly before I'd arrived. How much had she consumed that she was passed out already?

I glanced at the window near where she lay. The shade was down and the curtains closed. I could still see some light, though, which meant I couldn't have been gone long.

"This one did all the work for me," Van said with a grin in my direction. He released her and returned to me. "Feeling any better?"

"Still thirsty."

"I can fix that."

He helped me drink more of the second glass of water and tried to pet my hair again. This time, I jerked away. He grinned.

"The pills will kick in soon. Your tune will change then."

"What are you still doing in here?" Oscar demanded from the door.

"Just checking on our girls."

"You drug 'em?"

"Yep."

"Then leave 'em be."

I looked up at Oscar and found him studying me.

"Don't make any trouble, and you'll be fine," he said. "Make trouble, and your life will get a whole hell of a lot harder. Am I clear?"

I meekly nodded and remained quiet as the men left. They didn't close the door or force me to lie back down. Propped against the wall, I looked at the girl and winked, trying to let her know it would be okay.

She nodded and closed her eyes. Oscar and Van's conversation drifted into the room as I tried to figure a way out for the three of us. Hannah being passed out was a huge problem. I wasn't strong enough to carry her, and I sure as hell didn't want to leave her behind with them. But for the sake of the girl, I couldn't risk waiting for Hannah to get her act together, either.

"We need to be careful," Van said from the other room. "They found us once because of those grey bastards."

"That's on you," Oscar said, angrily. "I told you not to put her in the closet."

With growing horror, I glanced at the girl across from me. She didn't make a sound as I realized this wasn't her first kidnapping. In fact, she looked a lot calmer than she had a minute ago. Almost as soon as I thought it, I felt myself relax, too. It was like my emotions were a faucet, and someone had just turned the knobs until there was barely a trickle. My fear was still there—I knew we needed to run—but I felt disconnected from the moment.

"With the work on the gates, everyone will be on that side of town and not paying attention to this side," Oscar continued.

"Chuck's in place on the wall with the ropes. As long as we keep it quiet, we should be fine." Van chuckled. "I can't believe those grey bastards made our job even easier with these supplies." There was a shuffle of noise from the other room, like boxes being moved.

"It's only right after they took half of what we worked to gather. It'll help hold us over until we get settled again. You're sure the girls we took won't be noticed this time?" Oscar asked.

"They thought Tasha was hiding last time, and she was too scared to say any different. I doubt they'll search for her a second time, and she's got no family to care."

I glanced at the girl across from me. I knew I should pity her, but that feeling was just beyond my reach.

"And the drunk one was pissing off too many people for anyone to give a shit."

"We should have left Brenna," Oscar said. "Her ma came for her once."

"No. We're taking her. For all we know, she's already pregnant."

I snorted softly. That had been my biggest fear until I'd

gotten my period a week after leaving the bunker. Best period of my life.

"Fine," Oscar said. "We need to move soon. The longer we wait, the bigger the risk. We'll have to come back for one of the cows after we're settled, and they have the doors finished. I'll bring the next round of supplies to the wall. Leave them girls be until I get back."

The door closed, and I waited. It didn't take Van long to reappear.

"How you feeling?" he asked.

"Fine." My answer was slow and breathy.

He grinned.

"Yes, you are. Want me to untie your feet for you?"

I nodded.

He removed my boots before untying my ankles. When he finished, he didn't get up and move away; but then, I hadn't thought he would. With slow touches, he peeled back my socks and ran his fingers over my skin.

"You have no idea how much I've thought about you since they took you. They robbed us of the future we could have had." His fingers stroked the top of my bare feet then slid up my jeans to my knees, barely missing my stitches underneath. He gripped me firmly for a minute then glanced behind him at Tasha, who still had her eyes closed.

As soon as he faced me, I knew what he was thinking and felt no surprise when he tugged me down so my legs dangled off the bed. Even with the pills making everything swimmy, I felt the ache in my shoulders as I lay awkwardly on my bound arms.

"Do you know if it worked?" he asked softly, reaching for the button of my jeans.

"What?" I asked, feigning ignorance.

"Did my seed take? Are you pregnant?"

He unzipped my pants and started working them down my hips.

"My arms hurt. Can you tie them in front of me?" I asked.

He smiled, stopped what he was doing, and rolled me to my side.

"You're so sweet," he said. "Pretty. You talk nice. Not a mean bone in you."

He obviously had no idea who I really was. I'd been too afraid for Zach and traumatized after seeing my dad die to behave normally while I'd been at the bunker. But thanks to the drugs, I couldn't feel my fear now. I did, however, feel the rope loosen around my hands.

"I can't wait to sink inside you again. You were so tight and hot. It don't matter if you're not pregnant yet. You will be soon."

For all his words about me not being mean, he was careful to keep hold of my hands and press a knee into my legs to keep me down. Not that I did anything. It wasn't time. I was smart enough to know I needed to wait until he was distracted. Until he was in me like he wanted. I didn't let myself think about what he'd do to me, only what I'd do to him.

Turning me, he tied my hands in front of me, leaving a good six inches of rope between my wrists.

"That better, sweetheart?" he asked.

"Yes."

"Good."

He went back to tugging my pants down. I didn't make it easy for him and stayed limp the entire time. He didn't get angry or yell at me, though. He continued with a single-minded focus, his gaze continually flicking to my underwear until my jeans were off.

His fingers drifted over the skin near my exposed stitches.

"I'll take better care of you. You're too pretty for scars."

He had no idea. My scars weren't on the outside.

"This time's going to be a little rushed," he said, reaching for his pants. "Pa's going to be back quick. But I'll be gentle."

I kept my hands loose as I pictured how I'd twist and try to get the rope around his throat. The fey made it look so easy to kill someone, but I knew that I'd need every ounce of strength I possessed, and maybe more, to stop Van.

With his pants open, he reached for my underwear. The sound of the front door opening had him scrambling to his feet as he quickly did his pants back up. Oscar entered the room just as Van picked up my jeans.

"What the fuck are you doing, boy? I told you to leave them alone."

"She said she had to go to the bathroom."

Oscar looked at me. I didn't respond at all. That seemed to be enough for him to know Van was lying, though, because he walked into the room and grabbed the front of Van's shirt.

"Keep your dick to yourself until we're away from here. I need you focused, not distracted. Am I clear?"

Van nodded.

"Get those back on her, and if I see her without pants again, you're on your own."

"Pa..."

"Do it now."

Oscar released Van and left the room. I waited for Van to turn on me in anger, but he didn't. He carefully put my pants back on me.

"Soon," he said, with a brush of his hand over my crotch.

Then he, too, left.

Feet free and hands tied in front of me, I smiled and sat up. Sure, the door was open and both men were in the house, but I was in a better position than before. I could move a little, and I now knew what they planned. While they might be right about no one looking for Tasha or Hannah, they were wrong about me, and it wasn't my mom they needed to worry about.

Thallirin was probably already looking for me.

"You take the supplies this time," Oscar said from the living room.

Standing, I hurried over to Tasha. She opened her eyes as I sat beside her and didn't move as I leaned in close to her ear.

"Are you okay?" I asked, keeping my voice as soft and low as possible.

She nodded.

"Tap the outside wall. Quiet. Consistent. The fey will hear."

She nodded again, and I returned to my bed as a door closed. It would have been easy for me to tap the wall myself, but Van and Oscar were watching me a lot closer than the girl. And if they came back into the room, I didn't want to give them any reason to tie me up again. So, I sat in the same spot and leaned against the wall, hoping that I was making the right choices for all of us.

Oscar appeared in the doorway a few minutes after I was settled.

"How many pills he give you?" he asked.

I had to think about it for a second.

"Three, I think." My words were slow.

"You swallow them all."

I nodded.

His gaze flicked to my hands bound in front of me, and he swore under his breath.

"I hope any kids the two of you have get your brains," he said, coming toward me.

He untied my hands and leaned me forward to retie them behind me. I briefly thought of doing something, but looked at Tasha. She watched me closely, her eyes wide.

I mouthed the word "tap," and she nodded. If she was doing it, I couldn't hear it. Hopefully, the fey would.

Once I was bound to Oscar's satisfaction, he put my socks back on then hesitated with my boots.

"Harder to run off in socks," he said, taking my footwear with him.

I stared at the hallway in frustration. There were too many "ifs" for me to feel comfortable with the chance of a timely rescue just yet. If the house was close enough to the wall that the fey could hear us...If the fey were looking for us in the right area...If I wasn't overestimating their hearing abilities...

I could start screaming, but depending on how far away from the wall we were, any attempt to call for help would likely end with me unconscious and Tasha facing whatever happened next alone. That Oscar left me ungagged led me to believe we weren't close, so I couldn't do that to her. And I heard Oscar say the fey were still working on the wall, making the chances of a large search much lower. Where did that leave us? We were still in the house, which meant we had some time. Once Oscar and Van took us from Tenacity, though...I shivered. I couldn't let that happen.

A door in the other room opened.

"We're all set. Let's go," Van said.

Despite the drugs, I could feel panic starting to weigh my chest.

"Where are the girls?" a new voice asked.

"In the bedroom," Van said.

"How many we get?" the man asked.

"Three," Oscar said.

"That's not enough. You promised one for each of us."

"This is just the first round. Don't you worry. You'll get one. We can share one, like we did with May, until there's enough."

My stomach churned, and I looked around the room. Then

at the closed window. We were out of time. No more playing it safe.

Standing, I acted without fully thinking, and threw myself at the large window that almost went from floor to ceiling. The glass cracked under the layers of shade and curtain.

"What the hell was that?" Van said from the other room.

I took a few steps back and flew forward.

"Thallirin!" I screamed, hitting the window with my side.

Arms wrapped around me just as the glass gave way under my weight.

"Thallir—"

A hand clasped over my mouth. I bit down even as I was dragged away from the window.

"Son of a bitch!"

The hand lifted. I inhaled to scream again.

Crack.

My face exploded with pain.

"I thought you gave her the pills."

"I did!"

I inhaled again.

"Thall—!

A ball of cloth was shoved into my mouth.

Outside, something roared.

Behind the gag, I grinned.

Not something. Someone.

Thallirin.

Everyone in the room went still. My eyes swiveled to the window, and I laughed. I wouldn't be going anywhere with

Van. I could see that same realization, first in Oscar's eyes then Van's, only moments before wood splintered and something crashed in the other room.

In the next few seconds, chaos exploded around me.

I was shoved onto the bed, face first. There was a lot of swearing and sounds of movement. A gun went off. There were dull thumping sounds, a few grunts, then silence.

I lifted my head and looked at Thallirin, who stood in the bedroom doorway. The rage in his eyes should have made me quake in fear rather than wilt with relief.

"Brenna?" His low, deep voice shook with emotion.

I tried telling him I was fine, but the gag muffled the sound.

He lifted me gently onto his lap and pulled the cloth from my mouth.

"You have no idea how happy I am to see you," I said. "I'm guessing I just saw your angry face."

He set his forehead against mine. He didn't say anything, just stayed like that, holding me and shaking.

"My arms are getting sore. Can you untie me?"

He grunted and gently removed the rope. I rubbed my wrists and rolled my shoulders before sliding off his lap.

"Her too," I said, nodding toward Tasha.

The girl was watching us with wide, fearful eyes and shook her head.

"This is Thallirin," I said. "He looks different, but he's the nicest person I've met. He's not like these guys. He won't hurt us. He's here to make sure we stay free. Can he untie you?"

"My grandpa said they were bad," she said, speaking for the first time.

"I don't think your grandpa had a chance to meet Thallirin, then."

Thallirin waited until she nodded to free her. I went to Hannah, and tapped her cheek. She was still out cold.

"You're going to need to carry her," I said, looking up at Thallirin.

"No," Merdon said, appearing in the doorway. "Hannah is mine."

CHAPTER EIGHTEEN

I STAYED NEAR TASHA AS WE SAFELY WALKED WITHIN A CLUSTER of fey. They'd all volunteered to carry her, but I knew that would have scared her more than she already was. So, we shambled along like a pair of undead because of whatever pills Van had given us.

Van, Oscar, and Grady, a third guy I recognized from the bunker, remained passively trussed up, and each was slung over the shoulder of a fey. Hannah rested like a princess in Merdon's arms. I wasn't so sure that's how he thought of her, based on the angry looks he was giving her, but I knew looks could be deceiving.

Tasha stumbled beside me, and I caught her, almost sending myself to the ground as well.

"I should carry you," Thallirin said, yet again.

"I'm fine," I said. "So is Tasha. Walking will help us shake whatever they gave us."

A low rumbling growl was echoed by several members of our group.

"Guys, the growling is scaring Tasha. You have to stop doing that around her."

"Sorry, Tasha," rang out around us, making Tasha giggle then sniffle.

Seeing fey carrying the three gagged humans through town drew attention. By the time we reached the wall just before dusk, there was a crowd following us.

If Matt Davis was worried about seeing the trussed-up humans or the large group following us, he hid it well.

"What happened?" he asked.

The rest of the fey finishing up on the gate, along with Richard, Ryan, Garrett, and the remaining humans from Tolerance, came over to listen.

"These humans tied up Tasha, Hannah, and Brenna," Thallirin said. "They wanted to take the females."

Van made a few muffled noises before managing to spit out his gag.

"He's making it sound like kidnapping," Van said, arching to lift his head and look at Matt. "We were saving them."

Zach, recognizing Van, swore and started forward. Garrett locked an arm around him.

"That son of a bitch is a killer," Zach yelled.

Matt looked at me.

"These men are from the bunker," I said. His gaze lit with understanding. "They planned to take the three of us out of

Tenacity. This is the group who murdered my father and took Zach and me prisoner."

Uan, who was near Zach, growled menacingly.

"Why would humans want to take women?" someone behind me asked.

"Because they believe they have the right to take what they want," Matt said. "Including women to bear children. Only those women aren't given a choice. They're taken at gunpoint and forced to do whatever this group wants."

"That's worse than stealing food!" someone yelled. "Kick them out." More voices were added to the first.

Thallirin stepped forward, and the crowd's cries reduced to angry murmurs.

"Banishment is not enough. These humans came here even when they knew they shouldn't. If they leave, they will return again. We kill infected and hounds because they are a threat to the safety of the survivors. These humans have proven they are also a threat."

Oscar started making noise behind his gag, and Matt ordered it removed so he could speak. None of the fey looked happy about it.

"You can't kill us," Oscar said as soon as the gag was removed. "Every life has value. We were only trying to help humanity. We need to start having kids. And not with these abominations. Humans are close to extinction. We're doing what we need to do to ensure its survival."

His words made me sick. A few nods from the crowd, and the dark looks those nodders gave to the fey, made me sicker.

Matt studied Oscar, his expression impassive.

"Humanity as a whole has long struggled with the premise of betterment for mankind because everyone's idea of betterment is different. Through the zealous need to improve, there are always ripples of discord. If these conflicting ideals of betterment are not kept in check, they often result in war, each side fervently believing their cause more just than the other's.

"And in their heated defense, they forget the cornerstones that gave us the foundation for our beliefs. It's as simple as 'live and let live.'"

I wasn't sure how I felt about what Matt had just said. Yet, wasn't the morality of letting Van go the same thing I'd been struggling with?

"Wise words," Oscar said.

"Are they? Because you and your group killed to take Brenna once before, only preserving life when you thought it would benefit your ideals. While I will not order your deaths, I will not protect you within these walls." He looked at the men behind him. "Open our new gates."

"It's almost dark," Van said. "We'll never make it somewhere safe now."

"You were willing to leave before," I said.

"We had guns."

Oscar elbowed his son.

"Where are the guns?" Matt asked.

No one spoke.

"Chuck, another man from the bunker, was helping them

get supplies over the wall," I said. "They planned on coming back for a cow and more women."

That caused some more murmurs in the crowd, and Grady glared in my direction.

"Find him and the guns," Matt said to a few men behind him. They left, and the doors behind Matt started to swing open.

"Cut them free," he ordered with a nod to the bound trio.

The fey growled as a few of Matt's men followed his orders. I wanted to growl, also. I couldn't believe Matt was just going to banish the men. Sure, it was almost dark and we'd seen hellhounds only a few nights ago. But other than that, it'd been quiet, and this group was a bunch of hardened survivors. Thallirin was right, they'd be back.

Van, Oscar, and Grady stood tall and smirking at the rest of us. I put my arm around Tasha's shoulders so she wouldn't be afraid.

"You're making a wise choice, Matt," Oscar said. "Even if we don't exactly agree on how to preserve humanity, every life counts."

"What happens to these three outside this wall isn't my concern," Matt said, looking straight at Thallirin. "Chuck should be joining them soon."

Thallirin grunted, and he and several fey moved with speed to climb over the wall.

Realization of what Matt had just done registered with the gathered crowd. However, their low murmurs of surprise and worry were drowned out by Van's yell.

"You son of a bitch!"

Van surged forward, as if to go after Matt, but was stopped short by a man with a gun. The irony of the moment wasn't lost on me.

Forced at gunpoint, Van yelled at Matt's guards, who were herding them toward the gate. He was still yelling obscenities when the gates started to close, and Oscar told him to shut up.

After that, I strained to hear anything outside the wall. A scream. A shout. Anything. But there was only silence.

"You're welcome to stay until morning," Matt said.

"There's no need," Merdon said. "There's nothing beyond the wall we fear."

I looked at Tasha.

"Do you want to come with me? It's not scary in Tolerance. It's a town just like this one. There's an extra room in my house. My brother and my mom are both nice, and you'd have plenty to eat."

Something in her gaze shifted from fear to pain and longing.

"Your mom and brother are still alive?"

"Yes. Because of the fey."

She looked at the fey.

"They scare me."

"What's different always scares people. But don't let your fear keep you from leading a life you want."

"Can I come back here if I don't like it?"

"Always," Matt said. "And you're welcome to stay here. There are plenty of families who'd take you in."

She shook her head, and I gave her shoulders a reassuring squeeze.

"It's safer if the fey carry us because they can run really fast. But, don't worry. I'll be close by the whole time."

She didn't flinch away from Uan, who offered to carry her, and he made sure to stay close to me as we left Tenacity and Thallirin behind.

"ARE you sure you don't want the bed?" Tasha asked.

On the floor, I rolled to my side.

"I'm sure. You still hungry?"

"No. I had enough." There was a moment of silence. "Uan is a good cook."

Mom had taken our appearance just before dinner in stride. They'd made sure Tasha was fed, and Mom didn't ask questions when I said Tasha wanted to stay with us for a while. I hadn't missed Mom's questioning look and knew she'd want answers later. But for Tasha's sake, I was staying the night so she'd have someone familiar while she settled in.

I couldn't stop thinking about Thallirin, though. Was he home and wondering where I was? Would he come here, looking for me? He'd just rescued me, after all. I doubted he'd be okay with me disappearing again.

However, there were no crashing doors or roars of aggression. Just the quiet of a warm house at night.

"Your brother's nice," Tasha said.

"He can be until you catch him eating the last bag of chips. Then, you'll want to shoot him in the foot."

She snickered.

"Will he really show me how to use a bow?" she asked.

"He and Mom both will. Archery will be good for you. It's oddly calming."

She quieted again, and my mind drifted back to Thallirin. Had he killed Van? I held no disillusions about why he and the others had left. And, right or wrong, I hoped he'd tell me Van would never be coming back. Not just for my sake but for Tasha's and every other unprotected female still alive.

"They killed my grandpa," she said softly. "They found us in a house and killed him and took me. When they spotted the bigger group, Oscar said if I told anyone, he'd let the others have me." She paused. "I know what they wanted to do."

I sat up and leaned close so she'd see my face, even in the dark.

"Be sad. Be angry. Then, when enough time's passed, remember what it means to be you. Your grandpa wouldn't want you to waste any of your life fearing or hating the people who hurt you. Not when you can do so much more."

"Like what?"

"Start small. Tomorrow, you'll have waffles and syrup for breakfast and learn how to use a bow. You'll get to take a shower and put on clean clothes. You'll be able to walk around outside without a pinch of worry. And you'll be able to fall asleep in that same bed, with a full belly, knowing you're safe and have a family again. What you decide to do with your life from there will be up to you. Your choice."

She exhaled shakily.

"I want that so much."

"Which part?"

"All of it."

"It's yours. All you have to do is live it."

After that, her breathing evened out. Eventually, I fell asleep, too. It wasn't the best night's sleep, though. The floor was hard, and I missed Thallirin.

When I heard Uan moving around in the morning, I got up to help him. He already had the waffle iron out.

"Listening in?" I asked with a smile.

"Yes. How many waffles do children eat?"

"Probably only one or two. The waffles are pretty big. But make her four so she knows she can eat as many as she wants."

He grunted and started prepping the griddle as I made the just-add-water mix. Zach came stumbling out of his bedroom after Uan had the fourth waffle on a plate. My brother joined me, where I was frying some sausages, and forked one right out of the pan.

"Where'd we get these?" he asked, taking a bite.

"We traded for them yesterday."

He started setting the sausage down, and I stole it from the end of his fork.

"Feel guilty enough to make me a cake?" I asked playfully. "Something layered. With a custard and raspberry filling. And a whipped frosting."

He looked at me for a minute then shook his head and grinned.

"Nope. Not that guilty. Just don't go walking off by yourself, anymore, when you're at Tenacity. Those people have proven too many times they can't be trusted."

"I will watch her," Uan said. "She will never wander off again."

I rolled my eyes.

"Come on. I can't have you and Thallirin breathing down my neck. Besides, *Dad*, you have a new daughter to watch over."

Uan grunted.

"Yes. I will watch her, too."

Mom rolled out of her bedroom next, looking put together and alert.

"Uan filled me in," she said. "Do you think she'll stay?"

I opened my mouth to answer, but a quiet voice beat me.

"Do you want me to?"

We all turned toward Tasha, who was lingering in the hallway, half-hidden by the kitchen cabinets.

"I do," Mom said.

"Me, too," Zach said.

"I would like two daughters," Uan said. "Very much."

"Hey," Zach said, feigning indignation. "What about two sons?"

"Do you know of a boy child who needs a father? You can share a room."

I laughed as Zach sputtered at the idea of room sharing. When I met Tasha's gaze, she looked less uncertain.

"Come on," I said. "Uan made waffles."

While I sat through breakfast and did my best to help Tasha feel welcome and like part of the family, I couldn't stop glancing at the kitchen window and listening for the door.

"So how long are you staying with us?" Mom asked me, as blunt as ever.

"You don't live here?" Tasha asked.

"I did until recently. I met someone and moved in with him. But, I still come home for dinner."

She didn't seem too upset by the news that she'd have a room to herself.

As soon as Zach took her outside to introduce her to the world of archery, Mom shooed me from the house.

"We'll see you at dinner."

My steps were faster than usual as I crossed town.

I was expecting to see Thallirin in the kitchen, looking a little lost at the stove when I walked in. Instead, the house was quiet and still empty. I tried not to let his absence bother me and focused on taking care of myself.

After the hell I went through the day before and a night on the floor, I was ready for a hot shower and a change of clothes. And maybe some more pain reliever; everything was aching from all the manhandling I'd endured.

I dug some medicine out of the bathroom cabinet and drank from the sink. The mirror showed the barest hint of a bruise smudging my cheek from the smack I'd gotten for yelling Thallirin's name. I had a bruise on my shoulder, too, from hitting the window. Surprisingly, my leg wasn't too bad despite having my pants taken off and put back on with no regard to the stitches. My neck and throat were sore and bruised, but what hurt most were my shoulder and back muscles from having my hands bound behind me.

By the time I finished rinsing my hair in the shower, everything felt fine. Everything except for the ache in my chest that flared to life when I let myself wonder why Thallirin wasn't home yet. Tucking my towel around my torso, I left the bathroom.

The degree of worry that settled into my stomach surprised me a bit. Thallirin was strong, and the fey were immune. I shouldn't be worried. And when it came to Thallirin and his friends dealing with infected and hellhounds, I wasn't. I'd seen how they fought them. But, it wasn't infected that Thallirin had scaled the wall for. It'd been humans. The worst kind. I'd seen Van and Oscar's cruelty firsthand and knew not to trust them. What if they'd found a way to trick the fey? In spite of their strengths, I knew the fey could be hurt.

I took several of my calming breaths and focused on drying my hair.

Thallirin would be fine. He had to be.

That thought made me pause as I realized just how much I needed that to be true. Thallirin helped me feel safe in a world filled with creatures and people who wanted to destroy humanity as I knew it. Without him, I hated what the future might hold for me. Nothing but more anger and suffering. With him, though, I could be happy. He was gentle, despite all his roughness, and endearing, despite his sparse words.

A small smile lifted my lips as I understood what had happened. Somewhere along the way, I'd started to see past my fear of having my choices taken from me. Then, love had taken hold. It felt scary and fragile and, yet, so right.

I desperately wished Thallirin was there to hug at that moment.

Tossing my towel over the bathroom door, I glanced at myself in the mirror and really focused on me. The tank top and sleep shorts I wore hid nothing. I was bruised, stitched, emotionally scarred, and more than a few pounds shy of being overfed. But, I was also a strong, determined survivor. Like Thallirin.

"He'll be back," I whispered to myself. "Because if it were me out there, I'd find a way back, too."

Resolute in holding to my positive outlook, I went to the kitchen, foregoing my need for a nap, and set about making something to eat. I'd only just turned off the stove and moved to the table with my bowl of beans and franks when the door opened.

My heart leapt as I looked up at Thallirin.

He saw me immediately, his gaze tracking over my face then down to the bowl in my hands before he stepped inside and softly closed the door behind him.

"Why are you here?"

The near-crippling hurt I felt at such an unwelcoming and toneless question took a large amount of effort to ignore. Rather than feel attacked by the ugly words, I chose to believe I had misunderstood him.

"Because you want me here, and I want to be here. Why would you think I shouldn't be?"

His gaze drifted over my face again, and I could see the flicker of something in the depths of his eyes. Fear? Uncertainty? It was odd seeing either of those from him.

"Because I killed the humans. They didn't shoot at me. They screamed, and pled, and tried to run."

"Were you hurt?"

He looked down at the floor and smiled.

"They cannot hurt me."

I took a deep breath, set my bowl aside, and went to him.

"Only I can do that, right?"

He grunted in his non-committal way.

"I should feel bad that they're dead, but the only thing I feel is relief. Thank you for making sure they will never be back. I won't ever have to watch for their faces in any new people who join us. I'm just sorry you were the one who had to do it."

He reached up and tenderly ran a fingertip over the bruises circling my neck.

"I would do anything for you."

The simple words sent my heart racing.

"Do you mean that?"

"Yes."

I reached up, standing on my toes as I threaded my fingers in his hair, and slowly drew him to me. He didn't fight what I wanted. In fact, his hands settled on my sides, holding me in place as he leaned down to brush his lips against mine. The contact was all the sweeter for the briefness of it.

He set his forehead against mine, and I rubbed my nose against his.

"Then keep me safe forever," I said softly. "Make me immune."

He jerked as if I'd slapped him but didn't pull away.

"I know you think I'm too young. If it'd help, I'll ask Mom to bake me a cake and sing 'Happy Birthday' to me tonight. The truth is that I honestly don't know when I'll officially be eighteen. It could be next week or it could be a few weeks from now. But the actual date doesn't matter, Thallirin. The rule was made to protect the young and innocent. I don't believe it was meant to keep those who are too young to make their own intelligent and informed choices from making choices they might later come to regret. I think it was just to keep them innocent for as long as possible. I lost my virginity well before the earthquakes, and any remaining innocence was taken since then. Your hesitation isn't saving me anything but is putting me at risk.

"Let this be my choice. Let me choose you. You almost lost me, Thallirin, and I almost lost you. So much could have gone wrong. I love you and want to be with you. I don't know what else to say to you so you will understand that you've quietly claimed a piece of my heart, and every time you turn away from me, you break it."

Thallirin lifted his head from mine, and his gaze was intense as he stared down at me.

"You love me?"

"Yes."

"Forgive me," he whispered.

Before I could ask why, his lips crashed down upon mine. It was nothing like our prior kisses. His hands moved up my sides, skimming just below my breasts before he lifted me and wrapped my legs around his waist.

When he pulled back, I was panting and my lips felt puffy. His gaze skimmed over my face as he walked us down the hallway. He didn't speak. He didn't need to. I could see the hunger for me in his eyes, feel it in the grip of his hands. I grinned, understanding his apology. Thallirin was done waiting, and I couldn't have been any happier.

He growled at my smile, and before we reached the bed, he kissed me again, his fingers knotting in my hair as he lowered me. The mattress touched my back, and he pulled away. I watched with a racing heart as he stripped. Scars covered every inch of his body. I drank in the sight of the one on his hips then swallowed hard as my gaze dipped lower.

He was huge. Like, run-away-screaming huge. All the nice, tingly feelings those kisses had started faded a bit as I stared at what he planned to plant inside me.

"The choice will always be yours," he said.

Tearing my gaze from his overlarge equipment, I looked up at him. The hunger was still there in his gaze, but so was worry. He knew my past. He knew what I'd gone through, and he didn't want to be that for me. Because of his concern, he never would be.

I smiled at him again, loving him even more.

"I know. And right now, I choose yes."

I held out my hand, and he joined me on the bed. He was slow and sweet with his next kiss and trailed his fingers over my stomach. He took his time touching me, and I knew he was reveling in finally doing what he'd wanted to do all along. I enjoyed each lingering caress. Especially when he worked his way up my ribs, pushing my top higher.

Smiling, I sat up and removed my shirt first, then got to my knees and slowly removed my shorts and underwear. His ears darkened as he watched me, riveted to each small move I made. It was like all those full-frontal flashes I'd given him had never happened, and he was seeing me for the first time.

"Beautiful," he breathed when I settled next to him again.

He brushed his fingers over my nipple, then down to my navel and up again.

"Touches are good, but kisses are better," I said.

I lifted my lips to his, and he hungrily claimed them only to leave me panting as he trailed kisses from my neck down to my breast. His mouth on my nipple set fire to my insides. He took his sweet time there, not venturing any further south than my navel with his touches.

He was stalling.

Smiling, I pushed him onto his back and pressed my lips against the scar on his throat. Then the one covering his collarbone. My tongue flicked the one that bisected his nipple, and he groaned.

Continuing south, I took my time kissing and licking until I'd made certain he knew I was serious about having sex with him. When I reached his belly button, his shaft was safely cradled between my breasts. He arched into me, his fingers stroking my hair.

"Want me to stop?" I asked.

"Never stop," he rasped.

I slid lower and licked the clear bead of liquid shining at the end of his cock. He made a pained noise a moment before I was on my back, pinned under him.

"Maybe, sometimes stop," he said, setting his forehead against mine.

I giggled and wrapped my legs around his hips.

"Or maybe sometimes just hold on and enjoy the ride."

He kissed me hard and positioned himself at my entrance.

"Choose me," he said.

"I choose you."

He entered me slowly, one agonizing inch at a time. It burned as my channel tried to stretch to accommodate him. But, I knew he was so worried that he'd stop if I gave any indication it hurt. So, I tried to relax. It didn't help. He was just too big and wasn't getting anywhere because, thankfully, he wasn't forcing anything.

"I must do something," he said. "You're too small."

Before I could ask what he meant, he withdrew and had his face buried between my legs.

A strangled 'ah' escaped me with his first, unexpected lick. I buried my fingers in his hair and hung on as he brought me to the brink again and again.

"Please," I begged. "Stop teasing me."

"No," he mumbled against my clit, sending tingles of happiness through my vagina. "Teasing makes this better. Ghua told me."

I didn't have time to wonder what else Ghua had said because Thallirin made my eyes roll back into my head by sucking gently. One finger slipped inside me. Then two. Then three.

"Are you ready to try again, my Brenna?"

I nearly clawed him to get him back on top of me.

This time, there was no burn, only pleasure, as he slowly slid home. He growled low and withdrew to thrust deeply again. I lifted my hips, meeting his advance with enthusiasm. My orgasm hit me hard, and I cried out. Thallirin's pace doubled, sending me into a spiral. I didn't know what was up or down until he buried his face in my hair and was growling and groaning.

Each pulse of his shaft sent another wave of pleasure through me, and I pressed my mouth against his shoulder to muffle any noises I made. Thallirin was making enough for both of us. I grinned against his skin as the sound of his growls faded.

He didn't roll off or crush me with his weight. Pulling back a little, he looked down at me.

"The more we do this, the safer you will be," he said in all seriousness. "But it is your choice."

I grinned up at him.

"I have no other plans until dinner."

EPILOGUE

MOM'S WATCHFUL GAZE CAUGHT ME SHIFTING IN MY SEAT AGAIN, and a knowing smile made a flash appearance on her lips.

"Well, I'm glad you two finally figured out what's important," Mom said. "I was going to start baking cakes and singing 'Happy Birthday' to you until he pulled his head out of his ass."

"She does not mean that literally," Uan said to Thallirin. "She knows our heads cannot reach our butts."

Thallirin grunted and resumed eating while Mom, Zach, Tasha, and I started laughing.

"Would have been the perfect night for cake, too," Mom said with a nod to the bow on the counter. "It's beautiful."

Thallirin's gaze held mine for a moment before he looked at Mom.

"It will never replace the one that was taken from Brenna, and I am sorry for that."

He meant every word. His sweet apology, which had been given with the bow during one of our brief water breaks that afternoon, had brought me to tears. As had the bow he'd made. The carvings on it were beautiful. Trees and rocks and small animals decorated parts of the grip and limbs. He'd said they were of the caves, where he'd come from.

"And nothing will ever replace this one," I said. "It's the most beautiful bow I've ever owned. I can't wait to use it."

Under the table, I lifted my foot to trail a toe along Thallirin's thigh. His fork paused halfway to his mouth as his gaze locked with me.

I turned to Tasha.

"How was today?" I asked.

"Good. Zach says I'm a natural with the bow." She looked at Uan. "Can I have my own, too?"

"Of course. I will start on one tonight."

I didn't know where he'd get the wood from, but I knew that small detail wouldn't stand in the way of doing something that would make Tasha, his newest daughter, happy.

"Any word on how Hannah is doing?" I asked.

"She is sick," Thallirin said very seriously. "But Merdon is caring for her. He knows how to help her."

"Is she sick because they took her?" Tasha asked, worried.

"No, sweetie. She was sick before that," I said. "But Thallirin is right. With one of the fey looking out for her, she'll recover. Merdon will see to it."

I gave her a reassuring smile before meeting Thallirin's

gaze. The fey had a funny way of getting to women. It wasn't aggressive but it was persistent and endlessly patient. It sounded a little stalkerish when I thought of it like that, and I smiled slightly, thinking of all the times I'd thought of Thallirin as my stalker. He didn't feel like a stalker, now. I slid my foot a little higher up his thigh. In fact, he felt very much under my control.

He slowly set down his fork.

"Brenna is done eating and would like to leave now," he said, standing.

My grin widened as Mom snorted.

"Right. It's so obvious she wants nothing to do with that big, juicy steak on her plate. The steak that would give her hours and hours of energy."

Thallirin paused in the process of moving away from his place at the table, looking from the steak to me, before sitting down.

"Eat quickly," he said. He began eating his steak with a gusto that made the ache between my legs throb a little bit more in anticipation.

"Make sure to take a soak in a warm bath before bed," Mom said under her breath. "It helps."

Zach made gagging noises and started tugging on his ears.

"I think I just went deaf," he said loudly. "Can you hear me? I can't hear you."

I rolled my eyes at him and started eating.

I loved my family. We were uniquely diverse but better for

it. I could see in Mom's eyes that she was missing Dad at the moment. But I knew, without a doubt, he would have approved of the choices we'd made since his passing. After all, he'd given his life so we could live.

I was determined to do just that with Thallirin at my side.

AUTHOR'S NOTE

All the feels went into this story. Brenna survived so much that she was tough to write. Like a year, tough to write. Plus, (if you're in my fan group, you already know this) I thought I lost almost three chapters worth of words! Panic doesn't even begin to describe those terror filled minutes. Thankfully, I found what was missing and dedicated this book to what prevented a complete tragedy.

Speaking of tragedies...I cannot wait to dive into Hannah's book. That girl is a mess! You've been watching her shitstorm develop through other characters' eyes. The drinking. The propositioning fey to get what she needs. It's all going to end, and I'm pretty sure you can guess who's going to end it. I seriously cannot wait!

After Hannah, there's another story brewing. Yes, yes. I know you want Molev. But I'm pretty sure his story is going to be the end of the series because no one (my imaginary people) is talking to me after that. It makes me sad. I think ending the series would make you all sad too. So, I'm holding off for at least two more books (Hannah then Tor and a new girl). I'll have a clearer picture of the world in general after Hannah's book, though. Sometimes the characters who are talking are so loud drown out the rest. Also, there's a lot going on with the infected.

How fun was it to bring back some of the characters you didn't think you'd see again? Van and Oscar got what they had coming. Tasha, who you might remember as the little girl hiding in the attack from Eden's book, hasn't had the happiest journey, but have any of them? She's at least in a good home now with new parents who will love and protect her with their dying breaths.

They aren't the only past character's we've heard from either. If you've been waiting for Byllo's story, it's already available! You might have missed it if you're not subscribed to my newsletter. You can still grab it here, though: https://dl.bookfunnel.com/iaeqiqj17t

And, finally, if you'd like a sneak peak of Hannah's book, keep reading!

SNEAK PEEK OF DEMON DISGRACE

(BOOK 8)

Panic suffocated me, burning my lungs and straining my pulse.

They were behind us. The soft moans of the dozen infected were almost drowned out by our gasping breaths and the rustle of leaves under our feet, but even if we couldn't hear them, there was no doubting they were there. The stench of their rot carried on the wind that blew my hair into my face.

In front of us, the trees stretched endless, providing no protection.

My lungs burned with effort, and my side ached. I couldn't think. I didn't know what to do.

"Hannah," Katie panted. "I can't."

I tightened my hand on hers, pulling her along. Her weight dragged on my arm. She wasn't keeping up like she should.

"Keep going."

The moans were getting closer.

I glanced over my shoulder, catching so much detail in that brief look. Katie's wide, desperate eyes locked on me. The horde of infected barely fifty feet behind us and gaining.

I sat up, gasping and shaking. The memory coated my mind, an unwanted stain on my thoughts. Scrambling out of bed, I lay on my belly and searched frantically for another hidden bottle. There was no second miracle to be found, though. I curled in around myself, holding myself together while I desperately waited for the images to fade. They didn't, though. I saw it all play out again, and with a choked moan, pulled at my hair.

It wouldn't leave me. It wouldn't stop. Ever. This was my hell.

Sobbing softly, I heaved myself to my knees then stumbled to the window. The sash lifted soundlessly, and I slipped through the opening. The brisk air sent a shocked me enough to interrupt my tormented thoughts.

I looked over the quiet homes blanketed in white and focused on the lights illumining the dark above the wall. The lights kept the hellhounds out. Powered by batteries that were charged using the solar panels retrofitted on the homes, the lights wouldn't last forever. Then what? I didn't want to know. I didn't want to be here to find out.

Ignoring the bite of the snow on my bare feet, I climbed higher on the roof. Numbness wrapped around me. From the cold or my resolution, I couldn't be sure. I walked along the peak, waiting for some sense of calm to settle in my soul. It never came. I reached the edge and looked down at the dark yard below.

Hopefully, I was high enough. Even if I wasn't, I deserved whatever pain I had to endure until death claimed me.

I thought of my sister, closed my eyes, and stepped off.

Sign up for my newsletter to find out when this book releases! https://mjhaag.melissahaag.com/subscribe

SERIES READING ORDER

Resurrection Chronicles

Demon Ember

Demon Flames

Demon Ash

Demon Escape

Demon Deception

Demon Night

**More to come!*

Also by M.J. Haag

Beastly Tales

Depravity

Deceit

Devastation

Tales of Cinder

Disowned (Prequel)

Defiant

Damnation

Connect with the author

Website: MJHaag.melissahaag.com/

Newsletter: MJHaag.melissahaag.com/subscribe

Printed in Great Britain
by Amazon

47308974R00196